The Man Who Would Be King and other stories

Joseph Rudyard Kipling was born in 1865 in Bombay, where his father held a post at the School of Art. At the age of six, according to the normal custom of the time, he was taken home to England and spent several unhappy years in the charge of an unpleasant guardian before being sent to school at the United Services College in North Devon. His holidays were spent in the home of the artist Burne-Jones, his uncle by marriage. At seventeen he returned to India and joined the staff of a newspaper in Lahore, where his father was now curator of the government museum. Brilliant as a journalist, he soon began to write fiction and verse, publishing *Departmental Ditties* in 1886 and during the space of three years over seventy short stories. These included *Plain Tales from the Hills* and *Wee Willie Winkie*. In 1889 he travelled back to England by way of Japan and the United States and settled in London, where he produced some of his finest collections of stories. After his marriage in 1892 to an American girl he lived for four years in Vermont and wrote the famous *Jungle Books* there. In 1901 he published *Kim* and the following year, after the tragic death of his elder daughter, the *Just So Stories*, which he illustrated himself. From 1902 for the rest of his life his home was a seventeenth-century house at Burwash in Sussex, and there he wrote his historical tales for children, *Puck of Pook's Hill* and *Rewards and Fairies*. His only son was killed in the First World War.

Kipling was phenomenally popular in his own time. When only thirty he was offered the Poet Laureateship in succession to Tennyson but declined that honour, just as he thrice refused the Order of Merit. In 1907 he was awarded the Nobel Prize for Literature and he received many other distinctions including honorary degrees from such universities as Paris, Athens and McGill. He died in 1936 only two days before King George V, whose death seemed to mark the end of an epoch.

Kipling has been called the unofficial laureate of the British Empire: during his lifetime Britain attained the height of her imperial power. His mastery of the art of story-telling has never been surpassed and his vivid tales, especially of British India, have introduced countless readers to new realms of the imagination.

Rudyard Kipling
The Man Who Would Be King
and other stories

Pan Books in association with
Macmillan London

This selection published 1975 by Pan Books Ltd,
Cavaye Place, London SW10 9PG, in association with
Macmillan London Ltd
The stories are taken from:
Life's Handicap   First edition 1891
Many Inventions   First edition 1893
Wee Willie Winkie First edition 1895
The Day's Work   First edition 1898
This selection © 1975
ISBN 0 330 24662 3

Made and printed in Great Britain by
Cox & Wyman Ltd, London, Reading and Fakenham

Contents

The Man Who
Would Be King

Brother to a Prince and fellow to a beggar if he be found worthy.

The Law, as quoted, lays down a fair conduct of life, and one not easy to follow. I have been fellow to a beggar again and again under circumstances which prevented either of us finding out whether the other was worthy. I have still to be brother to a Prince, though I once came near to kinship with what might have been a veritable King, and was promised the reversion of a Kingdom – army, law-courts, revenue, and policy all complete. But, today, I greatly fear that my King is dead, and if I want a crown I must go hunt it for myself.

The beginning of everything was in a railway train upon the road to Mhow from Ajmir. There had been a Deficit in the Budget, which necessitated travelling, not Second-class, which is only half as dear as First-class, but by Intermediate, which is very awful indeed. There are no cushions in the Intermediate class, and the population are either Intermediate, which is Eurasian, or Native, which for a long night journey is nasty, or Loafer, which is amusing though intoxicated. Intermediates do not buy from refreshment-rooms. They carry their food in bundles and pots, and buy sweets from the native sweetmeat-sellers, and drink the roadside water. That is why in the hot weather Intermediates are taken out of the carriages dead, and in all weathers are most properly looked down upon.

My particular Intermediate happened to be empty till I reached Nasirabad, when a big black-browed gentleman in shirt-sleeves entered, and, following the custom of Intermediates, passed the time of day. He was a wanderer and a vagabond like myself, but with an educated taste for whisky.

He told tales of things he had seen and done, of out-of-the-way corners of the Empire into which he had penetrated, and of adventures in which he risked his life for a few days' food.

'If India was filled with men like you and me, not knowing more than the crows where they'd get their next day's rations, it isn't seventy millions of revenue the land would be paying – it's seven hundred millions,' said he; and as I looked at his mouth and chin I was disposed to agree with him.

We talked politics – the politics of Loaferdom, that sees things from the underside where the lath and plaster is not smoothed off – and we talked postal arrangements because my friend wanted to send a telegram back from the next station to Ajmir, the turning-off place from the Bombay to the Mhow line as you travel westward. My friend had no money beyond eight annas, which he wanted for dinner, and I had no money at all, owing to the hitch in the Budget before mentioned. Further, I was going into a wilderness where, though I should resume touch with the Treasury, there were no telegraph offices. I was, therefore, unable to help him in any way.

'We might threaten a Station-master, and make him send a wire on tick,' said my friend, 'but that'd mean inquiries for you and for me, and I've got my hands full these days. Did you say you are travelling back along this line within any days?'

'Within ten,' I said.

'Can't you make it eight?' said he. 'Mine is rather urgent business.'

'I can send your telegram within ten days if that will serve you,' I said.

'I couldn't trust the wire to fetch him, now I think of it. It's this way. He leaves Delhi on the 23rd for Bombay. That means he'll be running through Ajmir about the night of the 23rd.'

'But I'm going into the Indian Desert,' I explained.

'Well and good,' said he. 'You'll be changing at Marwar Junction to get into Jodhpore territory – you must do that – and he'll be coming through Marwar Junction in the early morning of the 24th by the Bombay Mail. Can you be at Marwar Junction on that time? 'Twon't be inconveniencing you because I know that there's precious few pickings to be got out of these Central India States – even though you pretend to be correspondent of the *Backwoodsman*.'

'Have you ever tried that trick?' I asked.

'Again and again, but the Residents find you out, and then you get escorted to the border before you've time to get your knife into them. But about my friend here. I *must* give him a word o' mouth to tell him what's come to me or else he won't know where to go. I would take it more than kind of you if you was to come out of Central India in time to catch him at Marwar Junction, and say to him: "He has gone South for the week." He'll know what that means. He's a big man with a red beard, and a great swell he is. You'll find him sleeping like a gentleman with all his luggage round him in a second-class compartment. But don't you be afraid. Slip down the window, and say: "He has gone South for the week," and he'll tumble. It's only cutting your time of stay in those parts by two days. I ask you as a stranger – going to the West,' he said with emphasis.

'Where have *you* come from?' said I.

'From the East,' said he, 'and I am hoping that you will give him the message on the Square – for the sake of my Mother as well as your own.'

Englishmen are not usually softened by appeals to the memory of their mothers, but for certain reasons, which will be fully apparent, I saw fit to agree.

'It's more than a little matter,' said he, 'and that's why I asked you to do it – and now I know that I can depend on you doing it. A second-class carriage at Marwar Junction, and a red-haired man asleep in it. You'll be sure to remember. I get out at the next station, and I must hold on there till he comes or sends me what I want.'

'I'll give the message if I catch him,' I said, 'and for the sake of your Mother as well as mine I'll give you a word of advice. Don't try to run the Central India States just now as the correspondent of the *Backwoodsman*. There's a real one knocking about there, and it might lead to trouble.'

'Thank you,' said he simply, 'and when will the swine be gone? I can't starve because he's ruining my work. I wanted to get hold of the Degumber Rajah down here about his father's widow, and give him a jump.'

'What did he do to his father's widow, then?'

'Filled her up with red pepper and slippered her to death as she hung from a beam. I found that out myself, and I'm the only man that would dare going into the State to get hush-money for it. They'll try to poison me, same as they did in Chortumna when I went on the loot there. But you'll give the man at Marwar Junction my message?'

He got out at a little roadside station, and I reflected. I had heard, more than once, of men personating correspondents of newspapers and bleeding small Native States with threats of exposure, but I had never met any of the caste before. They lead a hard life, and generally die with great suddenness. The Native States have a wholesome horror of English newspapers which may throw light on their peculiar methods of government, and do their best to choke correspondents with champagne, or drive them out of their mind with four-in-hand barouches. They do not understand that nobody cares a straw for the internal administration of Native States so long as oppression and crime are kept within decent limits, and the ruler is not drugged, drunk, or diseased from one end of the year to the other. They are the dark places of the earth, full of unimaginable cruelty, touching the Railway and the Telegraph on one side, and, on the other, the days of Harun-al-Raschid. When I left the train I did business with divers Kings, and in eight days passed through many changes of life. Sometimes I wore dress-clothes and consorted with Princes and Politicals, drinking from crystal and eating from silver. Sometimes I lay out upon the ground and devoured what I could get, from a plate made of leaves, and drank the running water, and slept under the same rug as my servant. It was all in the day's work.

Then I headed for the Great Indian Desert upon the proper

date, as I had promised, and the night mail set me down at Marwar Junction, where a funny, little, happy-go-lucky, native-managed railway runs to Jodhpore. The Bombay Mail from Delhi makes a short halt at Marwar. She arrived as I got in, and I had just time to hurry to her platform and go down the carriages. There was only one second-class on the train. I slipped the window and looked down upon a flaming red beard, half covered by a railway rug. That was my man, fast asleep, and I dug him gently in the ribs. He woke with a grunt, and I saw his face in the light of the lamps. It was a great and shining face.

'Tickets again?' said he.

'No,' said I. 'I am to tell you that he has gone South for the week. He has gone South for the week!'

The train had begun to move out. The red man rubbed his eyes. 'He has gone South for the week,' he repeated. 'Now that's just like his impidence. Did he say that I was to give you anything? Cause I won't.'

'He didn't,' I said, and dropped away, and watched the red lights die out in the dark. It was horribly cold because the wind was blowing off the sands. I climbed into my own train – not an Intermediate carriage this time – and went to sleep.

If the man with the beard had given me a rupee I should have kept it as a memento of a rather curious affair. But the consciousness of having done my duty was my only reward.

Later on I reflected that two gentlemen like my friends could not do any good if they forgathered and personated correspondents of newspapers, and might, if they blackmailed one of the little rat-trap states of Central India or Southern Rajputana, get themselves into serious difficulties. I therefore took some trouble to describe them as accurately as I could remember to people who would be interested in deporting them; and succeeded, so I was later informed, in having them headed back from the Degumber borders.

Then I became respectable, and returned to an office where there were no Kings and no incidents outside the daily manufacture of a newspaper. A newspaper office seems to attract every conceivable sort of person, to the prejudice of discipline. Zenana-mission ladies arrive, and beg that the Editor will instantly abandon all his duties to describe a Christian prize-giving in a back-slum of a perfectly inaccessible village; Colonels who have been overpassed for command sit down and sketch the outline of a series of ten, twelve, or twenty-four leading articles on Seniority *versus* Selection; Missionaries wish to know why they have not been permitted to escape from their regular vehicles of abuse and swear at a brother-missionary under special patronage of the editorial We; stranded theatrical companies troop up to explain that they cannot pay for their advertisements, but on their return from New Zealand or Tahiti will do so with interest; inventors of patent punkah-pulling machines, carriage couplings, and unbreakable swords and axle-trees, call with specifications in their pockets and hours at their disposal; tea-companies enter and elaborate their prospectuses with the office pens; secretaries of ball-committees clamour to have the glories of their last dance more fully described; strange ladies rustle in and say, 'I want a hundred lady's cards printed *at once*, please,' which is manifestly part of an Editor's duty; and every dissolute ruffian that ever tramped the Grand Trunk Road makes it his business to ask for employment as a proof-reader. And, all the time, the telephone-bell is ringing madly, and Kings are being killed on the Continent, and Empires are saying, 'You're another', and Mister Gladstone is calling down brimstone upon the British Dominions and the little black copy-boys are whining, '*kaa-pi chayha-yeh*' (copy wanted) like tired bees, and most of the paper is as blank as Modred's shield.

But that is the amusing part of the year. There are six other months when none ever comes to call, and the thermometer walks inch by inch up to the top of the glass, and the office is darkened to just above reading-light, and the press-machines are red-hot of touch, and nobody writes anything but accounts of amusements in the Hill-stations or obituary notices. Then the telephone becomes a tinkling terror, because it tells you of the sudden deaths of men and women that you knew intimately, and the prickly-heat covers you with a garment, and you sit down and write: 'A slight increase of sickness is reported from the Khuda Janta Khan District. The outbreak is purely sporadic in its nature, and, thanks to the energetic efforts of the District authorities, is now almost at an end. It is, however, with deep regret we record the death, etc.'

Then the sickness really breaks out, and the less recording and reporting the better for the peace of the subscribers. But the Empires and the Kings continue to divert themselves as selfishly as before, and the Foreman thinks that a daily paper really ought to come out once in twenty-four hours, and all the people at the Hill-stations in the middle of their amusements say: 'Good gracious! Why can't the paper be sparkling? I'm sure there's plenty going on up here.'

That is the dark half of the moon, and, as the advertisements say, 'must be experienced to be appreciated'.

It was in that season, and a remarkably evil season, that the paper began running the last issue of the week on Saturday night, which is to say Sunday morning, after the custom of a London paper. This was a great convenience, for immediately after the paper was put to bed, the dawn would lower the thermometer from 96° to almost 84° for half an hour, and in that chill – you have no idea how cold is 84° on the grass until you begin to pray for it – a very tired man could get off to sleep ere the heat roused him.

One Saturday night it was my pleasant duty to put the paper to bed alone. A King or a courtier or courtesan or a Community was going to die or get a new Constitution, or do something that was important on the other side of the world, and the paper was to be held open till the latest possible minute in order to catch the telegram.

It was a pitchy black night, as stifling as a June night can be, and the *loo*, the red-hot wind from the westward, was booming among the tinder-dry trees and pretending that the rain was on its heels. Now and again a spot of almost boiling water would fall on the dust with the flop of a frog, but all our weary world knew that was only pretence. It was a shade cooler in the press-room than the office, so I sat there, while the type ticked and clicked, and the night-jars hooted at the windows, and the all but naked compositors wiped the sweat from their foreheads, and called for water. The thing that was keeping us back, whatever it was, would not come off, though the *loo* dropped and the last type was set, and the whole round earth stood still in the choking heat, with its finger on its lip, to wait the event. I drowsed, and wondered whether the telegraph was a blessing, and whether this dying man, or struggling people might be aware of the inconvenience the delay was causing. There was no special reason beyond the heat and worry to make tension, but, as the clock-hands crept up to three o'clock, and the machines spun their fly-wheels two or three times to see that all was in order before I said the word that would set them off, I could have shrieked aloud.

Then the roar and rattle of the wheels shivered the quiet into little bits. I rose to go away, but two men in white clothes stood in front of me. The first one said: 'It's him!' The second said: 'So it is!' And they both laughed almost as loudly as the machinery roared, and mopped their foreheads. 'We seed there was a light burning across the road, and we were sleeping in that ditch there for coolness, and I said to my friend here, "The office is open. Let's come along and speak to him as turned us back from the Degumber State," ' said the smaller of the two. He was the man I had met in the Mhow train, and his fellow was the red-haired man of Marwar Junction. There was no mistaking the eyebrows of the one or the beard of the other.

I was not pleased, because I wished to go to sleep, not to squabble with loafers. 'What do you want?' I asked.

'Half an hour's talk with you, cool and comfortable, in the office,' said the red-bearded man. 'We'd *like* some drink – the Contrack doesn't begin yet, Peachey, so you needn't look – but what we really want is advice. We don't want money. We ask you as a favour, because we found out you did us a bad turn about Degumber State.'

I led from the press-room to the stifling office with the maps on the walls, and the red-haired man rubbed his hands. 'That's something like,' said he. 'This was the proper shop to come to. Now, sir, let me introduce to you Brother Peachey Carnehan, that's him, and Brother Daniel Dravot, that is *me*, and the less said about our professions the better, for we have been most things in our time. Soldier, sailor, compositor, photographer, proof-reader, street-preacher, *and* correspondent of the *Backwoodsman* when we thought the paper wanted one. Carnehan is sober, and so am I. Look at us first, and see that's sure. It will save you cutting into my talk. We'll take one of your cigars apiece, and you shall see us light up.'

I watched the test. The men were absolutely sober, so I gave them each a tepid whisky and soda.

'Well *and* good,' said Carnehan of the eyebrows, wiping the froth from his moustache. 'Let *me* talk now, Dan. We have been all over India, mostly on foot. We have been boiler-fitters, engine-drivers, petty contractors, and all that, and we have decided that India isn't big enough for such as us.'

They certainly were too big for the office. Dravot's beard seemed to fill half the room and Carnehan's shoulders the other half, as they sat on the big table. Carnehan continued: 'The country isn't half worked out because they that governs it won't let you touch it. They spend all their blessed time in governing it, and you can't lift a spade, nor chip a rock, nor look for oil, nor anything like that, without all the Government saying, "Leave it alone, and let us govern." Therefore, such *as* it is, we will let it alone, and go away to some other place where a man isn't crowded and can come to his own. We are not little men, and there is nothing that we are afraid of except Drink, and we have signed a Contrack on that. *Therefore*, we are going away to be Kings.'

'Kings in our own right,' muttered Dravot.

'Yes, of course,' I said. 'You've been tramping in the sun, and it's a very warm night, and hadn't you better sleep over the notion? Come tomorrow.'

'Neither drunk nor sunstruck,' said Dravot. 'We have slept over the notion half a year, and require to see Books and

Atlases, and we have decided that there is only one place now in the world that two strong men call Sar-a-*whack*. They call it Kafiristan. By my reckoning it's the top right-hand corner of Afghanistan, not more than three hundred miles from Pesha-wur. They have two-and-thirty heathen idols there, and we'll be the thirty-third and fourth. It's a mountainous country, and the women of those parts are very beautiful.'

'But that is provided against in the Contrack,' said Carne-han. 'Neither Woman nor Liqu-or, Daniel.'

'And that's all we know, except that no one has gone there, and they fight; and in any place where they fight, a man who knows how to drill men can always be a King. We shall go to those parts and say to any King we find – "D'you want to vanquish your foes?" and we will show him how to drill men; for that we know better than anything else. Then we will sub-vert that King and seize his Throne and establish a Dy-nasty.'

'You'll be cut to pieces before you're fifty miles across the Border,' I said. 'You have to travel through Afghanistan to get to that country. It's one mass of mountains and peaks and glaciers, and no Englishman has been through it. The people are utter brutes, and even if you reached them you couldn't do anything.'

'That's more like,' said Carnehan. 'If you could think us a little more mad we would be more pleased. We have come to you to know about this country, to read a book about it, and to be shown maps. We want you to tell us that we are fools and to show us your books.' He turned to the bookcases.

'Are you at all in earnest?' I said.

'A little,' said Dravot sweetly. 'As big a map as you have got, even if it's all blank where Kafiristan is, and any books you've got. We can read, though we aren't very educated.'

I uncased the big thirty-two-miles-to-the-inch map of India, and two smaller Frontier maps, hauled down volume INFKAN of the *Encyclopædia Britannica*, and the men consulted them.

'See here!' said Dravot, his thumb on the map. 'Up to Jagdallak, Peachey and me know the road. We was there with

Roberts' Army. We'll have to turn off to the right at Jagdallak through Laghman territory. Then we get among the hills – fourteen thousand feet – fifteen thousand – it will be cold work there, but it don't look very far on the map.'

I handed him Wood on the *Sources of the Oxus*. Carnehan was deep in the *Encyclopædia*.

'They're a mixed lot,' said Dravot reflectively; 'and it won't help us to know the names of their tribes. The more tribes the more they'll fight, and the better for us. From Jagdallak to Ashang – H'mm!'

'But all the information about the country is as sketchy and inaccurate as can be,' I protested. 'No one knows anything about it really. Here's the file of the *United Services' Institute*. Read what Bellew says.'

'Blow Bellew!' said Carnehan. 'Dan, they're a stinkin' lot of heathens, but this book here says they think they're related to us English.'

I smoked while the men pored over Raverty, Wood, the maps, and the *Encyclopædia*.

'There is no use your waiting,' said Dravot politely. 'It's about four o'clock now. We'll go before six o'clock if you want to sleep, and we won't steal any of the papers. Don't you sit up. We're two harmless lunatics, and if you come tomorrow evening down to the Serai we'll say good-bye to you.'

'You *are* two fools,' I answered. 'You'll be turned back at the Frontier or cut up the minute you set foot in Afghanistan. Do you want any money or a recommendation down-country? I can help you to the chance of work next week.'

'Next week we shall be hard at work ourselves, thank you,' said Dravot. 'It isn't so easy being a King as it looks. When we've got our Kingdom in going order we'll let you know, and you can come up and help us to govern it.'

'Would two lunatics make a Contrack like that?' said Carnehan, with subdued pride, showing me a greasy half-sheet of notepaper on which was written the following. I copied it, then and there, as a curiosity:

This Contract between me and you persuing witnesseth in the name of God – Amen and so forth.

(*One*) *That me and you will settle this matter together; i.e. to be Kings of Kafiristan.*

(*Two*) *That you and me will not, while this matter is being settled, look at any Liquor, nor any Woman black, white, or brown, so as to get mixed up with one or the other harmful.*

(*Three*) *That we conduct ourselves with Dignity and Discretion, and if one of us gets into trouble the other will stay by him.*

Signed by you and me this day.
Peachey Taliaferro Carnehan.
Daniel Dravot.
Both Gentlemen at Large.

'There was no need for the last article,' said Carnehan, blushing modestly; 'but it looks regular. Now you know the sort of men that loafers are – we *are* loafers, Dan, until we get out of India – and *do* you think that we would sign a Contrack like that unless we was in earnest? We have kept away from the two things that make life worth having.'

'You won't enjoy your lives much longer if you are going to try this idiotic adventure. Don't set the office on fire,' I said, 'and go away before nine o'clock.'

I left them still poring over the maps and making notes on the back of the 'Contrack'. 'Be sure to come down to the Serai tomorrow,' were their parting words.

The Kumharsen Serai is the great four-square sink of humanity where the strings of camels and horses from the North load and unload. All the nationalities of Central Asia may be found there, and most of the folk of India proper. Balkh and Bokhara there meet Bengal and Bombay, and try to draw eye-teeth. You can buy ponies, turquoises, Persian pussy-cats, saddle-bags, fat-tailed sheep and musk in the Kumharsen Serai and get many strange things for nothing. In the afternoon I went down to see whether my friends intended to keep their word or were lying there drunk.

A priest attired in fragments of ribbons and rags stalked up to me, gravely twisting a child's paper whirligig. Behind him was his servant bending under the load of a crate of mud toys. The two were loading up two camels, and the inhabitants of the Serai watched them with shrieks of laughter.

'The priest is mad,' said a horse-dealer to me. 'He is going up to Kabul to sell toys to the Amir. He will either be raised to honour or have his head cut off. He came in here this morning and has been behaving madly ever since.'

'The witless are under the protection of God,' stammered a flat-cheeked Uzbeg in broken Hindi. 'They foretell future events.'

'Would they could have foretold that my caravan would have been cut up by the Shinwaris almost within shadow of the Pass!' grunted the Yusufzai agent of a Rajputana trading-house whose goods had been diverted into the hands of other robbers just across the Border, and whose misfortunes were the laughing-stock of the bazaar. 'Ohé, priest, whence come you and whither do you go?'

'From Roum have I come,' shouted the priest, waving his whirligig; 'from Roum, blown by the breath of a hundred devils across the sea! O thieves, robbers, liars, the blessing of Pir Khan on pigs, dogs, and perjurers! Who will take the Protected of God to the North to sell charms that are never still to the Amir? The camels shall not gall, the sons shall not fall sick, and the wives shall remain faithful while they are away, of the men who give me place in their caravan. Who will assist me to slipper the King of the Roos with a golden slipper with a silver heel? The protection of Pir Khan be upon his labours!' He spread out the skirts of his gaberdine and pirouetted between the lines of tethered horses.

'There starts a caravan from Peshawur to Kabul in twenty days, *Huzrut*,' said the Yusufzai trader. 'My camels go therewith. Do thou also go and bring us good luck.'

'I will go even now!' shouted the priest. 'I will depart upon my winged camels, and be at Peshawur in a day! Ho! Hazar Mir Khan,' he yelled to his servant, 'drive out the camels, but let me first mount my own.'

He leaped on the back of his beast as it knelt, and, turning round to me, cried: 'Come thou also, Sahib, a little along the road, and I will sell thee a charm – an amulet that shall make thee King of Kafiristan.'

Then the light broke upon me, and I followed the two camels out of the Serai till we reached open road and the priest halted.

'What d'you think o' that?' said he in English. 'Carnehan can't talk their patter, so I've made him my servant. He makes a handsome servant. 'Tisn't for nothing that I've been knocking about the country for fourteen years. Didn't I do that talk neat? We'll hitch on to a caravan at Peshawur till we get to Jagdallak, and then we'll see if we can get donkeys for our camels, and strike into Kafiristan. Whirligigs for the Amir, oh, Lor! Put your hand under the camel-bags and tell me what you feel.'

I felt the butt of a Martini, and another and another.

'Twenty of 'em,' said Dravot placidly. 'Twenty of 'em and ammunition to correspond, under the whirligigs and the mud dolls.'

'Heaven help you if you are caught with those things!' I said. 'A Martini is worth her weight in silver among the Pathans.'

'Fifteen hundred rupees of capital – every rupee we could beg, borrow, or steal – are invested on these two camels,' said Dravot. 'We won't get caught. We're going through the Khyber with a regular caravan. Who'd touch a poor mad priest?'

'Have you got everything you want?' I asked, overcome with astonishment.

'Not yet, but we shall soon. Give us a memento of your kindness, *Brother*. You did me a service, yesterday, and that time in Marwar. Half my Kingdom shall you have, as the saying is.' I slipped a small charm compass from my watchchain and handed it up to the priest.

'Good-bye,' said Dravot, giving me hand cautiously. 'It's the last time we'll shake hands with an Englishman these many days. Shake hands with him, Carnehan,' he cried, as the second camel passed me.

Carnehan leaned down and shook hands. Then the camels passed away along the dusty road, and I was left alone to wonder. My eye could detect no failure in the disguises. The scene in the Serai proved that they were complete to the native mind. There was just the chance, therefore, that Carnehan and Dravot would be able to wander through Afghanistan without detection. But, beyond, they would find death – certain and awful death.

Ten days later a native correspondent, giving me the news of the day from Peshawur, wound up his letter with: 'There has been much laughter here on account of a certain mad priest who is going in his estimation to sell petty gauds and insignificant trinkets which he ascribes as great charms to H.H. the Amir of Bokhara. He passed through Peshawur and associated himself to the Second Summer caravan that goes to Kabul. The merchants are pleased because through superstition they imagine that such mad fellows bring good fortune.'

The two, then, were beyond the Border. I would have prayed for them, but, that night, a real King died in Europe, and demanded an obituary notice.

The wheel of the world swings through the same phases again and again. Summer passed and winter thereafter, and came and passed again. The daily paper continued and I with it, and upon the third summer there fell a hot night, a night-issue, and a strained waiting for something to be telegraphed from the other side of the world, exactly as had happened before. A few great men had died in the past two years, the machines worked with more clatter, and some of the trees in the office garden were a few feet taller. But that was all the difference.

I passed over to the press-room, and went through just such a scene as I have already described. The nervous tension was stronger than it had been two years before, and I felt the heat more acutely. At three o'clock I cried, 'Print off,' and turned to go, when there crept to my chair what was left of a man. He was bent into a circle, his head was sunk between his shoulders, and he moved his feet one over the other like a bear. I could hardly see whether he walked or crawled – this rag-wrapped, whining cripple who addressed me by name, crying that he was come back. 'Can you give me a drink?' he whimpered. 'For the Lord's sake, give me a drink!'

I went back to the office, the man following with groans of pain, and I turned up the lamp.

'Don't you know me?' he gasped, dropping into a chair, and he turned his drawn face, surmounted by a shock of grey hair, to the light.

I looked at him intently. Once before had I seen eyebrows that met over the nose in an inch-broad black band, but for the life of me I could not recall where.

'I don't know you,' I said, handing him the whisky. 'What can I do for you?'

He took a gulp of the spirit raw, and shivered in spite of the suffocating heat.

'I've come back,' he repeated; 'and I was the King of Kafiristan – me and Dravot – crowned Kings we was! In this office we settled it – you setting there and giving us the books. I am Peachey – Peachey Taliaferro Carnehan, and you've been setting here ever since – oh, Lord!'

I was more than a little astonished, and expressed my feelings accordingly.

'It's true,' said Carnehan, with a dry cackle, nursing his feet, which were wrapped in rags. 'True as gospel. Kings we were, with crowns upon our heads – me and Dravot – poor Dan – oh, poor, poor Dan, that would never take advice, not though I begged of him!'

'Take the whisky,' I said, 'and take your own time. Tell me all you can recollect of everything from beginning to end. You got across the Border on your camels, Dravot dressed as a mad priest and you his servant. Do you remember that?'

'I ain't mad – yet, but I shall be that way soon. Of course I remember. Keep looking at me, or maybe my words will go all to pieces. Keep looking at me in my eyes and don't say anything.'

I leaned forward and looked into his face as steadily as I

could. He dropped one hand upon the table and I grasped it by the wrist. It was twisted like a bird's claw, and upon the back was a ragged red diamond-shaped scar.

'No, don't look there. Look at *me*,' said Carnehan. 'That comes afterwards, but for the Lord's sake don't distrack me. We left with that caravan, me and Dravot playing all sorts of antics to amuse the people we were with. Dravot used to make us laugh in the evenings when all the people was cooking their dinners – cooking their dinners, and ... what did they do then? They lit little fires with sparks that went into Dravot's beard, and we all laughed – fit to die. Little red fires they was, going into Dravot's big red beard – so funny.' His eyes left mine and he smiled foolishly.

'You went as far as Jagdallak with that caravan,' I said at a venture, 'after you had lit those fires. To Jagdallak where you turned off to try to get into Kafiristan.'

'No, we didn't neither. What are you talking about? We turned off before Jagdallak, because we heard the roads was good. But they wasn't good enough for our two camels – mine and Dravot's. When we left the caravan, Dravot took off all his clothes and mine too, and said we would be heathen, because the Kafirs didn't allow Mohammedans to talk to them. So we dressed betwixt and between, and such a sight as Daniel Dravot I never saw yet nor expect to see again. He burned half his beard, and slung a sheep-skin over his shoulder, and shaved his head into patterns. He shaved mine too, and made me wear outrageous things to look like a heathen. That was in a most mountainous country, and our camels couldn't go along any more because of the mountains. They were tall and black, and coming home I saw them fight like wild goats – there are lots of goats in Kafiristan. And these mountains, they never keep still, no more than the goats. Always fighting they are, and don't let you sleep at night.'

'Take some more whisky,' I said very slowly. 'What did you and Daniel Dravot do when the camels could go no farther because of the rough roads that led into Kafiristan?'

'What did which do? There was a party called Peachey

Taliaferro Carnehan that was with Dravot. Shall I tell you about him? He died out there in the cold. Slap from the bridge fell old Peachey, turning and twisting in the air like a penny whirligig that you can sell to the Amir. — No; they was two for three-ha'pence, those whirligigs, or I am much mistaken and woeful sore ... And then these camels were no use, and Peachey said to Dravot — "For the Lord's sake let's get out of this before our heads are chopped off," and with that they killed the camels all among the mountains, not having anything in particular to eat, but first they took off the boxes with the guns and ammunition, till two men came along driving four mules. Dravot up and dances in front of them, singing: "Sell me four mules." Says the first man: "If you are rich enough to buy, you are rich enough to rob"; but before ever he could put his hand to his knife, Dravot breaks his neck over his knee, and the other party runs away. So Carnehan loaded the mules with the rifles that was taken off the camels, and together we starts forward into those bitter cold mountaineous parts, and never a road broader than the back of your hand.'

He paused for a moment, while I asked him if he could remember the nature of the country through which he had journeyed.

'I am telling you as straight as I can, but my head isn't as good as it might be. They drove nails through it to make me hear better how Dravot died. The country was mountaineous, and the mules were most contrary, and the inhabitants was dispersed and solitary. They went up and up, and down and down, and that other party, Carnehan, was imploring of Dravot not to sing and whistle so loud, for fear of bringing down the tremenjus avalanches. But Dravot says that if a King couldn't sing it wasn't worth being King, and whacked the mules over the rump, and never took no heed for ten cold days. We came to a big level valley all among the mountains, and the mules were near dead, so we killed them, not having anything in special for them or us to eat. We sat upon the boxes, and played odd and even with the cartridges that was jolted out.

'Then ten men with bows and arrows ran down that valley,

chasing twenty men with bows and arrows, and the row was tremenjus. They was fair men – fairer than you or me – with yellow hair and remarkable well built. Says Dravot, unpacking the guns: "This is the beginning of the business. We'll fight for the ten men," and with that he fires two rifles at the twenty men, and drops one of them at two hundred yards from the rock where he was sitting. The other men began to run, but Carnehan and Dravot sits on the boxes picking them off at all ranges, up and down the valley. Then we goes up to the ten men that had run across the snow too, and they fires a footy little arrow at us. Dravot he shoots above their heads and they all falls down flat. Then he walks over them and kicks them, and then he lifts them up and shakes hands all round to make them friendly like. He calls them and gives them the boxes to carry, and waves his hand for all the world as though he was King already. They takes the boxes and him across the valley and up the hill into a pine wood on the top, where there was half-a-dozen big stone idols. Dravot he goes to the biggest – a fellow they call Imbra – and lays a rifle and a cartridge at his feet, rubbing his nose respectful with his own nose, patting him on the head, and saluting in front of it. He turns round to the men and nods his head and says: "That's all right. I'm in the know too, and all these old jim-jams are my friends." Then he opens his mouth and points down it, and when the first man brings him food, he says: "No"; and when the second man brings him food, he says: "No"; but when one of the old priests and the boss of the village brings him food, he says: "Yes," very haughty, and eats it slow. That was how we came to our first village, without any trouble, just as though we had tumbled from the skies. But we tumbled from one of those damned rope-bridges, you see, and – you couldn't expect a man to laugh much after that?'

'Take some more whisky and go on,' I said. 'That was the first village you came into. How did you get to be King?'

'I wasn't King,' said Carnehan. 'Dravot he was the King, and a handsome man he looked with the gold crown on his head and all. Him and the other party stayed in that village, and every morning Dravot sat by the side of old Imbra, and the people came and worshipped. That was Dravot's order. Then a lot of men came into the valley, and Carnehan and Dravot picks them off with the rifles before they knew where they was and runs down into the valley and up again the other side and finds another village, same as the first one, and the people all falls down flat on their faces, and Dravot says: "Now what is the trouble between you two villages?" and the people points to a woman, as fair as you or me, that was carried off, and Dravot takes her back to the first village and counts up the dead – eight there was. For each dead man Dravot pours a little milk on the ground and waves his arms like a whirligig, and "That's all right," says he. Then he and Carnehan takes the big boss of each valley by the arm and walks them down into the valley, and shows them how to scratch a line with a spear right down the valley, and gives each a sod of turf from both sides of the line. Then all the people comes down and shouts like the devil and all, and Dravot says: "Go and dig the land, and be fruitful and multiply," which they did, though they didn't understand. Then we asks the names of things in their lingo – bread and water and fire and idols and such, and Dravot leads the priest of each village up to the idol, and says he must sit there and judge the people, and if anything goes wrong he is to be shot.

'Next week they was all turning up the land in the valley as quiet as bees and much prettier, and the priests heard all the complaints and told Dravot in dumb show what it was about. "That's just the beginning," says Dravot. "They think we're Gods." He and Carnehan picks out twenty good men and shows them how to click off a rifle, and form fours, and advance in line, and they was very pleased to do so, and clever to see the hang of it. Then he takes out his pipe and his baccy-pouch and leaves one at one village, and one at the other, and off we two goes to see what was to be done in the next valley. That was all rock, and there was a little village there, and Carnehan says: "Send 'em to the old valley to plant," and takes 'em there, and gives 'em some land that wasn't took before. They were a poor lot, and we blooded 'em with a kid before letting 'em into the new Kingdom. That was to impress the people, and then they settled down quiet, and Carnehan went back to Dravot, who had got into another valley, all snow and ice and most mountaineous. There was no people there and the Army got afraid, so Dravot shoots one of them, and goes on till he finds some people in a village, and the Army explains that unless the people wants to be killed they had better not shoot their little matchlocks; for they had matchlocks. We makes friends with the priest, and I stays there alone with two of the Army, teaching the men how to drill, and a thundering big Chief comes across the snow with kettle-drums and horns twanging, because he heard there was a new God kicking about. Carnehan sights for the brown of the men half a mile across the snow and wings one of them. Then he sends a message to the Chief that, unless he wished to be killed, he must come and shake hands with me and leave his arms behind. The Chief comes alone first, and Carnehan shakes hands with him and whirls his arms about, same as Dravot used, and very much surprised that Chief was, and strokes my eyebrows. Then Carnehan goes alone to the Chief, and asks him in dumb show if he had an enemy he hated. "I have," says the Chief. So Carnehan weeds out the pick of his men, and sets the two of the Army to show them drill, and at the end of two weeks the men can manœuvre about as well as Volunteers. So he marches with the Chief to a great big plain on the top of a mountain, and the Chief's men rushes into a village and takes it; we three Martinis firing into the brown of the enemy. So we took that village too, and I gives the Chief a rag from my coat and says, "Occupy till I come"; which was scriptural. By way of a reminder, when me and the Army was eighteen hundred yards away, I drops a bullet near him standing on the snow, and all the people falls flat on their faces. Then I sends a letter to Dravot wherever he be by land or by sea.'

At the risk of throwing the creature out of train I interrupted: 'How could you write a letter up yonder?'

'The letter? – Oh! – The letter! Keep looking at me

between the eyes, please. It was a string-talk letter, that we'd learned the way of it from a blind beggar in the Punjab.'

I remembered that there had once come to the office a blind man with a knotted twig and a piece of string which he wound round the twig according to some cipher of his own. He could, after the lapse of days or weeks, repeat the sentence which he had reeled up. He had reduced the alphabet to eleven primitive sounds, and tried to teach me his method, but I could not understand.

'I sent that letter to Dravot,' said Carnehan; 'and told him to come back because this Kingdom was growing too big for me to handle, and then I struck for the first valley, to see how the priests were working. They called the village we took along with the Chief, Bashkai, and the first village we took, Er-Heb. The priests at Er-Heb was doing all right, but they had a lot of pending cases about land to show me, and some men from another village had been firing arrows at night. I went out and looked for that village, and fired four rounds at it from a thousand yards. That used all the cartridges I cared to spend, and I waited for Dravot, who had been away two or three months, and I kept my people quiet.

'One morning I heard the devil's own noise of drums and horns, and Dan Dravot marches down the hill with his Army and a tail of hundreds of men, and, which was the most amazing, a great gold crown on his head. "My Gord, Carnehan," says Daniel, "this is a tremenjus business, and we've got the whole country as far as it's worth having. I am the son of Alexander by Queen Semiramis, and you're my younger brother and a God too! It's the biggest thing we've ever seen. I've been marching and fighting for six weeks with the Army, and every footy little village for fifty miles has come in rejoiceful; and more than that, I've got the key of the whole show, as you'll see, and I've got a crown for you! I told 'em to make two of 'em at a place called Shu, where the gold lies in the rock like suet in mutton. Gold I've seen, and turquoise I've kicked out of the cliffs, and there's garnets in the sands of the river, and here's a chunk of amber that a man brought me. Call up all the priests and, here, take your crown."

'One of the men opens a black hair bag, and I slips the crown on. It was too small and too heavy, but I wore it for the glory. Hammered gold it was – five pound weight, like a hoop of a barrel.

' "Peachey," says Dravot, "we don't want to fight no more. The Craft's the trick, so help me!" and he brings forward that same Chief that I left at Bashkai – Billy Fish we called him afterwards, because he was so like Billy Fish that drove the big tank-engine at Mach on the Bolan in the old days. "Shake hands with him," says Dravot, and I shook hands and nearly dropped, for Billy Fish gave me the Grip. I said nothing, but tried him with the Fellow Craft Grip. He answers all right, and I tried the Master's Grip, but that was a slip. "A Fellow Craft he is!" I says to Dan. "Does he know the Word?" – "He does," says Dan, "and all the priests know. It's a miracle! The Chiefs and the priests can work a Fellow Craft Lodge in a way that's very like ours, and they've cut the marks on the rocks, but they don't know the Third Degree, and they've come to find out. It's Gord's Truth! I've known these long years that the Afghans knew up to the Fellow Craft Degree, but this is a miracle. A God and a Grand-Master of the Craft am I, and a Lodge in the Third Degree I will open, and we'll raise the head priests and the Chiefs of the villages."

' "It's against all the law," I says, "holding a Lodge without warrant from any one; and you know we never held office in any Lodge."

' "It's a master-stroke o' policy," says Dravot. "It means running the country as easy as a four-wheeled bogie on a down grade. We can't stop to inquire now, or they'll turn against us. I've forty Chiefs at my heel, and passed and raised according to their merit they shall be. Billet these men on the villages, and see that we run up a Lodge of some kind. The temple of Imbra will do for the Lodge-room. The women must make aprons as you show them. I'll hold a levee of Chiefs tonight and Lodge tomorrow."

'I was fair run off my legs, but I wasn't such a fool as not to see what a pull this Craft business gave us. I showed the priests' families how to make aprons of the degrees, but for Dravot's apron the blue border and marks was made of turquoise lumps on white hide, not cloth. We took a great square stone in the temple for the Master's chair, and little stones for the officers' chairs, and painted the black pavement with white squares, and did what we could to make things regular.

'At the levee which was held that night on the hillside with big bonfires, Dravot gives out that him and me were Gods and sons of Alexander, and Past Grand-Masters in the Craft, and was come to make Kafiristan a country where every man should eat in peace and drink in quiet, and 'specially obey us. Then the Chiefs come round to shake hands, and they were so hairy and white and fair it was just shaking hands with old friends. We gave them names according as they was like men we had known in India – Billy Fish, Holly Dilworth, Pikky Kergan, that was Bazaar-master when I was at Mhow, and so on, and so on.

'*The* most amazing miracles was at Lodge next night. One of the old priests was watching us continuous, and I felt uneasy, for I knew we'd have to fudge the Ritual, and I didn't know what the men knew. The old priest was a stranger come in from beyond the village of Bashkai. The minute Dravot puts on the Master's apron that the girls had made for him, the priest fetches a whoop and a howl, and tries to overturn the stone that Dravot was sitting on. "It's all up now," I says. "That comes of meddling with the Craft without warrant!" Dravot never winked an eye, not when ten priests took and tilted over the Grand-Master's chair – which was to say the stone of Imbra. The priest begins rubbing the bottom end of it to clear away the black dirt, and presently he shows all the other priests the Master's Mark, same as was on Dravot's apron, cut into the stone. Not even the priests of the temple of Imbra knew it was there. The old chap falls flat on his face at Dravot's feet and kisses 'em. "Luck again," says Dravot, across the Lodge to me; "they say it's the missing Mark that no one could understand the why of. We're more than safe now." Then he bangs the butt of his gun for a gavel and says: "By virtue of the authority vested in me by my own right hand and the help of Peachey, I declare myself Grand-Master of all Freemasonry in Kafiristan in this the Mother Lodge o' the country, and King of Kafiristan equally with Peachey!" At that he puts on his crown and I puts on mine – I was doing Senior Warden – and we opens the Lodge in most ample form. It was a amazing miracle! The priests moved in Lodge through the first two degrees almost without telling, as if the memory was coming back to them. After that, Peachey and Dravot raised such as was worthy – high priests and Chiefs of far-off villages. Billy Fish was the first, and I can tell you we scared the soul out of him. It was not in any way according to Ritual, but it served our turn. We didn't raise more than ten of the biggest men, because we didn't want to make the Degree common. And they was clamouring to be raised.

' "In another six months," says Dravot, "we'll hold another Communication, and see how you are working." Then he asks them about their villages, and learns that they was fighting one against the other, and was sick and tired of it. And when they wasn't doing that they was fighting with the Mohammedans. "You can fight those when they come into our country," says Dravot. "Tell off every tenth man of your tribes for a Frontier guard, and send two hundred at a time to this valley to be drilled. Nobody is going to be shot or speared any more so long as he does well, and I know that you won't cheat me, because you're white people – sons of Alexander – and not like common, black Mohammedans. You are *my* people, and by God," says he, running off into English at the end, "I'll make a damned fine Nation of you, or I'll die in the making!"

'I can't tell all we did for the next six months, because Dravot did a lot I couldn't see the hang of, and he learned their lingo in a way I never could. My work was to help the people plough, and now and again go out with some of the Army and see what the other villages were doing, and make 'em throw rope-bridges across the ravines which cut up the country hor-

rid. Dravot was very kind to me, but when he walked up and
down in the pine-wood pulling that bloody red beard of his
with both fists I knew he was thinking plans I could not advise
about, and I just waited for orders.

'But Dravot never showed me disrespect before the people.
They were afraid of me and the Army, but they loved Dan. He
was the best of friends with the priests and the Chiefs; but any
one could come across the hills with a complaint, and Dravot
would hear him out fair, and call four priests together and say
what was to be done. He used to call in Billy Fish from Bashkai,
and Pikky Kergan from Shu, and an old Chief we called Kaf-
oozelum – it was like enough to his real name – and hold coun-
cils with 'em when there was any fighting to be done in small
villages. That was his Council of War, and the four priests of
Bashkai, Shu, Khawak, and Madora was his Privy Council. Between the lot of 'em they sent me, with forty men and twenty
rifles and sixty men carrying turquoises, into the Ghorband
country to buy those hand-made Martini rifles, that come out of
the Amir's workshops at Kabul, from one of the Amir's Herati
regiments that would have sold the very teeth out of their
mouths for turquoises.

'I stayed in Ghorband a month, and gave the Governor
there the pick of my baskets for hush-money, and bribed the
Colonel of the regiment some more, and, between the two and
the tribespeople, we got more than a hundred hand-made Martinis, a hundred good Kohat *jezails* that'll throw to six hundred
yards, and forty man-loads of very bad ammunition for the
rifles. I came back with what I had, and distributed 'em among
the men that the Chiefs sent in to me to drill. Dravot was too
busy to attend to those things, but the old Army that we first
made helped me, and we turned out five hundred men that
could drill, and two hundred that knew how to hold arms pretty
straight. Even those corkscrewed, hand-made guns was a
miracle to them. Dravot talked big about powder-shops and
factories, walking up and down in the pine-wood when the
winter was coming on.

' "I won't make a Nation," says he. "I'll make an Empire!

These men aren't niggers; they're English! Look at their eyes – look at their mouths. Look at the way they stand up. They sit on chairs in their own houses. They're the Lost Tribes, or something like it, and they've grown to be English. I'll take a census in the spring if the priests don't get frightened. There must be a fair two million of 'em in these hills. The villages are full o' little children. Two million people – two hundred and fifty thousand fighting men – and all English! They only want the rifles and a little drilling. Two hundred and fifty thousand men, ready to cut in on Russia's right flank when she tries for India! Peachey, man," he says, chewing his beard in great hunks, "we shall be Emperors – Emperors of the Earth! Rajah Brooke will be a suckling to us. I'll treat with the Viceroy on equal terms. I'll ask him to send me twelve picked English – twelve that I know of – to help us govern a bit. There's Mackray, Sergeant-pensioner at Segowli – many's the good dinner he's given me, and his wife a pair of trousers. There's Donkin, the Warder of Tounghoo Jail. There's hundreds that I could lay my hand on if I was in India. The Viceroy shall do it for me. I'll send a man through in the spring for those men, and I'll write for a Dispensation from the Grand Lodge for what I've done as Grand-Master. That – and all the Sniders that'll be thrown out when the native troops in India take up the Martini. They'll be worn smooth, but they'll do for fighting in these hills. Twelve English, a hundred thousand Sniders run through the Amir's country in driblets – I'd be content with twenty thousand in one year – and we'd be an Empire. When everything was ship-shape, I'd hand over the crown – this crown I'm wearing now – to Queen Victoria on my knees, and she'd say: 'Rise up, Sir Daniel Dravot.' Oh, it's big! It's big, I tell you! But there's so much to be done in every place – Bashkai, Khawak, Shu, and everywhere else."

' "What is it?" I says. "There are no more men coming in to be drilled this autumn. Look at those fat, black clouds. They're bringing the snow."

' "It isn't that," says Daniel, putting his hand very hard on my shoulder; "and I don't wish to say anything that's against you, for no other living man would have followed me and made me what I am as you have done. You're a first-class Commander-in-Chief, and the people know you; but – it's a big country, and somehow you can't help me, Peachey, in the way I want to be helped."

' " Go to your blasted priests, then!" I said, and I was sorry when I made that remark, but it did hurt me sore to find Daniel talking so superior, when I'd drilled all the men, and done all he told me.

' "Don't let's quarrel, Peachey," says Daniel without cursing. "You're a King too, and the half of this Kingdom is yours; but can't you see, Peachey, we want cleverer men than us now – three or four of 'em, that we can scatter about for our Deputies. It's a hugeous great State, and I can't always tell the right thing to do, and I haven't time for all I want to do, and here's winter coming on and all." He stuffed half his beard into his mouth, all red like the gold of his crown.

' "I'm sorry, Daniel," says I. "I've done all I could. I've drilled the men and shown the people how to stack their oats better; and I've brought in those tinware rifles from Ghorband – but I know what you're driving at. I take it Kings always feel oppressed that way."

' "There's another thing too," says Dravot, walking up and down. "The winter's coming and these people won't be giving much trouble, and if they do we can't move about. I want a wife."

' "For God's sake, leave the women alone!" I says. "We've both got all the work we can, though I *am* a fool. Remember the Contrack, and keep clear o' women."

' "The Contrack only lasted till such time as we was Kings; and Kings we have been these months past," says Dravot, weighing his crown in his hand. "You go get a wife, too, Peachey – a nice, strappin', plump girl that'll keep you warm in the winter. They're prettier than English girls, and we can take the pick of 'em. Boil 'em once or twice in hot water and they'll come out like chicken and ham."

' "Don't tempt me!" I says. "I will not have any dealings

with a woman not till we are a dam' sight more settled than we are now. I've been doing the work o' two men, and you've been doing the work o' three. Let's lie off a bit, and see if we can get some better tobacco from Afghan country and run in some good liquor; but no women."

' "Who's talking o' *women?*" says Dravot. "I said *wife* – a Queen to breed a King's son for the King. A Queen out of the strongest tribe, that'll make them your blood-brothers, and that'll lie by your side and tell you all the people thinks about you and their own affairs. That's what I want."

' "Do you remember that Bengali woman I kept at Mogul Serai when I was a platelayer?" says I. "A fat lot o' good she was to me. She taught me the lingo and one or two other things; but what happened? She ran away with the Station-master's servant and half my month's pay. Then she turned up at Dadur Junction in tow of a half-caste, and had the impidence to say I was her husband – all among the drivers in the running-shed too!"

' "We've done with that," says Dravot; "these women are whiter than you or me, and a Queen I will have for the winter months."

' "For the last time o' asking, Dan, do *not*," I says. "It'll only bring us harm. The Bible says that Kings ain't to waste their strength on women, 'specially when they've got a raw new Kingdom to work over."

' "For the last time of answering, I will," said Dravot, and he went away through the pine-trees looking like a big red devil, the sun being on his crown and beard and all.

'But getting a wife was not as easy as Dan thought. He put it before the Council, and there was no answer till Billy Fish said that he'd better ask the girls. Dravot damned them all round. "What's wrong with me?" he shouts, standing by the idol Imbra. "Am I a dog or am I not enough of a man for your wenches? Haven't I put the shadow of my hand over this country? Who stopped the last Afghan raid?" It was me really, but Dravot was too angry to remember. "Who bought your guns? Who repaired the bridges? Who's the Grand-Master of the Sign cut in the stone?" says he, and he thumped his hand on the block that he used to sit on in Lodge, and at Council, which opened like Lodge always. Billy Fish said nothing and no more did the others. "Keep your hair on, Dan," said I; "and ask the girls. That's how it's done at Home, and these people are quite English."

' "The marriage of the King is a matter of State," says Dan, in a red-hot rage, for he could feel, I hope, that he was going against his better mind. He walked out of the Council-room, and the others sat still, looking at the ground.

' "Billy Fish," says I to the Chief of Bashkai, "what's the difficulty here? A straight answer to a true friend."

' "You know," says Billy Fish. "How should a man tell you who knows everything? How can daughters of men marry Gods or Devils? It's not proper."

'I remembered something like that in the Bible; but if, after seeing us as long as they had, they still believed we were Gods, 'twasn't for me to undeceive them.

' "A God can do anything," says I. "If the King is fond of a girl he'll not let her die." – "She'll have to," says Billy Fish. "There are all sorts of Gods and Devils in these mountains, and now and again a girl marries one of them and isn't seen any more. Besides, you two know the Mark cut in the stone. Only the Gods know that. We thought you were men till you showed the Sign of the Master."

'I wished then that we had explained about the loss of the genuine secrets of a Master-Mason at the first go-off; but I said nothing. All that night there was a blowing of horns in a little dark temple half-way down the hill, and I heard a girl crying fit to die. One of the priests told us that she was being prepared to marry the King.

' "I'll have no nonsense of that kind," says Dan. "I don't want to interfere with your customs, but I'll take my own wife." – "The girl's a little bit afraid," says the priest. "She thinks she's going to die, and they are a-heartening of her up down in the temple."

' "Hearten her very tender, then," says Dravot, "or I'll

hearten you with the butt of a gun so you'll never want to be heartened again." He licked his lips, did Dan, and stayed up walking about more than half the night, thinking of the wife that he was going to get in the morning. I wasn't any means comfortable, for I knew that dealings with a woman in foreign parts, though you was a crowned King twenty times over, could not but be risky. I got up very early in the morning while Dravot was asleep, and I saw the priests talking together in whispers, and the Chiefs talking together too, and they looked at me out of the corners of their eyes.

' "What is up, Fish?" I says to the Bashkai man, who was wrapped up in his furs and looking splendid to behold.

' "I can't rightly say," says he; "but if you can make the King drop all this nonsense about marriage, you'll be doing him and me and yourself a great service."

' "That I do believe," says I. "But sure, you know, Billy, as well as me, having fought against and for us, that the King and me are nothing more than two of the finest men that God Almighty ever made. Nothing more, I do assure you."

' "That may be," says Billy Fish, "and yet I should be sorry if it was." He sinks his head upon his great fur cloak for a minute and thinks. "King," says he, "be you man or God or Devil, I'll stick by you today. I have twenty of my men with me, and they will follow me. We'll go to Bashkai until the storm blows over."

'A little snow had fallen in the night, and everything was white except them greasy fat clouds that blew down and down from the north. Dravot came out with his crown on his head, swinging his arms and stamping his feet, and looking more pleased than Punch.

' "For the last time, drop it, Dan," says I in a whisper. "Billy Fish here says that there will be a row."

' "A row among my people!" says Dravot. "Not much. Peachey, you're a fool not to get a wife too. Where's the girl?" says he with a voice as loud as the braying of a jackass. "Call up all the Chiefs and priests, and let the Emperor see if his wife suits him."

'There was no need to call any one. They were all there leaning on their guns and spears round the clearing in the centre of the pine-wood. A lot of priests went down to the little temple to bring up the girl, and the horns blew fit to wake the dead. Billy Fish saunters round and gets as close to Daniel as he could, and behind him stood his twenty men with matchlocks. Not a man of them under six feet. I was next to Dravot, and behind me was twenty men of the regular Army. Up comes the girl, and a strapping wench she was, covered with silver and turquoises, but white as death, and looking back every minute at the priests.

' "She'll do," said Dan, looking her over. "What's to be afraid of, lass? Come and kiss me." He puts his arm round her. She shuts her eyes, gives a bit of a squeak, and down goes her face in the side of Dan's flaming red beard.

' "The slut's bitten me!" says he, clapping his hand to his neck, and, sure enough, his hand was red with blood. Billy Fish and two of his matchlock-men catches hold of Dan by the shoulders and drags him into the Bashkai lot, while the priests howl in their lingo: "Neither God nor Devil but a man!" I was all taken aback, for a priest cut at me in front, and the Army behind began firing into the Bashkai men.

' "God A'mighty!" says Dan. "What is the meaning o' this?"

' "Come back! Come away!" says Billy Fish. "Ruin and Mutiny's the matter. We'll break for Bashkai if we can."

'I tried to give some sort of orders to my men – the men o' the regular Army – but it was no use, so I fired into the brown of 'em with an English Martini and drilled three beggars in a line. The valley was full of shouting, howling people, and every soul was shrieking, "Not a God nor a Devil but only a man!" The Bashkai troops stuck to Billy Fish all they were worth, but their matchlocks wasn't half as good as the Kabul breech-loaders, and four of them dropped. Dan was bellowing like a bull, for he was very wrathy; and Billy Fish had a hard job to prevent him running out at the crowd.

' "We can't stand," says Billy Fish. "Make a run for it down the valley! The whole place is against us." The matchlock-men ran, and we went down the valley in spite of Dravot. He was swearing horrible and crying out he was a King. The priests rolled great stones on us, and the regular Army fired hard, and there wasn't more than six men, not counting Dan, Billy Fish, and me, that came down to the bottom of the valley alive.

'Then they stopped firing and the horns in the temple blew again. "Come away – for God's sake come away!" says Billy Fish. "They'll send runners out to all the villages before ever we get to Bashkai. I can protect you there, but I can't do any-thing now."

'My own notion is that Dan began to go mad in his head from that hour. He stared up and down like a stuck pig. Then he was all for walking back alone and killing the priests with his bare hands; which he could have done. "An Emperor am I," says Daniel, "and next year I shall be a Knight of the Queen."

' "All right, Dan," says I; "but come along now while there's time."

' "It's your fault," says he, "for not looking after your Army better. There was mutiny in the midst, and you didn't know – you damned engine-driving, plate-laying, missionary's-pass-hunting hound!" He sat upon a rock and called me every name he could lay tongue to. I was too heart-sick to care, though it was all his foolishness that brought the smash.

' "I'm sorry, Dan," says I, "but there's no accounting for natives. This business is our 'Fifty-Seven. Maybe we'll make something out of it yet, when we've got to Bashkai."

' "Let's get to Bashkai, then," says Dan, "and, by God, when I come back here again I'll sweep the valley so there isn't a bug in a blanket left!"

'We walked all that day, and all that night Dan was stumping up and down on the snow, chewing his beard and muttering to himself.

' "There's no hope o' getting clear," said Billy Fish. "The priests will have sent runners to the villages to say that you are only men. Why didn't you stick on as Gods till things was more settled? I'm a dead man," says Billy Fish, and he throws himself down on the snow and begins to pray to his Gods.

'Next morning we was in a cruel bad country – all up and down, no level ground at all, and no food either. The six Bashkai men looked at Billy Fish hungry-ways as if they wanted to ask something, but they said never a word. At noon we came to the top of a flat mountain all covered with snow, and when we climbed up into it, behold, there was an Army in position waiting in the middle!

' "The runners have been very quick," says Billy Fish, with a little bit of a laugh. "They are waiting for us."

'Three or four men began to fire from the enemy's side, and a chance shot took Daniel in the calf of the leg. That brought him to his senses. He looks across the snow at the Army, and sees the rifles that we had brought into the country.

' "We're done for," says he. "They are Englishmen, these people – and it's my blasted nonsense that has brought you to this. Get back, Billy Fish, and take your men away. You've done what you could, and now cut for it. Carnehan," says he, "shake hands with me and go along with Billy. Maybe they won't kill you. I'll go and meet 'em alone. It's me that did it. Me, the King!"

' "Go!" says I. "Go to Hell, Dan! I'm with you here. Billy Fish, you clear out, and we two will meet those folk."

' "I'm a Chief," says Billy Fish, quite quiet. "I stay with you. My men can go."

'The Bashkai fellows didn't wait for a second word, but ran off, and Dan and me and Billy Fish walked across to where the drums were drumming and the horns were horning. It was cold – awful cold. I've got that cold in the back of my head now. There's a lump of it there.'

The punkah-coolies had gone to sleep. Two kerosene lamps were blazing in the office, and the perspiration poured down my face and splashed on the blotter as I leaned forward. Carnehan was shivering, and I feared that his mind might go. I wiped my face, took a fresh grip of the piteously mangled hands, and said: 'What happened after that?'

The momentary shift of my eyes had broken the clear current.

'What was you pleased to say?' whined Carnehan. 'They took them without any sound. Not a little whisper all along the snow, not though the King knocked down the first man that set hand on him – not though old Peachey fired his last cartridge into the brown of 'em. Not a single solitary sound did those swines make. They just closed up tight, and I tell you their furs stunk. There was a man called Billy Fish, a good friend of us all, and they cut his throat, sir, then and there, like a pig; and the King kicks up the bloody snow and says: "We've had a dashed fine run for our money. What's coming next?" But Peachey, Peachey Taliaferro, I tell you, sir, in confidence as betwixt two friends, he lost his head, sir. No, he didn't neither. The King lost his head, so he did, all along o' one of those cunning rope-bridges. Kindly let me have the paper-cutter, sir. It tilted this way. They marched him a mile across that snow to a rope-bridge over a ravine with a river at the bottom. You may have seen such. They prodded him behind like an ox. "Damn your eyes!" says the King. "D'you suppose I can't die like a gentleman?" He turns to Peachey – Peachey that was crying like a child. "I've brought you to this, Peachey," says he. "Brought you out of your happy life to be killed in Kafiristan, where you was late Commander-in-Chief of the Emperor's forces. Say you forgive me, Peachey." – "I do," says Peachey. "Fully and freely do I forgive you, Dan." – "Shake hands, Peachey," says he. "I'm going now." Out he goes, looking neither right nor left, and when he was plumb in the middle of those dizzy dancing ropes – "Cut, you beggars," he shouts; and they cut, and old Dan fell, turning round and round and round, twenty thousand miles, for he took half an hour to fall till he struck the water, and I could see his body caught on a rock with the gold crown close beside.

'But do you know what they did to Peachey between two pine-trees? They crucified him, sir, as Peachey's hands will show. They used wooden pegs for his hands and his feet; and he didn't die. He hung there and screamed, and they took him down next day, and said it was a miracle that he wasn't dead. They took him down – poor old Peachey that hadn't done them any harm – that hadn't done them any—'

He rocked to and fro and wept bitterly, wiping his eyes with the back of his scarred hands and moaning like a child for some ten minutes.

'They was cruel enough to feed him up in the temple, because they said he was more of a God than old Daniel that was a man. Then they turned him out on the snow, and told him to go home, and Peachey came home in about a year, begging along the roads quite safe; for Daniel Dravot he walked before and said: "Come along, Peachey. It's a big thing we're doing." The mountains they danced at night, and the mountains they tried to fall on Peachey's head, but Dan he held up his hand, and Peachey came along bent double. He never let go of Dan's hand, and he never let go of Dan's head. They gave it to him as a present in the temple, to remind him not to come again, and though the crown was pure gold, and Peachey was starving, never would Peachey sell the same. You knew Dravot, sir! You knew Right Worshipful Brother Dravot! Look at him now!'

He fumbled in the mass of rags round his bent waist; brought out a black horsehair bag embroidered with silver thread, and shook therefrom on to my table – the dried, withered head of Daniel Dravot! The morning sun that had long been paling the lamps struck the red beard and blind sunken eyes; struck, too, a heavy circlet of gold studded with raw turquoises, that Carnehan placed tenderly on the battered temples.

'You behold now,' said Carnehan, 'the Emperor in his habit as he lived – the King of Kafiristan with his crown upon his head. Poor old Daniel that was a monarch once!'

I shuddered, for, in spite of defacements manifold, I recognised the head of the man of Marwar Junction. Carnehan rose to go. I attempted to stop him. He was not fit to walk abroad. 'Let me take away the whisky, and give me a little money,' he gasped. 'I was a King once. I'll go to the Deputy-Commissioner and ask to set in the Poorhouse till I get my health.

No, thank you, I can't wait till you get a carriage for me. I've urgent private affairs – in the South – at Marwar.'

He shambled out of the office and departed in the direction of the Deputy-Commissioner's house. That day at noon I had occasion to go down the blinding hot Mall, and I saw a crooked man crawling along the white dust of the roadside, his hat in his hand, quavering dolorously after the fashion of street-singers at Home. There was not a soul in sight, and he was out of all possible earshot of the houses. And he sang through his nose, turning his head from right to left:

'The Son of God goes forth to war,
    A kingly crown to gain;
His blood-red banner streams afar!
    Who follows in his train?'

I waited to hear no more, but put the poor wretch into my carriage and drove him to the nearest missionary for eventual transfer to the Asylum. He repeated the hymn twice while he was with me, whom he did not in the least recognise, and I left him singing it to the missionary.

Two days later I inquired after his welfare of the Superintendent of the Asylum.

'He was admitted suffering from sunstroke. He died early yesterday morning,' said the Superintendent. 'Is it true that he was half an hour bare-headed in the sun at mid-day?'

'Yes,' said I, 'but do you happen to know if he had anything upon him by any chance when he died?'

'Not to my knowledge,' said the Superintendent.

And there the matter rests.

A Wayside Comedy

Because to every purpose there is time and judgment, therefore
the misery of man is great upon him. *Ecclesiastes* viii, 6

Fate and the Government of India have turned the Station of
Kashima into a prison; and, because there is no help for the
poor souls who are now lying there in torment, I write this
story, praying that the Government of India may be moved to
scatter the European population to the four winds.

Kashima is bounded on all sides by the rock-tipped circle of
the Dosehri hills. In spring, it is ablaze with roses. In summer,
the roses die and the hot winds blow from the hills. In autumn, the white mists from the *jhils* cover the place as with water,
and in winter, the frosts nip everything young and tender to
earth-level. There is but one view in Kashima – a stretch of perfectly flat pasture and plough-land, running up to the grey-blue
scrub of the Dosehri hills.

There are no amusements, except snipe and tiger shooting;
but the tigers have been long since hunted from their lairs in
the rock-caves, and the snipe only come once a year. Narkarra
– one hundred and forty-three miles by road – is the nearest
Station to Kashima. But Kashima never goes to Narkarra,
where there are at least twelve English people. It stays within
the circle of the Dosehri hills.

All Kashima acquits Mrs. Vansuythen of any intention to
do harm; but all Kashima knows that she, and she alone,
brought about their pain.

Boulte, the Engineer, Mrs. Boulte, and Captain Kurrell
know this. They are the English population of Kashima, if we
except Major Vansuythen, who is of no importance whatever,

and Mrs. Vansuythen, who is the most important of all.

You must remember, though you will not understand, that all laws weaken in a small and hidden community where there is no public opinion. When a man is absolutely alone in a Station he runs a certain risk of falling into evil ways. This risk is multiplied by every addition to the population up to twelve – the Jury-number. After that, fear and consequent restraint begin, and human action becomes less grotesquely jerky.

There was deep peace in Kashima till Mrs. Vansuythen arrived. She was a charming woman, every one said so everywhere; and she charmed every one. In spite of this, or, perhaps, because of this, since Fate is so perverse, she cared only for one man, and he was Major Vansuythen. Had she been plain or stupid, this matter would have been intelligible to Kashima. But she was a fair woman, with very still grey eyes, the colour of a lake just before the light of the sun touches it. No man who had seen those eyes could, later on, explain what fashion of woman she was to look upon. The eyes dazzled him. Her own sex said that she was 'not bad-looking, but spoilt by pretending to be so grave'. And yet her gravity was natural. It was not her habit to smile. She merely went through life, looking at those who passed; and the women objected while the men fell down and worshipped.

She knows and is deeply sorry for the evil she has done to Kashima; but Major Vansuythen cannot understand why Mrs. Boulte does not drop in to afternoon tea at least three times a week. 'When there are only two women in one Station, they ought to see a great deal of each other,' says Major Vansuythen.

Long and long before ever Mrs. Vansuythen came out of those far-away places where there is society and amusement, Kurrell had discovered that Mrs. Boulte was the one woman in the world for him and – you dare not blame them. Kashima was as out of the world as Heaven or the Other Place, and the Dosehri hills kept their secret well. Boulte had no concern in the matter. He was in camp for a fortnight at a time. He was a hard, heavy man, and neither Mrs. Boulte nor Kurrell pitied him. They had all Kashima and each other for their very, very own; and Kashima was the Garden of Eden in those days. When Boulte returned from his wanderings he would slap Kurrell between the shoulders and call him 'old fellow', and the three would dine together. Kashima was happy then when the Judgment of God seemed almost as distant as Narkarra or the railway that ran down to the sea. But the Government sent Major Vansuythen to Kashima, and with him came his wife.

The etiquette of Kashima is much the same as that of a desert island. When a stranger is cast away there, all hands go down to the shore to make him welcome. Kashima assembled at the masonry platform close to the Narkarra Road, and spread tea for the Vansuythens. That ceremony was reckoned a formal call, and made them free of the Station, its rights and privileges. When the Vansuythens settled down they gave a tiny house-warming to all Kashima; and that made Kashima free of their house, according to the immemorial usage of the Station.

Then the Rains came, when no one could go into camp, and the Narkarra Road was washed away by the Kasun River, and in the cup-like pastures of Kashima the cattle waded knee-deep. The clouds dropped down from the Dosehri hills and covered everything.

At the end of the Rains Boulte's manner towards his wife changed and became demonstratively affectionate. They had been married twelve years, and the change startled Mrs. Boulte, who hated her husband with the hate of a woman who has met with nothing but kindness from her mate, and, in the teeth of this kindness, has done him a great wrong. Moreover, she had her own trouble to fight with – her watch to keep over her own property, Kurrell. For two months the Rains had hidden the Dosehri hills and many other things besides; but, when they lifted, they showed Mrs. Boulte that her man among men, her Ted – for she called him Ted in the old days when Boulte was out of earshot – was slipping the links of the allegiance.

'The Vansuythen Woman has taken him,' Mrs. Boulte said to herself; and when Boulte was away, wept over her belief, in the face of the over-vehement blandishments of Ted. Sorrow in Kashima is as fortunate as Love because there is nothing to weaken it save the flight of Time. Mrs. Boulte had never breathed her suspicion to Kurrell because she was not certain; and her nature led her to be very certain before she took steps in any direction. That is why she behaved as she did.

Boulte came into the house one evening, and leaned against the door-post of the drawing-room, chewing his moustache. Mrs. Boulte was putting some flowers into a vase. There is a pretence of civilisation even in Kashima.

'Little woman,' said Boulte quietly, 'do you care for me?'

'Immensely,' said she, with a laugh. 'Can you ask it?'

'But I'm serious,' said Boulte. '*Do* you care for me?'

Mrs. Boulte dropped the flowers, and turned round quickly. 'Do you want an honest answer?'

'Ye-es, I've asked for it.'

Mrs. Boulte spoke in a low, even voice for five minutes, very distinctly, that there might be no misunderstanding her meaning. When Samson broke the pillars of Gaza, he did a little thing, and one not to be compared with the deliberate pulling down of a woman's homestead about her own ears. There was no wise female friend to advise Mrs. Boulte, the singularly cautious wife, to hold her hand. She struck at Boulte's heart, because her own was sick with suspicion of Kurrell, and worn out with the long strain of watching alone through the Rains. There was no plan or purpose in her speaking. The sentences made themselves; and Boulte listened, leaning against the door-post with his hands in his pockets. When all was over, and Mrs. Boulte began to breathe through her nose before breaking out into tears, he laughed and stared straight in front of him at the Dosehri hills.

'Is that all?' he said. 'Thanks, I only wanted to know, you know.'

'What are you going to do?' said the woman, between her sobs.

'Do! Nothing. What should I do? Kill Kurrell, or send you Home, or apply for leave to get a divorce? It's two days' *dâk* into Narkarra.' He laughed again and went on: 'I'll tell you what *you* can do. You can ask Kurrell to dinner tomorrow – no, on Thursday, that will allow you time to pack – and you can bolt with him. I give you my word I won't follow.'

He took up his helmet and went out of the room, and Mrs. Boulte sat till the moonlight streaked the floor, thinking and thinking and thinking. She had done her best upon the spur of the moment to pull the house down; but it would not fall. Moreover, she could not understand her husband, and she was afraid. Then the folly of her useless truthfulness struck her, and she was ashamed to write to Kurrell, saying, 'I have gone mad and told everything. My husband says that I am free to elope with you. Get a *dâk* for Thursday, and we will fly after dinner.' There was a cold-bloodedness about that procedure which did not appeal to her. So she sat still in her own house and thought.

At dinner-time Boulte came back from his walk, white and worn and haggard, and the woman was touched at his distress. As the evening wore on she muttered some expression of sorrow, something approaching to contrition. Boulte came out of a brown study and said, 'Oh, *that*! I wasn't thinking about that. By the way, what does Kurrell say to the elopement?'

'I haven't seen him,' said Mrs. Boulte. 'Good God, is that all?'

But Boulte was not listening, and her sentence ended in a gulp.

The next day brought no comfort to Mrs. Boulte, for Kurrell did not appear, and the new life that she, in the five minutes' madness of the previous evening, had hoped to build out of the ruins of the old, seemed to be no nearer.

Boulte ate his breakfast, advised her to see her Arab pony fed in the verandah, and went out. The morning wore through, and at mid-day the tension became unendurable. Mrs. Boulte could not cry. She had finished her crying in the night, and now she did not want to be left alone. Perhaps the Vansuythen Woman would talk to her; and, since talking opens the heart, perhaps there might be some comfort to be found in her company. She was the only other woman in the Station.

In Kashima there are no regular calling-hours. Every one can drop in upon every one else at pleasure. Mrs. Boulte put on a big *terai* hat, and walked across to the Vansuythens' house to borrow last week's *Queen*. The two compounds touched, and instead of going up the drive, she crossed through the gap in the cactus-hedge, entering the house from the back. As she passed through the dining-room, she heard, behind the *purdah* that cloaked the drawing-room door, her husband's voice, saying:

'But on my Honour! On my Soul and Honour, I tell you she doesn't care for me. She told me so last night. I would have told you then if Vansuythen hadn't been with you. If it is for *her* sake that you'll have nothing to say to me, you can make your mind easy. It's Kurrell—'

'What?' said Mrs. Vansuythen, with a hysterical little laugh. 'Kurrell! Oh, it can't be! You two must have made some horrible mistake. Perhaps you – you lost your temper, or misunderstood, or something. Things *can't* be as wrong as you say.'

Mrs. Vansuythen had shifted her defence to avoid the man's pleading and was desperately trying to keep him to a side-issue.

'There must be some mistake,' she insisted, 'and it can be all put right again.'

Boulte laughed grimly.

'It can't be Captain Kurrell! He told me that he had never taken the least – the least interest in your wife, Mr. Boulte. Oh, *do* listen! He said he had not. He swore he had not,' said Mrs. Vansuythen.

The *purdah* rustled, and the speech was cut short by the entry of a little thin woman, with big rings round her eyes. Mrs. Vansuythen stood up with a gasp.

'What was that you said?' asked Mrs. Boulte. 'Never mind that man. What did Ted say to you? What did he say to you? What did he say to you?'

Mrs. Vansuythen sat down helplessly on the sofa, overborne by the trouble of her questioner.

'He said – I can't remember exactly what he said – but I understood him to say – that is— But, really, Mrs. Boulte, isn't it rather a strange question?'

'*Will* you tell me what he said?' repeated Mrs. Boulte. Even a tiger will fly before a bear robbed of her whelps, and Mrs. Vansuythen was only an ordinarily good woman. She began in a sort of desperation: 'Well, he said that he never cared for you at all, and, of course, there was not the least reason why he should have, and – and – that was all.'

'You said he *swore* he had not cared for me. Was that true?'

'Yes,' said Mrs. Vansuythen very softly.

Mrs. Boulte wavered for an instant where she stood, and then fell forward fainting.

'What did I tell you?' said Boulte, as though the conversation had been unbroken. 'You can see for yourself. She cares for *him*.' The light began to break into his dull mind, and he went on: 'And he – what was *he* saying to you?'

But Mrs. Vansuythen, with no heart for explanations or impassioned protestations, was kneeling over Mrs. Boulte.

'Oh, you brute!' she cried. 'Are *all* men like this? Help me to get her into my room – and her face is cut against the table. Oh, *will* you be quiet, and help me to carry her? I hate you, and I hate Captain Kurrell. Lift her carefully, and now – go! Go away!'

Boulte carried his wife into Mrs. Vansuythen's bedroom, and departed before the storm of that lady's wrath and disgust, impenitent and burning with jealousy. Kurrell had been making love to Mrs. Vansuythen – would do Vansuythen as great a wrong as he had done Boulte, who caught himself considering whether Mrs. Vansuythen would faint if she discovered that the man she loved had forsworn her.

In the middle of these meditations, Kurrell came cantering along the road and pulled up with a cheery 'Good mornin'. Been mashing Mrs. Vansuythen as usual, eh? Bad thing for a sober, married man, that. What will Mrs. Boulte say?'

Boulte raised his head and said slowly: 'Oh, you liar!' Kurrell's face changed. 'What's that?' he asked quickly.

'Nothing much,' said Boulte. 'Has my wife told you that you two are free to go off whenever you please? She has been good enough to explain the situation to me. You've been a true friend to me, Kurrell – old man – haven't you?'

Kurrell groaned, and tried to frame some sort of idiotic sentence about being willing to give 'satisfaction'. But his interest in the woman was dead, had died out in the Rains, and, mentally he was abusing her for her amazing indiscretion. It would have been so easy to have broken off the thing gently and by degrees, and now he was saddled with— Boulte's voice recalled him.

'I don't think I should get any satisfaction from killing you, and I'm pretty sure you'd get none from killing me.'

Then in a querulous tone, ludicrously disproportioned to his wrongs, Boulte added:

'Seems rather a pity that you haven't the decency to keep to the woman, now you've got her. You've been a true friend to *her* too, haven't you?'

Kurrell stared long and gravely. The situation was getting beyond him.

'What do you mean?' he said.

Boulte answered, more to himself than the questioner: 'My wife came over to Mrs. Vansuythen's just now; and it seems you'd been telling Mrs. Vansuythen that you'd never cared for Emma. I suppose you lied, as usual. What had Mrs. Vansuythen to do with you, or you with her? Try to speak the truth for once in a way.'

Kurrell took the double insult without wincing, and replied by another question: 'Go on. What happened?'

'Emma fainted,' said Boulte simply. 'But, look here, what had you been saying to Mrs. Vansuythen?'

Kurrell laughed. Mrs. Boulte had, with unbridled tongue, made havoc of his plans; and he could at least retaliate by hurting the man in whose eyes he was humiliated and shown dishonourable.

'Saying to her? What *does* a man tell a lie like that for? I suppose I said pretty much what you've said, unless I'm a good deal mistaken.'

'I spoke the truth,' said Boulte, again more to himself than Kurrell. 'Emma told me she hated me. She has no right in me.'

'No! I suppose not. You're only her husband, y'know. And what did Mrs. Vansuythen say after you had laid your disengaged heart at her feet?'

Kurrell felt almost virtuous as he put the question.

'I don't think that matters,' Boulte replied; 'and it doesn't concern you.'

'But it does! I tell you it does—' began Kurrell shamelessly.

The sentence was cut by a roar of laughter from Boulte's lips. Kurrell was silent for an instant, and then he, too, laughed – laughed long and loudly, rocking in his saddle. It was an unpleasant sound – the mirthless mirth of these men on the long white line of the Narkarra Road. There were no strangers in Kashima, or they might have thought that captivity within the Dosehri hills had driven half the European population mad. The laughter ended abruptly, and Kurrell was the first to speak.

'Well, what are you going to do?'

Boulte looked up the road, and at the hills. 'Nothing,' said he quietly. 'What's the use? It's too ghastly for anything. We must let the old life go on. I can only call you a hound and a liar, and I can't go on calling you names for ever. Besides which, I don't feel that I'm much better. We can't get out of this place. What *is* there to do?'

Kurrell looked round the rat-pit of Kashima and made no reply. The injured husband took up the wondrous tale.

'Ride on, and speak to Emma if you want to. God knows *I* don't care what you do.'

He walked forward, and left Kurrell gazing blankly after him. Kurrell did not ride on either to see Mrs. Boulte or Mrs. Vansuythen. He sat in his saddle and thought, while his pony grazed by the roadside.

The whir of approaching wheels roused him. Mrs. Vansuythen was driving home Mrs. Boulte, white and wan, with a cut on her forehead.

'Stop, please,' said Mrs. Boulte. 'I want to speak to Ted.'

Mrs. Vansuythen obeyed, but as Mrs. Boulte leaned forward, putting her hand upon the splash-board of the dog-cart, Kurrell spoke.

'I've seen your husband, Mrs. Boulte.'

There was no necessity for any further explanation. The man's eyes were fixed, not upon Mrs Boulte, but her companion. Mrs. Boulte saw the look.

'Speak to him!' she pleaded, turning to the woman at her side. 'Oh, speak to him! Tell him what you told me just now. Tell him you hate him! Tell him you hate him!'

She bent forward and wept bitterly, while the *sais*, impassive, went forward to hold the horse. Mrs. Vansuythen turned scarlet and dropped the reins. She wished to be no party to such unholy explanations.

'I've nothing to do with it,' she began coldly; but Mrs. Boulte's sobs overcame her, and she addressed herself to the man. 'I don't know what I am to say, Captain Kurrell. I don't know what I can call you. I think you've – you've behaved abominably, and she has cut her forehead terribly against the table.'

'It doesn't hurt. It isn't anything,' said Mrs. Boulte feebly. '*That* doesn't matter. Tell him what you told me. Say you don't care for him. Oh, Ted, *won't* you believe her?'

'Mrs. Boulte has made me understand that you were – that you were fond of her once upon a time,' went on Mrs. Vansuythen.

'Well!' said Kurrell brutally. 'It seems to me that Mrs. Boulte had better be fond of her own husband first.'

'Stop!' said Mrs. Vansuythen. 'Hear me first. I don't care – I don't want to know anything about you and Mrs. Boulte; but I want *you* to know that I hate you, that I think you are a cur, and that I'll never, *never* speak to you again. Oh, I don't dare to say what I think of you, you — man!'

'I want to speak to Ted,' moaned Mrs. Boulte, but the dog-cart rattled on, and Kurrell was left on the road, shamed, and boiling with wrath against Mrs. Boulte.

He waited till Mrs. Vansuythen was driving back to her own

house, and, she being freed from the embarrassment of Mrs. Boulte's presence, he learned for the second time her opinion of himself and his actions.

In the evenings it was the wont of all Kashima to meet at the platform on the Narkarra Road, to drink tea and discuss the trivialities of the day. Major Vansuythen and his wife found themselves alone at the gathering-place for almost the first time in their remembrance; and the cheery Major, in the teeth of his wife's remarkably reasonable suggestion that the rest of the Station might be sick, insisted upon driving round to the two bungalows and unearthing the population.

'Sitting in the twilight!' said he, with great indignation, to the Boultes. 'That'll never do! Hang it all, we're one family here! You *must* come out, and so must Kurrell. I'll make him bring his banjo.'

So great is the power of honest simplicity and a good digestion over guilty consciences that all Kashima did turn out, even down to the banjo; and the Major embraced the company in one expansive grin. As he grinned, Mrs. Vansuythen raised her eyes for an instant and looked at all Kashima. Her meaning was clear. Major Vansuythen would never know anything. He was to be the outsider in that happy family whose cage was the Dosehri hills.

'You're singing villainously out of tune, Kurrell,' said the Major truthfully. 'Pass me that banjo.'

And he sang in excruciating wise till the stars came out and all Kashima went to dinner.

That was the beginning of the New Life of Kashima – the life that Mrs. Boulte made when her tongue was loosened in the twilight.

Mrs. Vansuythen has never told the Major; and since he insists upon keeping up a burdensome geniality, she has been compelled to break her vow of not speaking to Kurrell. This speech, which must of necessity preserve the semblance of politeness and interest, serves admirably to keep alight the flame of jealousy and dull hatred in Boulte's bosom, as it awakens the same passions in his wife's heart. Mrs. Boulte hates Mrs. Vansuythen because she has taken Ted from her, and, in some curious fashion, hates her because Mrs. Vansuythen – and here the wife's eyes see far more clearly than the husband's – detests Ted. And Ted – that gallant captain and honourable man – knows now that it is possible to hate a woman once loved, to the verge of wishing to silence her for ever with blows. Above all is he shocked that Mrs. Boulte cannot see the error of her ways.

Boulte and he go out tiger-shooting together in all friendship. Boulte has put their relationship on a most satisfactory footing.

'You're a blackguard,' he says to Kurrell, 'and I've lost any self-respect I may ever have had; but when you're with me, I can feel certain that you are not with Mrs. Vansuythen, or making Emma miserable.'

Kurrell endures anything that Boulte may say to him. Sometimes they are away for three days together, and then the Major insists upon his wife going over to sit with Mrs. Boulte; although Mrs. Vansuythen has repeatedly declared that she prefers her husband's company to any in the world. From the way in which she clings to him, she would certainly seem to be speaking the truth.

But of course, as the Major says, 'in a little Station we must all be friendly.'

In the *Rukh*

The Only Son lay down again and dreamed that he dreamed a
  dream.
The last ash dropped from the dying fire with the click of a
  falling spark,
And the Only Son woke up again and called across the dark: —
'Now, was I born of womankind and laid in a mother's breast?
For I have dreamed of a shaggy hide whereon I went to rest.
And was I born of womankind and laid on a father's arm?
For I have dreamed of long white teeth that guarded me from
  harm.
Oh, was I born of womankind and did I play alone?
For I have dreamed of playmates twain that bit me to the bone.
And did I break the barley bread and steep it in the tyre?
For I have dreamed of a youngling kid new riven from the byre.
An hour it lacks and an hour it lacks to the rising of the moon —
But I can see the black roof-beams as plain as it were noon!
'Tis a league and a league to the Lena Falls where the
  trooping sambhur go,
But I can hear the little fawn that bleats behind the doe!
'Tis a league and a league to the Lena Falls where the crop
  and the upland meet,
But I can smell the warm wet wind that whispers through the
  wheat!'

The Only Son

Of the wheels of public service that turn under the Indian
Government, there is none more important than the Department of Woods and Forests. The reboisement of all India is in

its hands; or will be when Government has the money to spend. Its servants wrestle with wandering sand-torrents and shifting dunes: wattling them at the sides, damming them in front, and pegging them down atop with coarse grass and spindling pine after the rules of Nancy. They are responsible for all the timber in the State forests of the Himalayas, as well as for the denuded hillsides that the monsoons wash into dry gullies and aching ravines; each cut a mouth crying aloud what carelessness can do. They experiment with battalions of foreign trees, and coax the blue gum to take root and, perhaps, dry up the Canal fever. In the plains the chief part of their duty is to see that the belt fire-lines in the forest reserves are kept clean, so that when drought comes and the cattle starve, they may throw the reserve open to the villager's herds and allow the man himself to gather sticks. They poll and lop for the stacked railway-fuel along the lines that burn no coal; they calculate the profit of their plantations to five points of decimals; they are the doctors and midwives of the huge teak forests of Upper Burma, the rubber of the Eastern Jungles, and the gall-nuts of the South; and they are always hampered by lack of funds. But since a Forest Officer's business takes him far from the beaten roads and the regular stations, he learns to grow wise in more than wood-lore alone; to know the people and the polity of the jungle; meeting tiger, bear, leopard, wild-dog, and all the deer, not once or twice after days of beating, but again and again in the execution of his duty. He spends much time in saddle or under canvas – the friend of newly-planted trees, the associate of uncouth rangers and hairy trackers – till the woods, that show his care, in turn set their mark upon him, and he ceases to sing the naughty French songs he learned at Nancy, and grows silent with the silent things of the underbrush.

Gisborne of the Woods and Forests had spent four years in the Service. At first he loved it without comprehension, because it led him into the open on horseback and gave him authority. Then he hated it furiously, and would have given a year's pay for one month of such society as India affords. That crisis over, the forests took him back again, and he was content to serve them, to deepen and widen his fire-lines, to watch the green mist of his new plantation against the older foliage, to dredge out the choked stream, and to follow and strengthen the last struggle of the forest where it broke down and died among the long pig-grass. On some still day that grass would be burned off, and a hundred beasts that had their homes there would rush out before the pale flames at high noon. Later the forest would creep forward over the blackened ground in orderly lines of saplings, and Gisborne, watching, would be well pleased. His bungalow, a thatched white-walled cottage of two rooms, was set at one end of the great *rukh* and overlooking it. He made no pretence at keeping a garden, for the *rukh* swept up to his door, curled over in a thicket of bamboo, and he rode from his verandah into its heart without the need of any carriage-drive.

Abdul Gafur, his fat Mohammedan butler, fed him when he was at home, and spent the rest of the time gossiping with the little band of native servants whose huts lay behind the bungalow. There were two grooms, a cook, a water-carrier, and a sweeper, and that was all. Gisborne cleaned his own guns and kept no dog. Dogs scared the game, and it pleased the man to be able to say where the subjects of his kingdom would drink at moonrise, eat before dawn, and lie up in the day's heat. The rangers and forest-guards lived in little huts far away in the *rukh*, only appearing when one of them had been injured by a falling tree or a wild beast. Thus Gisborne was alone.

In spring the *rukh* put out few new leaves, but lay dry and still untouched by the finger of the year, waiting for rain. Only there was then more calling and roaring in the dark on a quiet night; the tumult of a battle-royal among the tigers, the bellowing of arrogant buck, or the steady wood-chopping of an old boar sharpening his tushes against a bole. Then Gisborne laid aside his little-used gun altogether, for it was to him a sin to kill. In summer, through the furious May heats, the *rukh* reeled in the haze, and Gisborne watched for the first sign of curling smoke that should betray a forest fire. Then came the Rains with a roar, and the *rukh* was blotted out in fetch after fetch of warm mist, and the broad leaves drummed the night through under the big drops; and there was a noise of running water, and of juicy green stuff crackling where the wind struck it, and the lightning wove patterns behind the dense matting of the foliage, till the sun broke loose again and the *rukh* stood with hot flanks smoking to the newly-washed sky. Then the heat and the dry cold subdued everything to tiger-colour again. So Gisborne learned to know his *rukh* and was very happy. His pay came month by month, but he had very little need for money. The currency notes accumulated in the drawer where he kept his home-letters and the recapping-machine. If he drew anything, it was to make a purchase from the Calcutta Botanical Gardens, or to pay a ranger's widow a sum that the Government of India would never have sanctioned for her man's death.

Payment was good, but vengeance was also necessary, and he took that when he could. One night of many nights a runner, breathless and gasping, came to him with the news that a forest-guard lay dead by the Kanye stream, the side of his head smashed in as though it had been an egg-shell. Gisborne went out at dawn to look for the murderer. It is only travellers and now and then young soldiers who are known to the world as great hunters. The Forest Officers take their *shikar* as part of the day's work, and no one hears of it. Gisborne went on foot to the place of the kill: the widow was wailing over the corpse as it lay on a bedstead, while two or three men were looking at footprints on the moist ground. 'That is the Red One,' said a man. 'I knew he would turn to man in time, but surely there is game enough even for him. This must have been done for devilry.'

'The Red One lies up in the rocks at the back of the *sal* trees,' said Gisborne. He knew the tiger under suspicion.

'Not now, Sahib, not now. He will be raging and ranging to and fro. Remember that the first kill is a triple kill always. Our blood makes them mad. He may be behind us even as we speak.'

'He may have gone to the next hut,' said another. 'It is only four *koss*. Wallah, who is this?'

Gisborne turned with the others. A man was walking down the dried bed of the stream, naked except for the loin-cloth, but crowned with a wreath of the tasselled blossoms of the white convolvulus creeper. So noiselessly did he move over the little pebbles, that even Gisborne, used to the soft-footedness of trackers, started.

'The tiger that killed,' he began, without any salute, 'has gone to drink, and now he is asleep under a rock beyond that hill'. His voice was clear and bell-like, utterly different from the usual whine of the native, and his face as he lifted it in the sunshine might have been that of an angel strayed among the woods. The widow ceased wailing above the corpse and looked round-eyed at the stranger, returning to her duty with double strength.

'Shall I show the Sahib?' he said simply.

'If thou art sure—' Gisborne began.

'Sure indeed. I saw him only an hour ago – the dog. It is before his time to eat man's flesh. He has yet a dozen sound teeth in his evil head.'

The men kneeling above the footprints slunk off quietly, for fear that Gisborne should ask them to go with him, and the young man laughed a little to himself.

'Come, Sahib,' he cried, and turned on his heel, walking before his companion.

'Not so fast. I cannot keep that pace,' said the white man. 'Halt there. Thy face is new to me.'

'That may be. I am but newly come into this forest.'

'From what village?'

'I am without a village. I came from over there.' He flung out his arm towards the north.

'A gipsy then?'

'No, Sahib. I am a man without caste, and for matter of that without a father.'

'What do men call thee?'

'Mowgli, Sahib. And what is the Sahib's name?'

'I am the warden of this *rukh* – Gisborne is my name.'

'How? Do they number the trees and the blades of grass here?'

'Even so; lest such gipsy fellows as thou set them afire.'

'I! I would not hurt the jungle for any gift. That is my home.'

He turned to Gisborne with a smile that was irresistible, and held up a warning hand.

'Now, Sahib, we must go a little quietly. There is no need to wake the dog, though he sleeps heavily enough. Perhaps it were better if I went forward alone and drove him down wind to the Sahib.'

'Allah! Since when have tigers been driven to and fro like cattle by naked men?' said Gisborne, aghast at the man's audacity.

He laughed again softly. 'Nay, then, come along with me and shoot him in thy own way with the big English rifle.'

Gisborne stepped in his guide's track, twisted, crawled, and clomb and stooped and suffered through all the many agonies of a jungle-stalk. He was purple and dripping with sweat when Mowgli at the last bade him raise his head and peer over a blue baked rock near a tiny hill pool. By the waterside lay the tiger extended and at ease, lazily licking clean again an enormous elbow and fore-paw. He was old, yellow-toothed, and not a little mangy, but in that setting and sunshine, imposing enough.

Gisborne had no false ideas of sport where the man-eater was concerned. This thing was vermin, to be killed as speedily as possible. He waited to recover his breath, rested the rifle on the rock and whistled. The brute's head turned slowly not twenty feet from the rifle-mouth, and Gisborne planted his shots, business-like, one behind the shoulder and the other a little below the eye. At that range the heavy bones were no guard against the rending bullets.

'Well, the skin was not worth keeping at any rate,' said he, as the smoke cleared away and the beast lay kicking and gasping in the last agony.

'A dog's death for a dog,' said Mowgli quietly. 'Indeed there is nothing in that carrion worth taking away.'

'The whiskers. Dost thou not take the whiskers?' said Gisborne, who knew how the rangers valued such things.

'I? Am I a lousy *shikarri* of the jungle to paddle with a tiger's muzzle? Let him lie. Here come his friends already.'

A dropping kite whistled shrilly overhead, as Gisborne snapped out the empty shells, and wiped his face.

'And if thou art not a *shikarri*, where didst thou learn the knowledge of the tiger-folk?' said he. 'No tracker could have done better.'

'I hate all tigers,' said Mowgli curtly. 'Let the Sahib give me his gun to carry. Arré, it is a very fine one. And where does the Sahib go now?'

'To my house.'

'May I come? I have never yet looked within a white man's house.'

Gisborne returned to his bungalow, Mowgli striding noiselessly before him, his brown skin glistening in the sunlight.

He stared curiously at the verandah and the two chairs there, fingered the split bamboo shade curtains with suspicion, and entered, looking always behind him. Gisborne loosed a curtain to keep out the sun. It dropped with a clatter, but almost before it touched the flagging of the verandah Mowgli had leaped clear, and was standing with heaving chest in the open.

'It is a trap,' he said quickly.

Gisborne laughed. 'White men do not trap men. Indeed thou art altogether of the jungle.'

'I see,' said Mowgli, 'it has neither catch nor fall. I – I never beheld these things till today.'

He came in on tiptoe and stared with large eyes at the furniture of the two rooms. Abdul Gafur, who was laying lunch, looked at him with deep disgust.

'So much trouble to eat, and so much trouble to lie down after you have eaten!' said Mowgli with a grin. 'We do better in the jungle. It is very wonderful. There are very many rich things here. Is the Sahib not afraid that he may be robbed? I have never seen such wonderful things.' He was staring at a dusty Benares brass plate on a rickety bracket.

'Only a thief from the jungle would rob here,' said Abdul Gafur, setting down a plate with a clatter. Mowgli opened his eyes wide and stared at the white-bearded Mohammedan.

'In my country when goats bleat very loud we cut their throats,' he returned cheerfully. 'But have no fear, thou. I am going.'

He turned and disappeared into the *rukh*. Gisborne looked after him with a laugh that ended in a little sigh. There was not much outside his regular work to interest the Forest Officer, and this son of the forest, who seemed to know tigers as other people know dogs, would have been a diversion.

'He's a most wonderful chap,' thought Gisborne; 'he's like the illustrations in the Classical Dictionary. I wish I could have made him a gunboy. There's no fun in shikarring alone, and this fellow would have been a perfect *shikarri*. I wonder what in the world he is.'

That evening he sat on the verandah under the stars, smoking as he wondered. A puff of smoke curled from the pipe-bowl. As it cleared he was aware of Mowgli sitting with arms crossed on the verandah edge. A ghost could not have drifted up more noiselessly. Gisborne started and let the pipe drop.

'There is no man to talk to out there in the *rukh*,' said Mowgli; 'I came here, therefore.' He picked up the pipe and returned it to Gisborne.

'Oh,' said Gisborne, and after a long pause, 'What news is there in the *rukh*? Hast thou found another tiger?'

'The nilghai are changing their feeding-ground against the new moon, as is their custom. The pig are feeding near the Kanye river now, because they will not feed with the nilghai, and one of their sows has been killed by a leopard in the long grass at the water-head. I do not know any more.'

'And how didst thou know all these things?' said Gisborne, leaning forward and looking at the eyes that glittered in the starlight.

'How should I not know? The nilghai has his custom and his use, and a child knows that pig will not feed with him.'

'I do not know this,' said Gisborne.

'Tck! Tck! And thou art in charge – so the men of the huts tell me – in charge of all this *rukh*.' He laughed to himself.

'It is well enough to talk and to tell child's tales,' Gisborne retorted, nettled at the chuckle. 'To say that this and that goes on in the *rukh*. No man can deny thee.'

'As for the sow's carcase, I will show thee her bones to-morrow,' Mowgli returned, absolutely unmoved. 'Touching the matter of the nilghai, if the Sahib will sit here very still I will drive one nilghai up to this place, and by listening to the sounds carefully, the Sahib can tell whence that nilghai has been driven.'

'Mowgli, the jungle has made thee mad,' said Gisborne. 'Who can drive nilghai?'

'Still – sit still, then. I go.'

'Gad, the man's a ghost!' said Gisborne; for Mowgli had faded out into the darkness and there was no sound of feet. The *rukh* lay out in great velvety folds in the uncertain shimmer of the stardust – so still that the least little wandering wind among the tree-tops came up as the sigh of a child sleeping equably. Abdul Gafur in the cook-house was clicking plates together.

'Be still there!' shouted Gisborne, and composed himself to listen as a man can who is used to the stillness of the *rukh*. It had been his custom, to preserve his self-respect in his isolation, to dress for dinner each night, and the stiff white shirt-front creaked with his regular breathing till he shifted a little side-ways. Then the tobacco of a somewhat foul pipe began to purr, and he threw the pipe from him. Now, except for the night-breath in the *rukh*, everything was dumb.

From an inconceivable distance, and drawled through im-measurable darkness, came the faint, faint echo of a wolf's howl. Then silence again for, it seemed, long hours. At last, when his legs below the knees had lost all feeling, Gisborne heard something that might have been a crash far off through the undergrowth. He doubted till it was repeated again and yet again.

'That's from the west,' he muttered; 'there's something on foot there.' The noise increased – crash on crash, plunge on plunge – with the thick grunting of a hotly pressed nilghai, flying in panic terror and taking no heed to his course.

A shadow blundered out from between the tree-trunks, wheeled back, turned again grunting, and with a clatter on the bare ground dashed up almost within reach of his hand. It was a bull nilghai, dripping with dew – his withers hung with a torn trail of creeper, his eyes shining in the light from the house. The creature checked at sight of the man, and fled along the edge of the *rukh* till he melted in the darkness. The first idea in Gisborne's bewildered mind was the indecency of thus dragging out for inspection the big blue bull of the *rukh* – the putting him through his paces in the night which should have been his own.

Then said a smooth voice at his ear as he stood staring:

'He came from the water-head where he was leading the herd. From the west he came. Does the Sahib believe now, or shall I bring up the herd to be counted? The Sahib is in charge of this *rukh*.'

Mowgli had reseated himself on the verandah, breathing a little quickly. Gisborne looked at him with open mouth. 'How was that accomplished?' he said.

'The Sahib saw. The bull was driven – driven as a buffalo is. Ho! ho! He will have a fine tale to tell when he returns to the herd.'

'That is a new trick to me. Canst thou run as swiftly as the nilghai, then?'

'The Sahib has seen. If the Sahib needs more knowledge at any time of the movings of the game, I, Mowgli, am here. This is a good *rukh*, and I shall stay.'

'Stay then, and if thou hast need of a meal at any time my servants shall give thee one.'

'Yes, indeed, I am fond of cooked food,' Mowgli answered quickly. 'No man may say that I do not eat boiled and roast as much as any other man. I will come for that meal. Now, on my part, I promise that the Sahib shall sleep safely in his house by night, and no thief shall break in to carry away his so rich treasures.'

The conversation ended itself on Mowgli's abrupt departure.

Gisborne sat long smoking, and the upshot of his thoughts was that in Mowgli he had found at last that ideal ranger and forest-guard for whom he and the Department were always looking.

'I must get him into the Government service somehow. A man who can drive nilghai would know more about the *rukh* than fifty men. He's a miracle – a *lusus naturae* – but a forest-guard he must be if he'll only settle down in one place,' said Gisborne.

Abdul Gafur's opinion was less favourable. He confided to Gisborne at bedtime that strangers from God-knew-where were more than likely to be professional thieves, and that he personally did not approve of naked outcastes who had not the proper manner of addressing white people. Gisborne laughed and bade him go to his quarters, and Abdul Gafur retreated growling. Later in the night he found occasion to rise up and beat his thirteen-year-old daughter. Nobody knew the cause of dispute, but Gisborne heard the cry.

Through the days that followed Mowgli came and went like a shadow. He had established himself and his wild house-keeping close to the bungalow, but on the edge of the *rukh*, where Gisborne, going out on to the verandah for a breath of cool air, would see him sometimes sitting in the moonlight, his forehead on his knees, or lying out along the fling of a branch, closely pressed to it as some beast of the night. Thence Mowgli would throw him a salutation and bid him sleep at ease, or descending would weave prodigious stories of the manners of the beasts in the *rukh*. Once he wandered into the stables and was found looking at the horses with deep interest.

'That,' said Abdul Gafur pointedly, 'is sure sign that some day he will steal one. Why, if he lives about this house, does he not take an honest employment? But no, he must wander up and down like a loose camel, turning the heads of fools and opening the jaws of the unwise to folly.' So Abdul Gafur would give harsh orders to Mowgli when they met, would bid him fetch water and pluck fowls, and Mowgli, laughing unconcernedly, would obey.

'He has no caste,' said Abdul Gafur. 'He will do anything.

Look to it, Sahib, that he does not do too much. A snake is a snake, and a jungle-gipsy is a thief till the death.'

'Be silent, then,' said Gisborne. 'I allow thee to correct thy own household if there is not too much noise, because I know thy customs and use. My custom thou dost not know. The man is without doubt a little mad.'

'Very little mad indeed,' said Abdul Gafur. 'But we shall see what comes thereof.'

A few days later on his business took Gisborne into the *rukh* for three days. Abdul Gafur being old and fat was left at home. He did not approve of lying up in rangers' huts, and was inclined to levy contributions in his master's name of grain and oil and milk from those who could ill afford such benevolences. Gisborne rode off early one dawn a little vexed that his man of the woods was not at the verandah to accompany him. He liked him – liked his strength, fleetness, and silence of foot, and his ever-ready open smile; his ignorance of all forms of ceremony and salutations, and the child-like tales that he would tell (and Gisborne would credit now) of what the game was doing in the *rukh*. After an hour's riding through the greenery, he heard a rustle behind him, and Mowgli trotted at his stirrup.

'We have a three days' work toward,' said Gisborne, 'among the new trees.'

'Good,' said Mowgli. 'It is always good to cherish young trees. They make cover if the beasts leave them alone. We must shift the pig again.'

'Again? How?' Gisborne smiled.

'Oh, they were rooting and tusking among the young *sal* last night, and I drove them off. Therefore I did not come to the verandah this morning. The pig should not be on this side of the *rukh* at all. We must keep them below the head of the Kanye river.'

'If a man could herd clouds he might do that thing; but, Mowgli, if as thou sayest, thou art herder in the *rukh* for no gain and for no pay—'

'It is the Sahib's *rukh*,' said Mowgli, quickly looking up. Gisborne nodded thanks and went on: 'Would it not be better to work for pay from the Government? There is a pension at the end of long service.'

'Of that I have thought,' said Mowgli, 'but the rangers live in huts with shut doors, and all that is all too much a trap to me. Yet I think —'

'Think well then and tell me later. Here we will stay for breakfast.'

Gisborne dismounted, took his morning meal from his homemade saddle-bags, and saw the day open hot above the *rukh*. Mowgli lay in the grass at his side staring up to the sky.

Presently he said in a lazy whisper: 'Sahib, is there any order at the bungalow to take out the white mare today?'

'No, she is fat and old and a little lame besides. Why?'

'She is being ridden now and *not* slowly on the road that runs to the railway line.'

'Bah, that is two *koss* away. It is a wood-pecker.'

Mowgli put up his forearm to keep the sun out of his eyes.

'The road curves in with a big curve from the bungalow. It is not more than a *koss*, at the farthest, as the kite goes; and sound flies with the birds. Shall we see?'

'What folly! To run a *koss* in this sun to see a noise in the forest.'

'Nay, the pony is the Sahib's pony. I meant only to bring her here. If she is not the Sahib's pony, no matter. If she is, the Sahib can do what he wills. She is certainly being ridden hard.'

'And how wilt thou bring her here, madman?'

'Has the Sahib forgotten? By the road of the nilghai and no other.'

'Up then and run if thou art so full of zeal.'

'Oh, I do not run!' He put out his hand to sign for silence, and still lying on his back called aloud thrice – with a deep gurgling cry that was new to Gisborne.

'She will come,' he said at the end. 'Let us wait in the shade.' The long eyelashes drooped over the wild eyes as Mowgli began to doze in the morning hush. Gisborne waited patiently: Mowgli was surely mad, but as entertaining a companion as a lonely Forest Officer could desire.

'Ho! ho!' said Mowgli lazily, with shut eyes. 'He has dropped off. Well, first the mare will come and then the man.' Then he yawned as Gisborne's pony stallion neighed. Three minutes later Gisborne's white mare, saddled, bridled, but riderless, tore into the glade where they were sitting, and hurried to her companion.

'She is not very warm,' said Mowgli, 'but in this heat the sweat comes easily. Presently we shall see her rider, for a man goes more slowly than a horse – especially if he chance to be a fat man and old.'

'Allah! This is the devil's work,' cried Gisborne leaping to his feet, for he heard a yell in the jungle.

'Have no care, Sahib. He will not be hurt. He also will say that it is devil's work. Ah! Listen! Who is that?'

It was the voice of Abdul Gafur in an agony of terror, crying out upon unknown things to spare him and his gray hairs.

'Nay, I cannot move another step,' he howled. 'I am old and my turban is lost. Arré! Arré! But I will move. Indeed I will hasten. I will run! Oh, Devils of the Pit, I am a Mussulman!'

The undergrowth parted and gave up Abdul Gafur, turbanless, shoeless, with his waist-cloth unbound, mud and grass in his clutched hands, and his face purple. He saw Gisborne, yelled anew, and pitched forward, exhausted and quivering, at his feet. Mowgli watched him with a sweet smile.

'This is no joke,' said Gisborne sternly. 'The man is like to die, Mowgli.'

'He will not die. He is only afraid. There was no need that he should have come out of a walk.'

Abdul Gafur groaned and rose up, shaking in every limb.

'It was witchcraft – witchcraft and devildom!' he sobbed, fumbling with his hand in his breast. 'Because of my sin I have been whipped through the woods by devils. It is all finished. I repent. Take them, Sahib!' He held out a roll of dirty paper.

'What is the meaning of this, Abdul Gafur?' said Gisborne, already knowing what would come.

'Put me in the jail-khana – the notes are all here – but lock me up safely that no devils may follow. I have sinned against the Sahib and his salt which I have eaten; and but for those accursed wood-demons I might have bought land afar off and lived in peace all my days.' He beat his head upon the ground in an agony of despair and mortification. Gisborne turned the roll of notes over and over. It was his accumulated back-pay for the last nine months – the roll that lay in the drawer with the home-letters and the recapping machine. Mowgli watched Abdul Gafur, laughing noiselessly to himself. 'There is no need to put me on the horse again. I will walk home slowly with the Sahib, and then he can send me under guard to the jail-khana. The Government gives many years for this offence,' said the butler sullenly.

Loneliness in the *rukh* affects very many ideas about very many things. Gisborne stared at Abdul Gafur, remembering that he was a very good servant, and that a new butler must be broken into the ways of the house from the beginning, and at the best would be a new face and a new tongue.

'Listen, Abdul Gafur,' he said. 'Thou hast done great wrong, and altogether lost thy *izzat* and thy reputation. But I think that this came upon thee suddenly.'

'Allah! I had never desired the notes before. The Evil took me by the throat while I looked.'

'That also I can believe. Go then back to my house, and when I return I will send the notes by a runner to the Bank, and there shall be no more said. Thou art too old for the jail-khana. Also thy household is guiltless.'

For answer Abdul Gafur sobbed between Gisborne's cow-hide riding-boots.

'Is there no dismissal then?' he gulped.

'That we shall see. It hangs upon thy conduct when we return. Get upon the mare and ride slowly back.'

'But the devils! The *rukh* is full of devils.'

'No matter, my father. They will do thee no more harm unless, indeed, the Sahib's orders be not obeyed,' said Mowgli. 'Then, perchance, they may drive thee home – by the road of the nilghai.'

Abdul Gafur's lower jaw dropped as he twisted up his waist-cloth, staring at Mowgli.

'Are they *his* devils? His devils! And I had thought to return and lay the blame upon this warlock!'

'That was well thought of, Huzrut; but before we make a trap we see first how big the game is that may fall into it. Now I thought no more than that a man had taken one of the Sahib's horses. I did not know that the design was to make me a thief before the Sahib, or my devils had haled thee here by the leg. It is not too late now.'

Mowgli looked inquiringly at Gisborne; but Abdul Gafur waddled hastily to the white mare, scrambled on her back and fled, the woodways crashing and echoing behind him.

'That was well done,' said Mowgli. 'But he will fall again unless he holds by the mane.'

'Now it is time to tell me what these things mean,' said Gisborne a little sternly. 'What is this talk of thy devils? How can men be driven up and down the *rukh* like cattle? Give answer.'

'Is the Sahib angry because I have saved him his money?'

'No, but there is trick-work in this that does not please me.'

'Very good. Now if I rose and stepped three paces into the *rukh* there is no one, not even the Sahib, could find me till I chose. As I would not willingly do this, so I would not willingly tell. Have patience a little, Sahib, and some day I will show thee everything, for, if thou wilt, some day we will drive the buck together. There is no devil-work in the matter at all. Only ... I know the *rukh* as a man knows the cooking-place in his house.'

Mowgli was speaking as he would speak to an impatient child. Gisborne, puzzled, baffled, and a great deal annoyed, said nothing, but stared on the ground and thought. When he looked up the man of the woods had gone.

'It is not good,' said a level voice from the thicket, 'for friends to be angry. Wait till the evening, Sahib, when the air cools.'

Left to himself thus, dropped as it were in the heart of the *rukh*, Gisborne swore, then laughed, remounted his pony, and rode on. He visited a ranger's hut, overlooked a couple of new plantations, left some orders as to the burning of a patch of dry grass, and set out for a camping-ground of his own choice, a pile of splintered rocks roughly roofed over with branches and leaves, not far from the banks of the Kanye stream. It was twilight when he came in sight of his resting-place, and the *rukh* was waking to the hushed ravenous life of the night.

A camp-fire flickered on the knoll, and there was the smell of a very good dinner in the wind.

'Um,' said Gisborne, 'that's better than cold meat at any rate. Now the only man who'd be likely to be here'd be Muller, and, officially, he ought to be looking over the Changamanga *rukh*. I suppose that's why he's on my ground.'

The gigantic German who was the head of the Woods and Forests of all India, Head Ranger from Burma to Bombay, had a habit of flitting bat-like without warning from one place to another, and turning up exactly where he was least looked for. His theory was that sudden visitations, the discovery of short-comings and a word-of-mouth upbraiding of a subordinate were infinitely better than the slow processes of correspondence which might end in a written and official reprimand – a thing in after years to be counted against a Forest Officer's record. As he explained it: 'If I only talk to my boys like a Dutch uncle, dey say, "It was only dot damned old Muller," and dey do better next dime. But if my fat-head clerk he write and say dot Muller der Inspecdor-General fail to onderstand and is much annoyed, first dot does no goot because I am not dere, and, second, der fool dot comes after me he may say to my best boys: "Look here, you haf been wigged by my bredecessor." I tell you der big brass-hat pizness does not make der trees grow.'

Muller's deep voice was coming out of the darkness behind the firelight as he bent over the shoulders of his pet cook. 'Not so much sauce, you son of Belial! Worcester sauce he is a gondiment and not a fluid. Ah, Gisborne, you haf come to a very bad dinner. Where is your camp?' and he walked up to shake hands.

'I'm the camp, sir,' said Gisborne. 'I didn't know you were about here.'

Muller looked at the young man's trim figure. 'Goot! That is very goot! One horse and some cold things to eat. When I was young I did my camp so. Now you shall dine with me. I went into Headquarters to make up my rebort last month. I haf written half – ho! ho! – and der rest I haf leaved to my glerks and come out for a walk. Der Government is mad about dose reborts. I dold der Viceroy so at Simla.'

Gisborne chuckled, remembering the many tales that were told of Muller's conflicts with the Supreme Government. He was the chartered libertine of all the offices, for as a Forest Officer he had no equal.

'If I find you, Gisborne, sitting in your bungalow und hatching reborts to me about der blantations instead of riding der blantations, I will dransfer you to der middle of der Bikaneer Desert to reforest *him*. I am sick of reborts und chewing paper when we should do our work.'

'There's not much danger of my wasting time over my annuals. I hate them as much as you do, sir.'

The talk went over at this point to professional matters. Muller had some questions to ask, and Gisborne orders and hints to receive, till dinner was ready. It was the most civilised meal Gisborne had eaten for months. No distance from the base of supplies was allowed to interfere with the work of Muller's cook; and that table spread in the wilderness began with devilled small fresh-water fish, and ended with coffee and cognac.

'Ah!' said Muller at the end, with a sigh of satisfaction as he lighted a cheroot and dropped into his much worn camp-chair. 'When I am making reborts I am Freethinker und Atheist, but here in der *rukh* I am more than Christian. I am Bagan also.' He rolled the cheroot-butt luxuriously under his tongue, dropped his hands on his knees, and stared before him into the dim shifting heart of the *rukh*, full of stealthy noises; the snapping of twigs like the snapping of the fire behind him; the sigh and rustle of a heat-bended branch recovering her straightness in the cool night; the incessant mutter of the Kanye stream, and the undernote of the many-peopled grass uplands out of sight beyond a swell of hill. He blew out a thick puff of smoke, and began to quote Heine to himself.

'Yes, it is very goot. Very goot. "Yes, I work miracles, and, by Gott, dey come off too." I remember when dere was no *rukh* more big than your knee, from here to der plough-lands, und in drought-time der cattle ate bones of dead cattle up and down. Now der trees haf come back. Dey were planted by a Freethinker, because he know just de cause dot made der effect. But der trees dey had der cult of der old gods – "und der Christian Gods howl loudly." Dey could not live in der *rukh*, Gisborne.'

A shadow moved in one of the bridle-paths – moved and stepped out into the starlight.

'I haf said true. Hush! Here is Faunus himself come to see der Insbector-General. Himmel, he is der god! Look!'

It was Mowgli, crowned with his wreath of white flowers and walking with a half-peeled branch – Mowgli, very mistrustful of the fire-light and ready to fly back to the thicket on the least alarm.

'That's a friend of mine,' said Gisborne. 'He's looking for me. Ohé, Mowgli!'

Muller had barely time to gasp before the man was at Gisborne's side, crying: 'I was wrong to go. I was wrong, but I did not know then that the mate of him that was killed by this river was awake looking for thee. Else I should not have gone away. She tracked thee from the back-ranges, Sahib.'

'He is a little mad,' said Gisborne, 'and he speaks of all the beasts about here as if he was a friend of theirs.'

'Of course – of course. If Faunus does not know, who should know?' said Muller gravely. 'What does he say about tigers – dis god who knows you so well?'

Gisborne relighted his cheroot, and before he had finished the story of Mowgli and his exploits it was burned down to moustache-edge. Muller listened without interruption. 'Dot is not madness,' he said at last when Gisborne had described the driving of Abdul Gafur. 'Dot is not madness at all.'

'What is it, then? He left me in a temper this morning because I asked him to tell how he did it. I fancy the chap's possessed in some way.'

'No, dere is no bossession, but it is most wonderful. Normally they die young – dese beople. Und you say now dot your thief-servant did not say what drove der poney, and of course der nilghai he could not speak.'

'No, but, confound it, there wasn't anything. I listened, and I can hear most things. The bull and the man simply came headlong – mad with fright.'

For answer Muller looked Mowgli up and down from head to foot, then beckoned him nearer. He came as a buck treads a tainted trail.

'There is no harm,' said Muller in the vernacular. 'Hold out an arm.'

He ran his hand down to the elbow, felt that, and nodded. 'So I thought. Now the knee.' Gisborne saw him feel the kneecap and smile. Two or three white scars just above the ankle caught his eye.

'Those came when thou wast very young?' he said.

'Ay,' Mowgli answered with a smile. 'They were love-tokens from the little ones.' Then to Gisborne over his shoulder, 'This Sahib knows everything. Who is he?'

'That comes after, my friend. Now where are *they*?' said Muller.

Mowgli swept his hand round his head in a circle.

'So! And thou canst drive nilghai? See! There is my mare in her pickets. Canst thou bring her to me without frightening her?'

'Can I bring the mare to the Sahib without frightening her!' Mowgli repeated, raising his voice a little above its normal pitch. 'What is more easy if the heel-ropes are loose?'

'Loosen the head and heel-pegs,' shouted Muller to the groom. They were hardly out of the ground before the mare, a huge black Australian, flung up her head and cocked her ears.

'Careful! I do not wish her driven into the *rukh*,' said Muller.

Mowgli stood still fronting the blaze of the fire – in the very form and likeness of that Greek god who is so lavishly described in the novels. The mare whickered, drew up one hind leg, found that the heel-ropes were free, and moved swiftly to her master, on whose bosom she dropped her head, sweating lightly.

'She came of her own accord. My horses will do that,' cried Gisborne.

'Feel if she sweats,' said Mowgli.

Gisborne laid a hand on the damp flank.

'It is enough,' said Muller.

'It is enough,' Mowgli repeated, and a rock behind him threw back the word.

'That's uncanny, isn't it?' said Gisborne.

'No, only wonderful – most wonderful. Still you do not know, Gisborne?'

'I confess I don't.'

'Well then, I shall not tell. He says dot some day he will show you what it is. It would be gruel if I told. But why he is not dead I do not understand. Now listen thou.' Muller faced Mowgli, and returned to the vernacular. 'I am the head of all the *rukhs* in the country of India and others across the Black Water. I do not know how many men be under me – perhaps five thousand, perhaps ten. Thy business is this – to wander no more up and down the *rukh* and drive beasts for sport or for show, but to take service under me, who am the Government in the matter of Woods and Forests, and to live in this *rukh* as a forest guard; to drive the villagers' goats away when there is no order to feed them in the *rukh*; to admit them when there is an order; to keep down, as thou canst keep down, the boar and the nilghai when they become too many; to tell Gisborne Sahib how and where tigers move, and what game there is in the forests; and to give sure warning of all the fires in the *rukh*, for thou canst give warning more quickly than any other. For that work there is a payment each month in silver, and at the end, when thou hast gathered a wife and cattle and, may be, children, a pension. What answer?'

'That's just what I —' Gisborne began.

'My Sahib spoke this morning of such a service. I walked all day alone considering the matter, and my answer is ready here. I serve, *if* I serve in this *rukh* and no other: *with* Gisborne Sahib and with no other.'

'It shall be so. In a week comes the written order that pledges the honour of the Government for the pension. After that thou wilt take up thy hut where Gisborne Sahib shall appoint.'

'I was going to speak to you about it,' said Gisborne.

'I did not want to be told when I saw dot man. Dere will never be a forest-guard like him. He is a miracle. I tell you, Gisborne, some day you will find it so. Listen, he is blood-brother to every beast in der *rukh*!'

'I should be easier in my mind if I could understand him.'

'Dot will come. Now I tell you dot only once in my service, and dot is thirty years, haf I met a boy dot began as this man began. Und he died. Sometimes you hear of dem in der census reports, but dey all die. Dis man haf lived, and he is an anachronism, for he is before der Iron Age, and der Stone Age. Look here, he is at der beginnings of der history of man – Adam in der Garden, und now we want only an Eva! No! He is older than dot child-tale, shust as der *rukh* is older dan der gods. Gisborne, I am a Bagan now, once for all.'

Through the rest of the long evening Muller sat smoking and smoking and staring and staring into the darkness, his lips moving in multiplied quotations, and great wonder upon his face. He went to his tent, but presently came out again in his majestic pink sleeping-suit, and the last words that Gisborne heard him address to the *rukh* through the deep hush of midnight were these, delivered with immense emphasis:

'Dough we shivt und bedeck und bedrape us,
    Dou art noble und nude und andeek;
 Libidina dy moder, Briapus
    Dy fader, a God und a Greek.

Now I know dot, Bagan *or* Christian, I shall nefer know der inwardness of der *rukh*!'

*   *   *

It was midnight in the bungalow a week later when Abdul
Gafur, ashy gray with rage, stood at the foot of Gisborne's bed
and whispering bade him awake.

'Up, Sahib,' he stammered. 'Up and bring thy gun. Mine
honour is gone. Up and kill before any see.'

The old man's face had changed, so that Gisborne stared
stupidly.

'It was for this, then, that that jungle outcaste helped me to
polish the Sahib's table, and drew water and plucked fowls.
They have gone off together for all my beatings, and now he sits
among his devils dragging her soul to the Pit. Up, Sahib, and
come with me!'

He thrust a rifle into Gisborne's half-wakened hand and
almost dragged him from the room on to the verandah.

'They are there in the *rukh*; even within gunshot of the house.
Come softly with me.'

'But what is it? What is the trouble, Abdul?'

'Mowgli, and his devils. Also my own daughter,' said Abdul
Gafur. Gisborne whistled and followed his guide. Not for
nothing, he knew, had Abdul Gafur beaten his daughter of
nights, and not for nothing had Mowgli helped in the house-
work a man whom his own powers, whatever those were, had
convicted of theft. Also, a forest wooing goes quickly.

There was the breathing of a flute in the *rukh*, as it might
have been the song of some wandering wood-god, and, as they
came nearer, a murmur of voices. The path ended in a little
semicircular glade walled partly by high grass and partly by
trees. In the centre, upon a fallen trunk, his back to the watch-
ers and his arm round the neck of Abdul Gafur's daughter, sat
Mowgli, newly crowned with flowers, playing upon a rude
bamboo flute, to whose music four huge wolves danced sol-
emnly on their hind legs.

'Those are his devils,' Abdul Gafur whispered. He held a
bunch of cartridges in his hand. The beasts dropped to a long-
drawn quavering note and lay still with steady green eyes,
glaring at the girl.

'Behold,' said Mowgli, laying aside the flute. 'Is there anything of fear in that? I told thee, little Stout-heart, that there was not, and thou didst believe. Thy father said – and oh, if thou couldst have seen thy father being driven by the road of the nilghai! – thy father said that they were devils; and by Allah, who is thy God, I do not wonder that he so believed.'

The girl laughed a little rippling laugh, and Gisborne heard Abdul grind his few remaining teeth. This was not at all the girl that Gisborne had seen with a half-eye slinking about the compound veiled and silent, but another – a woman full blown in a night as the orchid puts out in an hour's moist heat.

'But they are my playmates and my brothers, children of that mother that gave me suck, as I told thee behind the cook-house,' Mowgli went on. 'Children of the father that lay between me and the cold at the mouth of the cave when I was a little naked child. Look' – a wolf raised his gray jowl, slavering at Mowgli's knee – 'my brother knows that I speak of them. Yes, when I was a little child he was a cub rolling with me on the clay.'

'But thou hast said that thou art human-born,' cooed the girl, nestling closer to the shoulder. 'Thou art human-born?'

'Said! Nay, I know that I am human-born, because my heart is in thy hold, little one.' Her head dropped under Mowgli's chin. Gisborne put up a warning hand to restrain Abdul Gafur, who was not in the least impressed by the wonder of the sight.

'But I was a wolf among wolves none the less till a time came when Those of the jungle bade me go because I was a man.'

'Who bade thee go? That is not like a true man's talk.'

'The very beasts themselves. Little one, thou wouldst never believe that telling, but so it was. The beasts of the jungle bade me go, but these four followed me because I was their brother. Then was I a herder of cattle among men, having learned their language. Ho! ho! The herds paid toll to my brothers, till a woman, an old woman, beloved, saw me playing by night with my brethren in the crops. They said that I was possessed of devils, and drove me from that village with sticks and stones, and the four came with me by stealth and not openly. That was when I had learned to eat cooked meat and to talk boldly. From village to village I went, heart of my heart, a herder of cattle, a tender of buffaloes, a tracker of game, but there was no man that dared lift a finger against me twice.' He stooped down and patted one of the heads. 'Do thou also like this. There is neither hurt nor magic in them. See, they know thee.'

'The woods are full of all manner of devils,' said the girl with a shudder.

'A lie. A child's lie,' Mowgli returned confidently. 'I have lain out in the dew under the stars and in the dark night, and I know. The jungle is my house. Shall a man fear his own roof-beams or a woman her man's hearth? Stoop down and pat them.'

'They are dogs and unclean,' she murmured, bending forward with averted head.

'Having eaten the fruit, now we remember the Law!' said Abdul Gafur bitterly. 'What is the need of this waiting, Sahib? Kill!'

'H'sh, thou. Let us learn what has happened,' said Gisborne.

'That is well done,' said Mowgli, slipping his arm round the girl again. 'Dogs or no dogs, they were with me through a thousand villages.'

'Ahi, and where was thy heart then? Through a thousand villages. Thou hast seen a thousand maids. I – that am – that am a maid no more, have I thy heart?'

'What shall I swear by? By Allah, of whom thou speakest?'

'Nay, by the life that is in thee, and I am well content. Where was thy heart in those days?'

Mowgli laughed a little. 'In my belly, because I was young and always hungry. So I learned to track and to hunt, sending and calling my brothers back and forth as a king calls his armies. Therefore I drove the nilghai for the foolish young Sahib, and the big fat mare for the big fat Sahib, when they questioned my power. It were as easy to have driven the men themselves. Even now,' – his voice lifted a little – 'even now I know that behind me stand thy father and Gisborne Sahib. Nay, do not run, for no ten men dare move a pace forward.

Remembering that thy father beat thee more than once, shall I give the word and drive him again in rings through the *rukh*?' A wolf stood up with bared teeth.

Gisborne felt Abdul Gafur tremble at his side. Next, his place was empty, and the fat man was skimming down the glade.

'Remains only Gisborne Sahib,' said Mowgli, still without turning; 'but I have eaten Gisborne Sahib's bread, and presently I shall be in his service, and my brothers will be his servants to drive game and carry the news. Hide thou in the grass.'

The girl fled, the tall grass closed behind her and the guardian wolf that followed, and Mowgli turning with his three retainers faced Gisborne as the Forest Officer came forward.

'That is all the magic,' he said, pointing to the three. 'The fat Sahib knew that we who are bred among wolves run on our elbows and our knees for a season. Feeling my arms and legs, he felt the truth which thou didst not know. Is it so wonderful, Sahib?'

'Indeed it is all more wonderful than magic. These then drove the nilghai?'

'Ay, as they would drive Eblis if I gave the order. They are my eyes and feet to me.'

'Look to it, then, that Eblis does not carry a double rifle. They have yet something to learn, thy devils, for they stand one behind the other, so that two shots would kill the three.'

'Ah, but they know they will be thy servants as soon as I am a forest-guard.'

'Guard or no guard, Mowgli, thou hast done a great shame to Abdul Gafur. Thou hast dishonoured his house and blackened his face.'

'For that, it was blackened when he took thy money, and made blacker still when he whispered in thy ear a little while since to kill a naked man. I myself will talk to Abdul Gafur, for I am a man of the Government service, with a pension. He shall make the marriage by whatsoever rite he will, or he shall run once more. I will speak to him in the dawn. For the rest, the Sahib has his house and this is mine. It is time to sleep again, Sahib.'

Mowgli turned on his heel and disappeared into the grass, leaving Gisborne alone. The hint of the wood-god was not to be mistaken; and Gisborne went back to the bungalow, where Abdul Gafur, torn by rage and fear, was raving in the verandah.

'Peace, peace,' said Gisborne, shaking him, for he looked as though he were going to have a fit. 'Muller Sahib has made the man a forest-guard, and as thou knowest, there is a pension at the end of that business, and it is Government service.'

'He is an outcaste – a *mlech* – a dog among dogs; an eater of carrion! What pension can pay for that?'

'Allah knows; and thou hast heard that the mischief is done. Wouldst thou blaze it to all the other servants? Make the *shadi* swiftly, and the girl will make him a Mussulman. He is very comely. Canst thou wonder that after thy beatings she went to him?'

'Did he say that he would chase me with his beasts?'

'So it seemed to me. If he be a wizard, he is at least a very strong one.'

Abdul Gafur thought awhile, and then broke down and howled, forgetting that he was a Mussulman:

'Thou art a Brahmin. I am thy cow. Make thou the matter plain, and save my honour if it can be saved!'

A second time then Gisborne plunged into the *rukh* and called Mowgli. The answer came from high overhead, and in no submissive tones.

'Speak softly,' said Gisborne, looking up. 'There is yet time to strip thee of thy place and hunt thee with thy wolves. The girl must go back to her father's house tonight. Tomorrow there will be the *shadi*, by the Mussulman law, and then thou canst take her away. Bring her to Abdul Gafur.'

'I hear.' There was a murmur of two voices conferring among the leaves. 'Also, we will obey – for the last time.'

A year later Muller and Gisborne were riding through the *rukh* together, talking of their business. They came out among the rocks near the Kanye stream; Muller riding a little in advance. Under the shade of a thorn thicket sprawled a naked brown baby, and from the brake immediately behind him peered the head of a gray wolf. Gisborne had just time to strike up Muller's rifle, and the bullet tore spattering through the branches above.

'Are you mad?' thundered Muller. 'Look!'

'I see,' said Gisborne quietly. 'The mother's somewhere near. You'll wake the whole pack, by Jove!'

The bushes parted once more, and a woman unveiled snatched up the child.

'Who fired, Sahib?' she cried to Gisborne.

'This Sahib. He had not remembered thy man's people.'

'Not remembered? But indeed it may be so, for we who live with them forget that they are strangers at all. Mowgli is down the stream catching fish. Does the Sahib wish to see him? Come out, ye lacking manners. Come out of the bushes, and make your service to the Sahibs.'

Muller's eyes grew rounder and rounder. He swung himself off the plunging mare and dismounted, while the jungle gave up four wolves who fawned round Gisborne. The mother stood nursing her child and spurning them aside as they brushed against her bare feet.

'You were quite right about Mowgli,' said Gisborne. 'I meant to have told you, but I've got so used to these fellows in the last twelve months that it slipped my mind.'

'Oh, don't apologise,' said Muller. 'It's nothing. Gott in Himmel! "Und I work miracles – und dey come off too!" '

At the Pit's Mouth

Men say it was a stolen tide—
   The Lord that sent it He knows all,
But in mine ear will aye abide
   The message that the bells let fall,
And awesome bells they were to me,
That in the dark rang 'Enderby'.

Jean Ingelow

Once upon a time there was a Man and his Wife and a Tertium Quid.

All three were unwise, but the Wife was the unwisest. The Man should have looked after his Wife, who should have avoided the Tertium Quid, who, again, should have married a wife of his own, after clean and open flirtations, to which nobody can possibly object, round Jakko or Observatory Hill. When you see a young man with his pony in a white lather and his hat on the back of his head, flying downhill at fifteen miles an hour to meet a girl who will be properly surprised to meet him, you naturally approve of that young man, and wish him Staff appointments, and take an interest in his welfare, and, as the proper time comes, give them sugar-tongs or side-saddles according to your means and generosity.

The Tertium Quid flew downhill on horseback, but it was to meet the Man's Wife; and when he flew uphill it was for the same end. The Man was in the Plains, earning money for his Wife to spend on dresses and four-hundred-rupee bracelets, and inexpensive luxuries of that kind. He worked very hard, and sent her a letter or a postcard daily. She also wrote to him daily, and said that she was longing for him to come up to Simla. The Tertium Quid used to lean over her shoulder and laugh as she wrote the notes. Then the two would ride to the Post Office together.

Now, Simla is a strange place and its customs are peculiar; nor is any man who has not spent at least ten seasons there qualified to pass judgment on circumstantial evidence, which is the most untrustworthy in the Courts. For these reasons, and for others which need not appear, I decline to state positively whether there was anything irretrievably wrong in the relations between the Man's Wife and the Tertium Quid. If there was, and hereon you must form your own opinion, it was the Man's Wife's fault. She was kittenish in her manners, wearing generally an air of soft and fluffy innocence. But she was deadlily learned and evil-instructed; and, now and again, when the mask dropped, men saw this, shuddered and – almost drew back. Men are occasionally particular, and the least particular men are always the most exacting.

Simla is eccentric in its fashion of treating friendships. Certain attachments which have set and crystallised through half-a-dozen seasons acquire almost the sanctity of the marriage bond, and are revered as such. Again, certain attachments equally old, and, to all appearance, equally venerable, never seem to win any recognised official status; while a chance-sprung acquaintance, not two months born, steps into the place which by right belongs to the senior. There is no law reducible to print which regulates these affairs.

Some people have a gift which secures them infinite toleration, and others have not. The Man's Wife had not. If she looked over the garden wall, for instance, women taxed her with stealing their husbands. She complained pathetically that she was not allowed to choose her own friends. When she put up her big white muff to her lips, and gazed over it and under her eyebrows at you as she said this thing, you felt that she had been infamously misjudged, and that all the other women's instincts were all wrong. Which was absurd. She was not allowed to own the Tertium Quid in peace; and was so strangely constructed that she would not have enjoyed peace had she been so permitted. She preferred some semblance of intrigue to cloak even her most commonplace actions.

After two months of riding, first round Jakko, then Elysium, then Summer Hill, then Observatory Hill, then under Jutogh, and lastly up and down the Cart Road, as far as the Tara Devi gap in the dusk, she said to the Tertium Quid, 'Frank, people say we are too much together, and people are so horrid.'

The Tertium Quid pulled his moustache, and replied that horrid people were unworthy of the consideration of nice people.

'But they have done more than talk – they have written – written to my hubby – I'm sure of it,' said the Man's Wife, and she pulled a letter from her husband out of her saddle-pocket and gave it to the Tertium Quid.

It was an honest letter, written by an honest man, then stewing in the Plains on two hundred rupees a month (for he allowed his wife eight hundred and fifty), and in a silk singlet and cotton trousers. It said that, perhaps, she had not thought of the unwisdom of allowing her name to be so generally coupled with the Tertium Quid's; that she was too much of a child to understand the dangers of that sort of thing; that he, her husband, was the last man in the world to interfere jealously with her little amusements and interests, but that it would be better were she to drop the Tertium Quid quietly and for her husband's sake. The letter was sweetened with many pretty little pet names, and it amused the Tertium Quid considerably. He and She laughed over it, so that you, fifty yards away, could see their shoulders shaking while the horses slouched along side by side.

Their conversation was not worth repeating. The upshot of it was that, next day, no one saw the Man's Wife and the Tertium Quid together. They had both gone down to the Cemetery, which, as a rule, is only visited officially by the inhabitants of Simla.

A Simla funeral with the clergyman riding, the mourners riding, and the coffin creaking as it swings between the bearers, is one of the most depressing things on this earth, particularly when the procession passes under the wet, dank dip beneath the Rockcliffe Hotel, where the sun is shut out, and all the hill streams are wailing and weeping together as they go down the valleys.

Occasionally folk tend the graves, but we in India shift and are transferred so often that, at the end of the second year, the Dead have no friends – only acquaintances who are far too busy amusing themselves up the hill to attend to old partners. The idea of using a Cemetery as a rendezvous is distinctly a feminine one. A man would have said simply, 'Let people talk. We'll go down the Mall.' A woman is made differently, especially if she be such a woman as the Man's Wife. She and the Tertium Quid enjoyed each other's society among the graves of men and women whom they had known and danced with aforetime.

They used to take a big horse-blanket and sit on the grass a little to the left of the lower end, where there is a dip in the ground, and where the occupied graves stop short and the ready-made ones are not ready. Each well-regulated Indian Cemetery keeps half-a-dozen graves permanently open for contingencies and incidental wear and tear. In the Hills these are more usually baby's size, because children who come up weakened and sick from the Plains often succumb to the effects of the Rains in the Hills or get pneumonia from their *ayahs* taking them through damp pinewoods after the sun has set. In cantonments, of course, the man's size is more in request; these arrangements varying with the climate and population.

One day when the Man's Wife and the Tertium Quid had just arrived in the Cemetery, they saw some coolies breaking ground. They had marked out a full-size grave, and the Tertium Quid asked them whether any Sahib was sick. They said that they did not know; but it was an order that they should dig a Sahib's grave.

'Work away,' said the Tertium Quid, 'and let's see how it's done.'

The coolies worked away, and the Man's Wife and the

Tertium Quid watched and talked for a couple of hours while
the grave was being deepened. Then a coolie, taking the earth
in baskets as it was thrown up, jumped over the grave.

'That's queer,' said the Tertium Quid. 'Where's my ulster?'

'What's queer?' said the Man's Wife.

'I have got a chill down my back – just as if a goose had
walked over my grave.'

'Why do you look at the thing, then?' said the Man's Wife.
'Let us go.'

The Tertium Quid stood at the head of the grave, and stared
without answering for a space. Then he said, dropping a pebble
down, 'It is nasty – and cold: horribly cold. I don't think I
shall come to the Cemetery any more. I don't think grave-
digging is cheerful.'

The two talked and agreed that the Cemetery was depressing.
They also arranged for a ride next day out from the Cemetery
through the Mashobra Tunnel up to Fagoo and back, because
all the world was going to a garden-party at Viceregal Lodge,
and all the people of Mashobra would go too.

Coming up the Cemetery road, the Tertium Quid's horse
tried to bolt uphill, being tired with standing so long, and
managed to strain a back sinew.

'I shall have to take the mare tomorrow,' said the Tertium
Quid, 'and she will stand nothing heavier than a snaffle.'

They made their arrangements to meet in the Cemetery,
after allowing all the Mashobra people time to pass into Simla.
That night it rained heavily, and, next day, when the Tertium
Quid came to the trysting-place, he saw that the new grave
had a foot of water in it, the ground being a tough and sour
clay.

'Jove! That looks beastly,' said the Tertium Quid. 'Fancy
being boarded up and dropped into that well!'

They then started off to Fagoo, the mare playing with the
snaffle and picking her way as though she were shod with satin,
and the sun shining divinely. The road below Mashobra to
Fagoo is officially styled the Himalayan-Tibet Road; but in
spite of its name it is not much more than six feet wide in most

places, and the drop into the valley below may be anything between one and two thousand feet.

'Now we're going to Tibet,' said the Man's Wife merrily, as the horses drew near to Fagoo. She was riding on the cliff side.

'Into Tibet,' said the Tertium Quid, 'ever so far from people who say horrid things, and hubbies who write stupid letters. With you – to the end of the world!'

A coolie carrying a log of wood came round a corner, and the mare went wide to avoid him – forefeet in and haunches out, as a sensible mare should go.

'To the world's end,' said the Man's Wife, and looked unspeakable things over her near shoulder at the Tertium Quid.

He was smiling, but, while she looked, the smile froze stiff, as it were, on his face, and changed to a nervous grin – the sort of grin men wear when they are not quite easy in their saddles. The mare seemed to be sinking by the stern, and her nostrils cracked while she was trying to realise what was happening. The rain of the night before had rotted the drop-side of the Himalayan-Tibet Road, and it was giving way under her. 'What are you doing?' said the Man's Wife. The Tertium Quid gave no answer. He grinned nervously and set his spurs into the mare, who rapped with her forefeet on the road, and the struggle began. The Man's Wife screamed, 'Oh, Frank, get off!'

But the Tertium Quid was glued to the saddle – his face blue and white – and he looked into the Man's Wife's eyes. Then the Man's Wife clutched at the mare's head and caught her by the nose instead of the bridle. The brute threw up her head and went down with a scream, the Tertium Quid upon her, and the nervous grin still set on his face.

The Man's Wife heard the tinkle-tinkle of little stones and loose earth falling off the roadway, and the sliding roar of the man and horse going down. Then everything was quiet, and she called on Frank to leave his mare and walk up. But Frank did not answer. He was underneath the mare, nine hundred feet below, spoiling a patch of Indian corn.

As the revellers came back from Viceregal Lodge in the mists of the evening, they met a temporarily insane woman, on a temporarily mad horse, swinging round the corners, with her eyes and her mouth open, and her head like the head of a Medusa. She was stopped by a man at the risk of his life, and taken out of the saddle, a limp heap, and put on the bank to explain herself. This wasted twenty minutes, and then she was sent home in a lady's 'rickshaw, still with her mouth open and her hands picking at her riding-gloves.

She was in bed through the following three days, which were rainy; so she missed attending the funeral of the Tertium Quid, who was lowered into eighteen inches of water, instead of the twelve to which he had first objected.

My Lord the Elephant

'Less you want your toes trod off you'd better get back at once,
    For the bullocks are walkin' two by two,
    The *byles* are walkin' two by two,
    The bullocks are walkin' two by two,
An' the elephants bring the guns!
      Ho! Yuss!
Great – big – long – black forty-pounder guns:
    Jiggery-jolty to and fro,
    Each as big as a launch in tow—
Blind – dumb – broad-breeched beggars o' batterin' guns!

Barrack-Room Ballad

Touching the truth of this tale there need be no doubt at all,
for it was told to me by Mulvaney at the back of the elephant-
lines, one warm evening when we were taking the dogs out for
exercise. The twelve Government elephants rocked at their
pickets outside the big mud-walled stables (one arch, as wide
as a bridge-arch, to each restless beast), and the mahouts
were preparing the evening meal. Now and again some impatient youngster would smell the cooking flour-cakes and
squeal; and the naked little children of the elephant-lines would
strut down the row shouting and commanding silence, or,
reaching up, would slap at the eager trunks. Then the elephants
feigned to be deeply interested in pouring dust upon their
heads, but, so soon as the children passed, the rocking,
fidgeting, and muttering broke out again.

The sunset was dying, and the elephants heaved and swayed
dead black against the one sheet of rose-red low down in the

dusty gray sky. It was at the beginning of the hot weather, just after the troops had changed into their white clothes, so Mulvaney and Ortheris looked like ghosts walking through the dusk. Learoyd had gone off to another barrack to buy sulphur ointment for his last dog under suspicion of mange, and with delicacy had put his kennel into quarantine at the back of the furnace where they cremate the anthrax cases.

'*You* wouldn't like mange, little woman?' said Ortheris, turning my terrier over on her fat white back with his foot. 'You're no end bloomin' partic'lar, you are. 'Oo wouldn't take no notice o' me t'other day 'cause she was goin' 'ome all alone in 'er dorg-cart, eh? Settin' on the box-seat like a bloomin' little tart, you was, Vicky. Now you run along an' make them 'uttees 'oller. Sick 'em, Vicky, loo!'

Elephants loathe little dogs. Vixen barked herself down the pickets, and in a minute all the elephants were kicking and squealing and clucking together.

'Oh, you soldier-men,' said a mahout angrily, 'call off your she-dog. She is frightening our elephant-folk.'

'Rummy beggars!' said Ortheris meditatively. ' 'Call 'em people, same as if they was. An' they are too. Not so bloomin' rummy when you come to think of it, neither.'

Vixen returned yapping to show that she could do it again if she liked, and established herself between Ortheris's knees, smiling a large smile at his lawful dogs who dared not fly at her.

' 'Seed the battery this mornin'?' said Ortheris. He meant the newly arrived elephant-battery; otherwise he would have said simply 'guns'. Three elephants harnessed tandem go to each gun, and those who have not seen the big forty-pounders of position trundling along in the wake of their gigantic teams have yet something to behold. The lead-elephant had behaved very badly on parade; had been cut loose, sent back to the lines in disgrace, and was at that hour squealing and lashing out with his trunk at the end of the line; a picture of blind, bound, bad temper. His mahout, standing clear of the flail-like blows, was trying to soothe him.

'That's the beggar that cut up on p'rade. 'E's *must*,' said

Ortheris, pointing. 'There'll be murder in the lines soon, and then, per'aps, 'e'll get loose an' we'll 'ave to be turned out to shoot 'im, same as when one o' they native king's elephants *musted* last June. 'Ope 'e will.'

'*Must* be sugared!' said Mulvaney contemptuously from his resting-place on the pile of dried bedding. 'He's no more than in a powerful bad timper wid bein' put upon. I'd lay my kit he's new to the gun-team, an' by natur' he hates haulin'. Ask the mahout, sorr.'

I hailed the old white-bearded mahout who was lavishing pet words on his sulky red-eyed charge.

'He is not *musth*,' the man replied indignantly; 'only his honour has been touched. Is an elephant an ox or a mule that he should tug at a trace? His strength is in his head – Peace, peace, my Lord! It was not *my* fault that they yoked thee this morning! – Only a low-caste elephant will pull a gun, and *he* is a Kumeria of the Doon. It cost a year and the life of a man to break him to burden. They of the Artillery put him in the gun-team because one of their base-born brutes has gone lame. No wonder that he was, and is wroth.'

'Rummy! Most unusual rum,' said Ortheris. 'Gawd, 'e is in a temper, though! S'pose 'e got loose!'

Mulvaney began to speak but checked himself, and I asked the mahout what would happen if the heel-chains broke.

'God knows, who made elephants,' he said simply. 'In his now state peradventure he might kill you three, or run at large till his rage abated. He would not kill me except he were *musth*. *Then* would he kill me before any one in the world, because he loves me. Such is the custom of the elephant-folk; and the custom of us mahout-people matches it for foolishness. We trust each our own elephant, till our own elephant kills us. Other castes trust women, but we the elephant-folk. I have seen men deal with enraged elephants and live; but never was man yet born of woman that met my lord the elephant in his *musth* and lived to tell of the taming. They are enough bold who meet him angry.'

I translated. Then said Terence: 'Ask the heathen if he iver saw a man tame an elephint – anyways – a white man.'

'Once,' said the mahout, 'I saw a man astride of such a beast in the town of Cawnpore; a bare-headed man, a white man, beating it upon the head with a gun. It was said he was possessed of devils or drunk.'

'Is ut like, think you, he'd be doin' it sober?' said Mulvaney after interpretation, and the chained elephant roared.

'There's only one man top of earth that would be the partic'lar kind o' sorter bloomin' fool to do it!' said Ortheris. 'When was that, Mulvaney?'

'As the naygur sez, in Cawnpore; an' I was that fool – in the days av my youth. But it came about as naturil as wan thing leads to another – me an' the elephint, and the elephint and me; an' the fight betune us was the most naturil av all.'

'That's just wot it would ha' been,' said Ortheris. 'Only you must ha' been more than usual full. You done one queer trick with an elephant that I know of, why didn't you never tell us the other one?'

'Bekase, onless you had heard the naygur here say what he has said spontaneous, you'd ha' called me for a liar, Stanley, my son, an' it would ha' bin my duty an' my delight to give you the father an' mother av a beltin'! There's only wan fault about you, little man, an' that's thinking you know all there is in the world, an' a little more. 'Tis a fault that has made away wid a few orf'cers I've served undher, not to spake av ivry man but two that I iver thried to make into a privit.'

'Ho!' said Ortheris with ruffled plumes, 'an' 'oo was your two bloomin' little Sir Garnets, eh?'

'Wan was mesilf,' said Mulvaney with a grin that darkness could not hide; 'an' – seein' that he's not here there's no harm speakin' av' him – t'other was Jock.'

'Jock's no more than a 'ayrick in trousies. 'E be'aves *like* one; an' 'e can't *'it* one at a 'undred; 'e was born *on* one, an' s'welp me 'e'll die *under* one for not bein' able to say wot 'e wants in a Christian lingo,' said Ortheris, jumping up from the piled fodder only to be swept off his legs. Vixen leaped upon his stomach, and the other dogs followed and sat down there.

'I know what Jock is like,' I said. 'I want to hear about the elephant, though.'

'It's another o' Mulvaney's bloomin' panoramas,' said Ortheris, gasping under the dogs. "'Im an' Jock for the 'ole bloomin' British Army! You'll be sayin' you won Waterloo next – you an' Jock. Garn!'

Neither of us thought it worth while to notice Ortheris. The big gun-elephant threshed and muttered in his chains, giving tongue now and again in crashing trumpet-peals, and to this accompaniment Terence went on: 'In the beginnin',' said he, 'me bein' what I was, there was a misunderstandin' wid my sergeant that was then. He put his spite on me for various reasons—'

The deep-set eyes twinkled above the glow of the pipe-bowl, and Ortheris grunted, 'Another petticoat!'

'—For various an' promiscuous reasons; an' the upshot av it was that he come into barricks wan afternoon whin I was settlin' my cowlick before goin' walkin', called me a big baboon (which I was not), an' a demoralisin' beggar (which I was), an' bid me go on fatigue thin an' there, helpin' shift E.P. tents, fourteen av thim from the rest-camps. At that, me bein' set on my walk—'

'Ah!' from under the dogs, "'e's a Mormon, Vic. Don't you 'ave nothin' to do with 'im, little dorg.'

'—Set on my walk, I tould him a few things that came up in my mind, an' wan thing led on to another, an' betune talkin' I made time for to hit the nose av him so that he'd be no Venus to any woman for a week to come. 'Twas a fine big nose, and well it paid for a little groomin'. Afther that I was so well pleased wid my handicraftfulness that I niver raised fist on the gyard that came to take me to Clink. A child might ha' led me along, for I knew old Kearney's nose was ruined. That summer the Ould Rig'ment did not use their own Clink, bekase the cholera was hangin' about there like Mildew on wet boots, an' 'twas murdher to confine in ut. We borrowed the Clink that belonged to the Holy Christians (the rig'ment that has never seen service yet), and that lay a matther av a mile away, acrost two p'rade-grounds an' the main road, an' all the ladies av Cawnpore goin' out for their afternoon dhrive. So I moved in the best av society, my shadow dancin' along forninst me, an' the gyard as solemn as putty, the bracelets on my wrists, an' my heart full contint wid the notion av Kearney's pro – pro – probosculum in a shling.

'In the middle av ut all I perceived a gunner-orf'cer in full rig'mentals perusin' down the road, hell-for-leather, wid his mouth open. He fetched wan woild despairin' look on the dog-kyarts an' the polite society av Cawnpore, an' thin he dived like a rabbut into a dhrain by the side av the road.

' "Bhoys," sez I, "that orf'cer's dhrunk. 'Tis scand'lus. Let's take him to Clink too."

'The corp'ril of the gyard made a jump for me, unlocked my stringers, an' he sez: "If it comes to runnin', run for your life. If it doesn't, I'll trust your honour. Anyways," sez he, "come to Clink whin you can."

'Then I behild him runnin' wan way, stuffin' the bracelets in his pocket, they bein' Gov'ment property and the gyard runnin' another, an' all the dog-kyarts runnin' all ways to wanst, an' me alone lookin' down the red bag av a mouth av an elephint forty-two feet high at the shoulder, tin feet wide, wid tusks as long as the Ochterlony Monumint. That was my first reconnaissance. Maybe he was not quite so contagious, nor quite so tall, but I didn't stop to throw out pickets. Mother av Hiven, how I ran down the road! The baste began to inveshtigate the dhrain wid the gunner-orf'cer in ut; an' that was the makin' av me. I tripped over wan av the rifles that my gyard had discarded (onsoldierly blackguards they was!), and whin I got up I was facin' t'other way about an' the elephint was huntin' for the gunner-orf'cer. I can see his big fat back yet. Excipt that he didn't dig, he car'ied on for all the world like little Vixen here at a rat-hole. He put his head down (by my sowl he nearly stood on ut!) to shquint down the dhrain; thin he'd grunt, and run round to the other ind in case the orf'cer was gone out by the back door; an' he'd shtuff his trunk down the flue an' get ut filled wid mud, an' blow ut out, an' grunt, an' swear! My troth, he swore all hiven down upon that orf'cer; an' what a commissariat elephint had to do wid a gunner-orf'cer passed me. Me havin' nowhere to go except to Clink, I stud in the road wid the rifle, a Snider an' no amm'nition, philosophisin' upon the rear ind av the animal. All round me, miles and miles, there was howlin' desolation, for ivry human sowl wid two legs, or four for the matther av that, was ambuscadin', an' this ould rapparee stud on his head tuggin' and gruntin' above the dhrain, his tail stickin' up to the sky, an' he thryin' to thrumpet through three feet av road-sweepin's up his thrunk. Begad, 'twas wickud to behold!

'Subsequint he caught sight av me standin' alone in the wide, wide world lanin' on the rifle. That dishcomposed him, bekase he thought I was the gunner-orf'cer got out unbeknownst. He looked betune his feet at the dhrain, an' he looked at me, an' I sez to myself: "Terence, my son, you've been watchin' this Noah's ark too long. Run for your life!" Dear knows I wanted to tell him I was only a poor privit on my way to Clink, an' no orf'cer at all, at all; but he put his ears forward av his thick head, an' I rethreated down the road grippin' the rifle, my back as cowld as a tombstone, and the slack av my trousies, where I made sure he'd take hould, crawlin' wid – wid invidjus apprehension.

'I might ha' run till I dhropped, bekase I was betune the two straight lines av the road, an' a man, or a thousand men for the matther av that, are the like av sheep in keepin' betune right an' left marks.'

'Same as canaries,' said Ortheris from the darkness. 'Draw a line on a bloomin' little board, put their bloomin' little beakses there; stay so for hever and hever, amen, they will. 'Seed a 'ole reg'ment, I 'ave, walk crabways along the edge of a two-foot water-cut 'stid o' thinkin' to cross it. Men *is* sheep – bloomin' sheep. Go on.'

'But I saw his shadow wid the tail av my eye,' continued the man of experiences, 'an' "Wheel," I sez, "Terence, wheel!" an' I wheeled. 'Tis truth that I cud hear the shparks flyin' from my heels; an' I shpun into the nearest compound, fetched wan jump from the gate to the verandah av the house, an' fell over a tribe of naygurs wid a half-caste boy at a desk, all manu-facturin' harness. 'Twas Antonio's Carriage Emporium at Cawnpore. You know ut, sorr?

'Ould Grambags must ha' wheeled abreast wid me, for his trunk came lickin' into the verandah like a belt in a barrick-room row, before I was in the shop. The naygurs an' the half-caste boy howled an' wint out at the backdoor, an' I stud lone as Lot's wife among the harness. A powerful thirsty thing is harness, by reason av the smell to ut.

'I wint into the back room, nobody bein' there to invite, an' I found a bottle av whisky and a goglet av wather. The first an' the second dhrink I never noticed bein' dhry, but the fourth an' the fifth tuk good hould av me an' I began to think scornful av elephints. "Take the upper ground in manœ'vrin', Terence," I sez; "an' you'll be a gen'ral yet," sez I. An' wid that I wint up to the flat mud roof av the house an' looked over the edge av the parapit, threadin' delicate. Ould Barrel-belly was in the compound, walkin' to an' fro, pluckin' a piece av grass here an' a weed there, for all the world like our colonel that is now whin his wife's given him a talkin' down an' he's prom'nadin' to ease his timper. His back was to me, an' by the same token, I hiccupped. He checked in his walk, wan ear forward like a deaf ould lady wid an ear-thrumpet, an' his thrunk hild out in a kind av fore-reaching hook. Thin he wagged his ear sayin', "Do my sinses deceive me?" as plain as print, an' he recomminst promenadin'. You know Antonio's compound? 'Twas as full thin as 'tis now av new kyarts and ould kyarts, an' second-hand kyarts an' kyarts for hire – landos, an' b'rooshes, an' brooms, an' wag'nettes av ivry description. Thin I hiccupped again, an' he began to study the ground beneath him, his tail whistlin' wid emotion. Thin he lapped his thrunk round the shaft av a wag'nette an' dhrew it out circumspectuous an' thoughtful. "He's not there," he sez, fumblin' in the cush-ions wid his thrunk. Thin I hiccupped again, an' wid that he lost his patience good an' all, same as this wan in the lines here.'

The gun-elephant was breaking into peal after peal of indignant trumpetings, to the disgust of the other animals who had finished their food and wished to drowse. Between the outcries we could hear him picking restlessly at his ankle ring.

'As I was sayin',' Mulvaney went on, 'he behaved dishgraceful. He let out wid his fore-fut like a steam-hammer, bein' convinced that I was in ambuscade adjacent; an' that wag'nette ran back among the other carriages like a field-gun in charge. Thin he hauled ut out again an' shuk ut, an' by nature it came all to little pieces. Afther that he went sheer damn, slam, dancin', lunatic, double-shuffle demented wid the whole av Antonio's shtock for the season. He kicked, an' he straddled, and he stamped, an' he pounded all at wanst, his big bald head bobbin' up an' down, solemn as a rigadoon. He tuk a new shiny broom an' kicked ut on wan corner, an' ut opened out like a blossomin' lily; an' he shtuck wan fool-foot through the flure av ut an' a wheel was shpinnin' on his tusk. At that he got scared, an' by this an' that he fair sat down plump among the carriages, an' they pricked 'im wid splinters till he was a boundin' pincushin. In the middle av the mess, whin the kyarts was climbin' wan on top av the other, an' rickochettin' off the mud walls, an' showin' their agility, wid him tearin' their wheels off, I heard the sound av distrestful wailin' on the housetops, an' the whole Antonio firm an' fam'ly was cursin' me an' him from the roof next door; me bekase I'd taken refuge wid them, and he bekase he was playin' shtep-dances wid the carriages av the aristocracy.

' "Divart his attention," sez Antonio, dancin' on the roof in his big white waistcoat. "Divart his attention," he sez, "or I'll prosecute you." An' the whole fam'ly shouts, "Hit him a kick, mister soldier."

' "He's divartin' himself," I sez, for it was just the worth av a man's life to go down into the compound. But by way av makin' show I threw the whisky-bottle ('twas not full whin I came there) at him. He shpun round from what was left av the last kyart, an' shtuck his head into the verandah not three feet below me. Maybe 'twas the temptin'ness av his back or the whisky. Anyways, the next thing I knew was me, wid my hands full av mud an' mortar, all fours on his back, an' the Snider just slidin' off the slope av his head. I grabbed that an' scuffled on his neck, dhruv my knees undher his big flappin' ears, an' we wint to glory out av that compound wid a shqueal that crawled up my back an' down my belly. Thin I remimbered the Snider, an' I grup ut by the muzzle an' hit him on the head. 'Twas most forlorn – like tappin' the deck av a throopship wid a cane to stop the engines whin you're sea-sick. But I parsevered till I sweated, an' at last from takin' no notice at all he began to grunt. I hit wid the full strength that was in me in those days, an' it might ha' discommoded him. We came back to the p'rade-groun' forty miles an hour, trumpetin' vainglorious. I never stopped hammerin' him for a minut'; 'twas by way av divartin' him from runnin' undher the trees an' scrapin' me off like a poultice. The p'rade-groun' an' the road was all empty, but the throops was on the roofs av the barricks, an' betune Ould Thrajectory's gruntin' an' mine (for I was winded wid my stone-breakin'), I heard them clappin' an' cheerin'. He was growin' more confused an' tuk to runnin' in circles.

' "Begad," sez I to mesilf, "there's dacincy in all things, Terence. 'Tis like you've shplit his head, and whin you come out av Clink you'll be put under stoppages for killin' a Gov'ment elephint." At that I caressed him.'

''Ow the devil did you do that? Might as well pat a barrick,' said Ortheris.

'Thried all manner av endearin' epitaphs, but bein' more than a little shuk up I disremimbered what the divil would answer to. So, "Good dog," I sez; "Pretty puss," sez I; "Whoa mare," I sez; an' at that I fetched him a shtroke av the butt for to conciliate him, an' he stud still among the barricks.

' "Will no one take me off the top av this murderin' volcano?" I sez at the top av my shout; an' I heard a man yellin', "Hould on, faith an' patience, the other elephints are comin'." "Mother av Glory," I sez, "will I rough-ride the whole stud? Come an' take me down, ye cowards!"

'Thin a brace av fat she-elephints wid mahouts an' a commissariat sergint came shuffling round the corner av the barricks; an' the mahouts was abusin' ould Potiphar's mother an' blood-kin.

' "Observe my reinforcemints," I sez. "They're goin' to take you to Clink, my son;" an' the child av calamity put his ears forward an' swung head on to those females. The pluck av him, afther my oratorio on his brain-pan, wint to the heart av me. "I'm in dishgrace mesilf," I sez, "but I'll do what I can for ye. Will ye go to Clink like a man, or fight like a fool whin there's no chanst?" Wid that I fetched him wan last lick on the head, an' he fetched a tremenjus groan an' dhropped his thrunk. "Think," sez I to him, an' "Halt!" I sez to the mahouts. They was anxious so to do. I could feel the ould reprobit meditating undher me. At last he put his thrunk straight out an' gave a most melancholious toot (the like av a sigh wid an elephant); an' by that I knew the white flag was up an' the rest was no more than considherin' his feelin's.

' "He's done," I sez. "Kape open ordher left an' right alongside. We'll go to Clink quiet."

'Sez the commissariat sergeant to me from his elephant, "Are you a man or a mericle?" sez he.

' "I'm betwixt an' betune," I sez, thryin' to set up stiff-back. "An' what," sez I, "may ha' set this animal off in this opprobrious shtyle?" I sez, the gun-butt light an' easy on my hip an' my left hand dhropped, such as throopers behave. We was bowlin' on to the elephint-lines under escort all this time.

' "I was not in the lines whin the throuble began," sez the sergeant. "They tuk him off carryin' tents an' such like, an' put him to the gun-team. I knew he would not like ut, but by token it fair tore his heart out."

' "Faith, wan man's meat is another's poison," I sez. "'Twas bein' put on to carry tents that was the ruin av me." An' my heart warrumed to Ould Double Ends bekase he had been put upon.

' "We'll close on him here," sez the sergeant, whin we got to the elephint-lines. All the mahouts an' their childher was round the pickets cursin' my poney from a mile to hear. "You skip off on to my elephint's back," he sez. "There'll be throuble."

' "Sind that howlin' crowd away," I sez, "or he'll thrample the life out av thim." I cud feel his ears beginnin' to twitch. "An' do you an' your immoril she-elephints go well clear away. I will get down here. He's an Irishman," I sez, "for all his long Jew's nose, an' he shall be threated like an Irishman."

' "Are ye tired av life?" sez the sergeant.

' "Divil a bit," I sez; "but wan av us has to win, an' I'm av opinion 'tis me. Get back," I sez.

'The two elephints wint off, an' Smith O'Brine came to a halt dead above his own pickuts. "Down," sez I, whackin' him on the head, an' down he wint, shouldher over shouldher like a hill-side slippin' afther rain. "Now," sez I, slidin' down his nose an' runnin' to the front av him, "you will see the man that's betther than you."

'His big head was down betune his big fore-feet, an' they was twisted in sideways like a kitten's. He looked the picture av innocince an' forlornsomeness, an' by this an' that his big hairy undherlip was tremblin', an' he winked his eyes together to kape from cryin'. "For the love av God," I sez, clean forgettin' he was a dumb baste, "don't take ut to heart so! Aisy, be aisy," I sez; an' wid that I rubbed his cheek an' betune his eyes an' the top av his thrunk, talkin' all the time. "Now," sez I, "I'll make you comfortable for the night. Send wan or two childher here," I sez to the sergeant, who was watchin' for to see me killed. "He'll rouse at the sight av a man." '

'You got bloomin' clever all of a sudden,' said Ortheris. ''Ow did you come to know 'is funny little ways that soon?'

'Bekase,' said Terence with emphasis, 'bekase I had conquered the beggar, my son.'

'Ho!' said Ortheris between doubt and derision. 'G'on.'

'His mahout's child an' wan or two other line-babies came runnin' up, not bein' afraid av anything, an' some got wather, an' I washed the top av his poor sore head (begad, I had done him to a turn!), an' some picked the pieces av carts out av his hide, an' we scraped him, an' handled him all over, an' we put a thunderin' big poultice av neem-leaves (the same that we stick on a pony's gall) on his head, an' it looked like a smokin'-cap, an' we put a pile av young sugar-cane forninst him, an' he began to pick at ut. "Now," sez I, settin' down on his fore-foot, "we'll have a dhrink, an' let bygones be." I sent a naygur-child for a quart av arrack an' the sergeant's wife she sint me out four fingers av whisky, an' when the liquor came I cud see by the twinkle in Ould Typhoon's eye that he was no more a stranger to ut than me – worse luck, than me! So he tuk his quart like a Christian, an' *thin* I put his shackles on, chained him fore an' aft to the pickets, an' gave him my blessin' and wint back to barricks.'

'And after?' I said in the pause.

'Ye can guess,' said Mulvaney. 'There was confusion, an' the colonel gave me ten rupees, an' the adj'tant gave me five, an' my comp'ny captain gave me five, an' the men carried me round the barricks shoutin'.'

'Did you go to Clink?' said Ortheris.

'I niver heard a word more about the misundherstandin' wid Kearney's beak, if that's what you mane; but sev'ril av the bhoys was tuk off sudden to the Holy Christians' Hotel that night. Small blame to thim – they had twenty rupees in dhrinks. I wint to lie down an' sleep ut off, for I was as done an' double done as him there in the lines. 'Tis no small thing to go ride elephints.

'Subsequint, me an' the Venerable Father av Sin became mighty friendly. I wud go down to the lines, whin I was in dishgrace, an' spend an afthernoon collogin' wid him; he chewin' wan stick av sugar-cane an' me another, as thick as thieves. He'd take all I had out av my pockets an' put ut back again, an' now an' thin I'd bring him beer for his dijistin', an' I'd give him advice about bein' well behaved an' keepin' off the books. Afther that he wint the way av the Army, an' that's bein' thransferred as soon as you've made a good friend.'

'So you never saw him again?' I demanded.

'Do you belave the first half av the affair?' said Terence.

'I'll wait till Learoyd comes,' I said evasively. Except when he was carefully tutored by the other two and the immediate money-benefit explained, the Yorkshireman did not tell lies; and Terence, I knew, had a profligate imagination.

'There's another part still,' said Mulvaney. 'Ortheris was in that.'

'Then I'll believe it all,' I answered, not from any special belief in Ortheris's word, but from desire to learn the rest. Ortheris stole a pup from me when our acquaintance was new, and with the little beast stifling under his overcoat, denied not only the theft, but that he ever was interested in dogs.

'That was at the beginnin' av the Afghan business,' said Mulvaney; 'years afther the men that had seen me do the thrick was dead or gone home. I came not to speak av ut at the last – bekase I do *not* care to knock the face av ivry man that calls me a liar. At the very beginnin' av the marchin' I wint sick like a fool. I had a boot-gall, but I was all for keepin' up wid the rig'mint and such like foolishness. So I finished up wid a hole in my heel that you cud ha' dhruv a tent-peg into. Faith, how often have I preached that to recruities since, for a warnin' to thim to look afther their feet! Our docthor, who knew our business as well as his own, he sez to me, in the middle av the Tangi Pass it was: "That's sheer damned carelessness," sez he. "How often have I tould you that a marchin' man is no stronger than his feet – his feet – his feet!" he sez. "Now to hospital you go," he sez, "for three weeks, an expense to your Quane an' a nuisince to your counthry. Next time," sez he, "perhaps you'll put some av the whisky you pour down your throat, an' some av the tallow you put into your hair, into your socks," sez he. Faith he was a just man. So soon as we come to the head av the Tangi I wint to hospital, hoppin' on wan fut, woild wid disappointment. 'Twas a field-hospital (all flies an' native apothecaries an' liniment) dhropped, in a way av speakin', close by the head av the Tangi. The hospital guard was ravin' mad wid us sick for keepin' thim there, an' we was ravin' mad at bein' kept; an' through the Tangi, day an' night an' night an' day, the fut an' horse an' guns an' commissariat an' tents an' followers av the brigades was pourin' like a coffee-mill. The doolies

came dancin' through, scores an' scores av thim, an' they'd
turn up the hill to hospital wid their sick, an' I lay in bed nursin'
my heel, an' hearin' the men bein' tuk out. I remember wan
night (the time I was tuk wid fever) a man came rowlin' through
the tents an', "Is there any room to die here?" he sez; "there's
none wid the columns"; an' at that he dhropped dead acrost
a cot, an' thin the man in ut began to complain against dyin' all
alone in the dust undher dead men. Thin I must ha' turned
mad wid the fever, an' for a week I was prayin' the saints to
stop the noise av the columns movin' through the Tangi. Gun-
wheels it was that wore my head thin. Ye know how 'tis wid
fever?'

We nodded; there was no need to explain.

'Gun-wheels an' feet an' people shoutin', but mostly gun-
wheels. 'Twas neither night nor day to me for a week. In the
mornin' they'd rowl up the tent-flies, an' we sick cud look at
the Pass an' considher what was comin' next. Horse, fut, or
guns, they'd be sure to dhrop wan or two sick wid us an' we'd
get news. Wan mornin', whin the fever hild off of me, I was
watchin' the Tangi, an' 'twas just like the picture on the back-
side av the Afghan medal – men an' elephints an' guns comin'
wan at a time crawlin' out of a dhrain.'

'It were a dhrain,' said Ortheris with feeling. 'I've fell out an'
been sick in the Tangi twice; an' wot turns my innards ain't no
bloomin' vi'lets neither.'

'The Pass gave a twist at the ind, so everything shot out
suddint an' they'd built a throop-bridge (mud an' dead mules)
over a nullah at the head av ut. I lay an' counted the elephints
(gun-elephints) thryin' the bridge wid their thrunks an' rolling
out sagacious. The fifth elephint's head came round the corner,
an' he threw up his thrunk, an' he fetched a toot, an' there he
shtuck at the head of the Tangi like a cork in a bottle. "Faith,"
thinks I to mesilf, "he will not thrust the bridge; there will be
throuble." '

'Trouble! My Gawd!' said Ortheris. 'Terence, I was be'ind
that blooming 'uttee up to my stock in dust. Trouble!'

'Tell on then, little man; I only saw the hospital ind av ut.'

Mulvaney knocked the ashes out of his pipe, as Ortheris heaved the dogs aside and went on.

'We was escort to them guns, three comp'nies of us,' he said. 'Dewcy was our major, an' our orders was to roll up anything we come across in the Tangi an' shove it out t'other end. Sort o' pop-gun picnic, see? We'd rolled up a lot o' lazy beggars o' native followers, an' some commissariat supplies that was bivoo-whackin' for ever seemin'ly, an' all the sweepin's of 'arf a dozen things what ought to 'ave bin at the front weeks ago, an' Dewcy, he sez to us: "You're most 'eart-breakin' sweeps," 'e sez. "For 'eving's sake," sez 'e, "do a little sweepin' now." So we swep' – s'welp me, 'ow we did sweep 'em along! There was a full reg'ment be'ind us; most anxious to get on they was; an' they kep' on sendin' to us with the colonel's compliments, an' what in 'ell was we stoppin' the way for, please? Oh, they was partic'lar polite! So was Dewcy! 'E sent 'em back wot-for, an' 'e give us wot-for, an' we give the guns wot-for, an' they give the commissariat wot-for, an' the commissariat give first-class extry wot-for to the native followers, an' on we'd go again till we was stuck, an' the 'ole Pass 'ud be swimmin' Allelujah for a mile an' a 'arf. We 'adn't no tempers, nor no seats to our trousies, an' our coats an' our rifles was chucked in the carts, so as we might ha' been cut up any minute, an' we was doin' drover-work. That was wot it was; drovin' on the Islin'ton road!

'I was close up at the 'ead of the column when we saw the end of the Tangi openin' out ahead of us, an' I sez: "The door's open, boys. 'Oo'll git to the gall'ry fust?" I sez. Then I saw Dewcy screwin' 'is bloomin' eyeglass in 'is eye an' lookin' straight on. "Propped – *ther* beggar!" he sez; an' the be'ind end o' that bloomin' old 'uttee was shinin' through the dust like a bloomin' old moon made o' tarpaulin. Then we 'alted, all chock-a-block, one atop o' the other, an' right at the back o' the guns there sails in a lot o' silly grinnin' camels, wot the com-missariat was in charge of – sailin' away as if they was at the Zoological Gardens an' squeezin' our men most awful. The dust was that up you couldn't see your 'and; an' the more we 'it 'em on the 'ead the more their drivers sez, "Accha! Accha!" an' by Gawd it was "at yer" before you knew where you was. An' that 'uttee's be'ind end stuck in the Pass good an' tight, an' no one knew wot for.

'Fust thing we 'ad to do was to fight they bloomin' camels. I wasn't goin' to be eat by no bull-*oont*; so I 'eld up my trousies with one 'and, standin' on a rock, an' 'it away with my belt at every nose I saw bobbin' above me. Then the camels fell back, an' they 'ad to fight to keep the rear-guard an' the native followers from crushin' into them; an' the rear-guard 'ad to send down the Tangi to warn the other reg'ment that we was blocked. I 'eard the mahouts shoutin' in front that the 'uttee wouldn't cross the bridge; an' I saw Dewcy skippin' about through the dust like a musquito-worm in a tank. Then our comp'nies got tired o' waitin' an' begun to mark time, an' some goat struck up *Tommy, make room for your Uncle.* After *that,* you couldn't neither see nor breathe nor 'ear; an' there we was, singin' bloomin' serenades to the end of a' elephant that don't care for tunes! I sung too; I couldn't do nothin' else. They was strengthenin' the bridge in front, all for the sake of the 'uttee. By an' by a' orf'cer caught me by the throat an' choked the sing out of me. So I caught the next man I could see by the throat an' choked the sing out of '*im.*'

'What's the difference between being choked by an officer and being hit?' I asked, remembering a little affair in which Ortheris's honour had been injured by his lieutenant.

'One's a bloomin' lark, an' one's a bloomin' insult!' said Ortheris. 'Besides, we was on service, an' no one cares what an orf'cer does then, s'long as 'e gets our rations an' don't get us unusual cut up. After that we got quiet, an' I 'eard Dewcy say that 'e'd court-martial the lot of us soon as we was out of the Tangi. Then we give three cheers for Dewcy an' three more for the Tangi; an' the 'uttee's be'ind end was stickin' in the Pass, so we cheered *that.* Then they said the bridge had been strengthened, an' we give three cheers for the bridge; but the 'uttee wouldn't move a bloomin' hinch. Not 'im! Then we cheered 'im again, an' Kite Dawson, that was corner-man at all the sing-songs ('e died on the way down), began to give a nigger lecture on the be'ind ends of elephants, an' Dewcy, 'e tried to keep 'is face for a minute, but, Lord, you couldn't do such when Kite was playin' the fool an' askin' whether 'e mightn't 'ave leave to rent a villa an' raise 'is orphan children in the Tangi, 'cos 'e couldn't get 'ome no more. Then up come a orf'cer (mounted, like a fool, too) from the reg'mint at the back with some more of his colonel's pretty little compliments, an' what was this delay, please? We sung 'im *There's another bloomin' row downstairs* till 'is 'orse bolted, an' then we give 'im three cheers; an' Kite Dawson sez 'e was going to write to *The Times* about the awful state of the streets in Afghanistan. The 'uttee's be'ind end was stickin' in the Pass all the time. At last one o' the mahouts came to Dewcy an' sez something. "Oh Lord!" sez Dewcy, "*I* don't know the beggar's visiting-list! I'll give 'im another ten minutes an' then I'll shoot 'im." Things was gettin' pretty dusty in the Tangi, so we all listened. "'E wants to see a friend," sez Dewcy out loud to the men, an' 'e mopped 'is forehead an' sat down on a gun-trail.

'I leave it to you to judge 'ow the reg'ment shouted. "That's all right," we sez. "Three cheers for Mister Winterbottom's friend," sez we. "Why didn't you say so at first? Pass the word for old Swizzletail's wife" – and such like. Some o' the men they didn't laugh. They took it same as if it might have been a' introduction like, 'cos they knew about 'uttees. Then we all run forward over the guns an' in an' out among the elephants' legs – Lord, I wonder 'arf the comp'nies wasn't squashed – an' the next thing I saw was Terence 'ere, lookin' like a sheet o' wet paper, comin' down the 'illside wid a sergeant. "'Strewth," I sez. "I might ha' knowed 'e'd be at the bottom of any cat's trick," sez I. Now you tell wot 'appened your end?'

'I lay by the same as you did, little man, listenin' to the noises an' the bhoys singin'. Presently I heard whisperin' an' the doctor sayin', "Get out av this, wakin' my sick wid your jokes about elephints." An' another man sez, all angry: "'Tis a joke that is stoppin' two thousand men in the Tangi. That son av sin av a haybag av an elephint sez, or the mahouts sez for him, that he wants to see a friend, an' he'll not lift hand or fut till he finds him. I'm wore out wid inthrojucin' sweepers an' coolies to him, an' his hide's as full o' bay'net pricks as a musquito-net av holes, an' I'm here undher ordhers, doctor dear, to ask if any one, sick or well, or alive or dead, knows an elephint. I'm not mad," he sez, settin' on a box av medical comforts. "'Tis my ordhers, an' 'tis my mother," he sez, "that would laugh at me for the father av all fools today. Does any wan here know an elephint?" We sick was all quiet.

'"Now you've had your answer," sez the doctor. "Go away."

'"Hould on," I sez, thinkin' mistiways in my cot, an' I did not know my own voice. "I'm by way av bein' acquainted wid an elephint, myself," I sez.

'"That's delirium," sez the doctor. "See what you've done, sergeant. Lie down, man," he sez, seein' me thryin' to get up.

'"'Tis not," I sez. "I rode him round Cawnpore barricks. He will not ha' forgotten. I bruk his head wid a rifle."

'"Mad as a coot," sez the doctor, an' thin he felt my head. "It's quare," sez he. "Man," he sez, "if you go, d'you know 'twill either kill or cure?"

'"What do I care?" sez I. "If I'm mad, 'tis better dead."

'"Faith, that's sound enough," sez the doctor. "You've no fever on you now."

'"Come on," sez the sergeant. "We're all mad today, an' the throops are wantin' their dinner." He put his arm round av me an' I came into the sun, the hills an' the rocks skippin' big giddy-go-rounds. "Seventeen years have I been in the army," sez the sergeant, "an' the days av mericles are not done. They'll be givin' us more pay next. Begad," he sez, "the brute knows you!"

'Ould Obstructionist was screamin' like all possist whin I came up, an' I heard forty million men up the Tangi shoutin', "He knows him!" Thin the big thrunk came round me an' I was nigh faintin' wid weakness. "Are you well, Malachi?" I sez, givin' him the name he answered to in the lines. "Malachi, my son, are you well?" sez I, "for I am not." At that he thrumpeted again till the Pass rang to ut, an' the other elephints

tuk it up. Thin I got a little strength back. "Down, Malachi,"
I sez, "an' put me up, but touch me tendher for I am not good."
He was on his knees in a minut an' he slung me up as gentle as
a girl. "Go on now, my son," I sez. "You're blockin' the road."
He fetched wan more joyous toot, an' swung grand out av the
head av the Tangi, his gun-rear clankin' on his back; an' at the
back av him there wint the most amazin' shout I iver heard.
An' thin I felt my head shpin, an' a mighty sweat bruk out on
me, an' Malachi was growin' taller an' taller to me settin' on
his back, an' I sez, foolish-like an' weak, smilin' all round an'
about, "Take me down," I sez, "or I'll fall."

'The next I remimber was lyin' in my cot again, limp as a
chewed rag, but cured av the fever, an' the Tangi as empty as
the back av my hand. They'd all gone up to the front, an' ten
days later I wint up too, havin' blocked an' unblocked an entire
army corps. What do you think av ut, sorr?'

'I'll wait till I see Learoyd,' I repeated.

'Ah'm here,' said a shadow from among the shadows. 'Ah've
heard t' tale too.'

'Is it true, Jock?'

'Ay; true as t'owd bitch has getten t'mange. Orth'ris, yo'
maun't let t'dawgs hev owt to do wi' her.'

Wee Willie Winkie

An officer and a gentleman.

His full name was Percival William Williams, but he picked up the other name in a nursery-book, and that was the end of the christened titles. His mother's *ayah* called him Willie-*baba*, but as he never paid the faintest attention to anything that the *ayah* said, her wisdom did not help matters.

His father was the Colonel of the 195th, and as soon as Wee Willie Winkie was old enough to understand what Military Discipline meant, Colonel Williams put him under it. There was no other way of managing the child. When he was good for a week, he drew good-conduct pay; and when he was bad, he was deprived of his good-conduct stripe. Generally he was bad, for India offers many chances of going wrong to little six-year-olds.

Children resent familiarity from strangers, and Wee Willie Winkie was a very particular child. Once he accepted an acquaintance, he was graciously pleased to thaw. He accepted Brandis, a subaltern of the 195th, on sight. Brandis was having tea at the Colonel's, and Wee Willie Winkie entered strong in the possession of a good-conduct badge won for not chasing the hens round the compound. He regarded Brandis with gravity for at least ten minutes, and then delivered himself of his opinion.

'I like you,' said he slowly, getting off his chair and coming over to Brandis. 'I like you. I shall call you Coppy, because of your hair. Do you *mind* being called Coppy? It is because of ve hair, you know.'

Here was one of the most embarrassing of Wee Willie

Winkie's peculiarities. He would look at a stranger for some time, and then, without warning or explanation, would give him a name. And the name stuck. No regimental penalties could break Wee Willie Winkie of this habit. He lost his good-conduct badge for christening the Commissioner's wife 'Pobs'; but nothing that the Colonel could do made the Station forgo the nickname, and Mrs. Collen remained 'Pobs' till the end of her stay. So Brandis was christened 'Coppy', and rose, therefore, in the estimation of the Regiment.

If Wee Willie Winkie took an interest in any one, the fortunate man was envied alike by the officers and the rank and file. And in their envy lay no suspicion of self-interest. 'The Colonel's son' was idolised on his own merits entirely. Yet Wee Willie Winkie was not lovely. His face was permanently freckled, as his legs were permanently scratched, and in spite of his mother's almost tearful remonstrances he had insisted upon having his long yellow locks cut short in the military fashion. 'I want my hair like Sergeant Tummil's,' said Wee Willie Winkie, and, his father abetting, the sacrifice was accomplished.

Three weeks after the bestowal of his youthful affections on Lieutenant Brandis – henceforward to be called 'Coppy' for the sake of brevity – Wee Willie Winkie was destined to behold strange things and far beyond his comprehension.

Coppy returned his liking with interest. Coppy had let him wear for five rapturous minutes his own big sword – just as tall as Wee Willie Winkie. Coppy had promised him a terrier puppy; and Coppy had permitted him to witness the miraculous operation of shaving. Nay, more – Coppy had said that even he, Wee Willie Winkie, would rise in time to the ownership of a box of shiny knives, a silver soap-box, and a silver-handled 'sputter-brush', as Wee Willie Winkie called it. Decidedly, there was no one except his father, who could give or take away good-conduct badges at pleasure, half so wise, strong, and valiant as Coppy with the Afghan and Egyptian medals on his breast. Why, then, should Coppy be guilty of the unmanly weakness of kissing – vehemently kissing – a 'big girl', Miss Allardyce to wit? In the course of a morning ride Wee Willie Winkie had seen Coppy so doing, and, like the gentleman he was, had promptly wheeled round and cantered back to his groom, lest the groom should also see.

Under ordinary circumstances he would have spoken to his father, but he felt instinctively that this was a matter on which Coppy ought first to be consulted.

'Coppy,' shouted Wee Willie Winkie, reining up outside that subaltern's bungalow early one morning – 'I want to see you, Coppy!'

'Come in, young 'un,' returned Coppy, who was at early breakfast in the midst of his dogs. 'What mischief have you been getting into now?'

Wee Willie Winkie had done nothing notoriously bad for three days, and so stood on a pinnacle of virtue.

'*I*'ve been doing nothing bad,' said he, curling himself into a long chair with a studious affectation of the Colonel's languor after a hot parade. He buried his freckled nose in a tea-cup and, with eyes staring roundly over the rim, asked: 'I say, Coppy, is it pwoper to kiss big girls?'

'By Jove! You're beginning early. Who do you want to kiss?'

'No one. My muvver's always kissing me if I don't stop her. If it isn't pwoper, how was you kissing Major Allardyce's big girl last morning, by ve canal?'

Coppy's brow wrinkled. He and Miss Allardyce had with great craft managed to keep their engagement secret for a fortnight. There were urgent and imperative reasons why Major Allardyce should not know how matters stood for at least another month, and this small marplot had discovered a great deal too much.

'I saw you,' said Wee Willie Winkie calmly. 'But ve *sais* didn't see. I said, "*Hut jao*!"'

'Oh, you had that much sense, you young rip,' groaned poor Coppy, half amused and half angry. 'And how many people may you have told about it?'

'Only me myself. You didn't tell ven I twied to wide ve

buffalo ven my pony was lame; and I fought you wouldn't like.'

'Winkie,' said Coppy enthusiastically, shaking the small hand, 'you're the best of good fellows. Look here, you can't understand all these things. One of these days – hang it, how can I make you see it? – I'm going to marry Miss Allardyce, and then she'll be Mrs. Coppy, as you say. If your young mind is so scandalised at the idea of kissing big girls, go and tell your father.'

'What will happen?' said Wee Willie Winkie, who firmly believed that his father was omnipotent.

'I shall get into trouble,' said Coppy, playing his trump card with an appealing look at the holder of the ace.

'Ven I won't,' said Wee Willie Winkie briefly. 'But my faver says it's un-man-ly to be always kissing, and I didn't fink *you*'d do vat, Coppy.'

'I'm not always kissing, old chap. It's only now and then, and when you're bigger you'll do it too. Your father meant it's not good for little boys.'

'Ah!' said Wee Willie Winkie, now fully enlightened. 'It's like ve sputter-brush?'

'Exactly,' said Coppy gravely.

'But I don't fink I'll ever want to kiss big girls, nor no one, 'cept my muvver. And I *must* vat, you know.'

There was a long pause, broken by Wee Willie Winkie.

'Are you fond of vis big girl, Coppy?'

'Awfully!' said Coppy.

'Fonder van you are of Bell or ve Butcha – or me?'

'It's in a different way,' said Coppy. 'You see, one of these days Miss Allardyce will belong to me, but you'll grow up and command the Regiment and – all sorts of things. It's quite different, you see.'

'Very well,' said Wee Willie Winkie, rising. 'If you're fond of ve big girl I won't tell any one. I must go now.'

Coppy rose and escorted his small guest to the door, adding: 'You're the best of little fellows, Winkie. I tell you what. In thirty days from now you can tell if you like – tell any one you like.'

Thus the secret of the Brandis–Allardyce engagement was dependent on a little child's word. Coppy, who knew Wee Willie Winkie's idea of truth, was at ease, for he felt that he would not break promises. Wee Willie Winkie betrayed a special and unusual interest in Miss Allardyce, and, slowly revolving round that embarrassed young lady, was used to regard her gravely with unwinking eye. He was trying to discover why Coppy should have kissed her. She was not half so nice as his own mother. On the other hand, she was Coppy's property, and would in time belong to him. Therefore it behoved him to treat her with as much respect as Coppy's big sword or shiny pistol.

The idea that he shared a great secret in common with Coppy kept Wee Willie Winkie unusually virtuous for three weeks. Then the Old Adam broke out, and he made what he called a 'camp-fire' at the bottom of the garden. How could he have foreseen that the flying sparks would have lighted the Colonel's little hay-rick and consumed a week's store for the horses? Sudden and swift was the punishment – deprivation of the good-conduct badge and, most sorrowful of all, two days' confinement to barracks – the house and veranda – coupled with the withdrawal of the light of his father's countenance.

He took the sentence like the man he strove to be, drew himself up with a quivering under-lip, saluted, and, once clear of the room, ran to weep bitterly in his nursery – called by him 'my quarters'. Coppy came in the afternoon and attempted to console the culprit.

'I'm under awwest,' said Wee Willie Winkie mournfully, 'and I didn't ought to speak to you.'

Very early the next morning he climbed on to the roof of the house – that was not forbidden – and beheld Miss Allardyce going for a ride.

'Where are you going?' cried Wee Willie Winkie.

'Across the river,' she answered, and trotted forward.

Now the cantonment in which the 195th lay was bounded on the north by a river – dry in the winter. From his earliest years, Wee Willie Winkie had been forbidden to go across the river, and had noted that even Coppy – the almost almighty Coppy – had never set foot beyond it. Wee Willie Winkie had once been read to, out of a big blue book, the history of the Princess and the Goblins – a most wonderful tale of a land where the Goblins were always warring with the children of men until they were defeated by one Curdie. Ever since that date it seemed to him that the bare black and purple hills across the river were inhabited by Goblins, and, in truth, every one had said that there lived the Bad Men. Even in his own house the lower halves of the windows were covered with green paper on account of the Bad Men who might, if allowed clear view, fire into peaceful drawing-rooms and comfortable bedrooms. Certainly, beyond the river, which was the end of all the Earth, lived the Bad Men. And here was Major Allardyce's big girl, Coppy's property, preparing to venture into their borders! What would Coppy say if anything happened to her? If the Goblins ran off with her as they did with Curdie's Princess? She must at all hazards be turned back.

The house was still. Wee Willie Winkie reflected for a moment on the very terrible wrath of his father; and then – broke his arrest! It was a crime unspeakable. The low sun threw his shadow, very large and very black, on the trim garden-paths, as he went down to the stables and ordered his pony. It seemed to him in the hush of the dawn that all the big world had been bidden to stand still and look at Wee Willie Winkie guilty of mutiny. The drowsy *sais* gave him his mount, and, since the one great sin made all others insignificant, Wee Willie Winkie said that he was going to ride over to Coppy Sahib, and went out at a foot-pace, stepping on the soft mould of the flower-borders.

The devastating track of the pony's feet was the last misdeed that cut him off from all sympathy of Humanity. He turned into the road, leaned forward, and rode as fast as the pony could put foot to the ground in the direction of the river.

But the liveliest of twelve-two ponies can do little against the long canter of a Waler. Miss Allardyce was far ahead, had passed through the crops, beyond the Police-posts, where all the guards were asleep, and her mount was scattering the pebbles of the river-bed as Wee Willie Winkie left the cantonment and British India behind him. Bowed forward and still flogging, Wee Willie Winkie shot into Afghan territory, and could just see Miss Allardyce, a black speck, flickering across the stony plain. The reason of her wandering was simple enough. Coppy, in a tone of too-hastily-assumed authority, had told her overnight that she must not ride out by the river. And she had gone to prove her own spirit and teach Coppy a lesson.

Almost at the foot of the inhospitable hills, Wee Willie Winkie saw the Waler blunder and come down heavily. Miss Allardyce struggled clear, but her ankle had been severely twisted, and she could not stand. Having fully shown her spirit, she wept, and was surprised by the apparition of a white, wide-eyed child in khaki, on a nearly spent pony.

'Are you badly, badly hurted?' shouted Wee Willie Winkie, as soon as he was within range. 'You didn't ought to be here.'

'I don't know,' said Miss Allardyce ruefully, ignoring the reproof. 'Good gracious, child, what are *you* doing here?'

'You said you was going acwoss ve wiver,' panted Wee Willie Winkie, throwing himself off his pony. 'And nobody – not even Coppy – must go acwoss ve wiver, and I came after you ever so hard, but you wouldn't stop, and now you've hurted yourself, and Coppy will be angwy wiv me, and – I've bwoken my awwest! I've bwoken my awwest!'

The future Colonel of the 195th sat down and sobbed. In spite of the pain in her ankle the girl was moved.

'Have you ridden all the way from cantonments, little man? What for?'

'You belonged to Coppy. Coppy told me so!' wailed Wee Willie Winkie disconsolately. 'I saw him kissing you, and he said he was fonder of you van Bell or ve Butcha or me. And so I came. You must get up and come back. You didn't ought to be here. Vis is a bad place, and I've bwoken my awwest.'

'I can't move, Winkie,' said Miss Allardyce, with a groan. 'I've hurt my foot. What shall I do?'

She showed a readiness to weep anew, which steadied Wee Willie Winkie, who had been brought up to believe that tears were the depth of unmanliness. Still, when one is as great a sinner as Wee Willie Winkie, even a man may be permitted to break down.

'Winkie,' said Miss Allardyce, 'when you've rested a little, ride back and tell them to send out something to carry me back in. It hurts fearfully.'

The child sat still for a little time and Miss Allardyce closed her eyes; the pain was nearly making her faint. She was roused by Wee Willie Winkie tying up the reins on his pony's neck and setting it free with a vicious cut of his whip that made it whicker. The little animal headed towards the cantonments.

'Oh, Winkie, what are you doing?'

'Hush!' said Wee Willie Winkie. 'Vere's a man coming – one of ve Bad Men. I must stay wiv you. My faver says a man must *always* look after a girl. Jack will go home, and ven vey'll come and look for us. Vat's why I let him go.'

Not one man but two or three had appeared from behind the rocks of the hills, and the heart of Wee Willie Winkie sank within him, for just in this manner were the Goblins wont to steal out and vex Curdie's soul. Thus had they played in Curdie's garden – he had seen the picture – and thus had they frightened the Princess's nurse. He heard them talking to each other, and recognised with joy the bastard Pushtu that he had picked up from one of his father's grooms lately dismissed. People who spoke that tongue could not be the Bad Men. They were only natives after all.

They came up to the boulders on which Miss Allardyce's horse had blundered.

Then rose from the rock Wee Willie Winkie, child of the Dominant Race, aged six and three-quarters, and said briefly and emphatically, '*Jao!*' The pony had crossed the river-bed.

The men laughed, and laughter from natives was the one thing Wee Willie Winkie could not tolerate. He asked them what they wanted and why they did not depart. Other men with most evil faces and crooked-stocked guns crept out of the shadows of the hills, till, soon, Wee Willie Winkie was face to face with an audience some twenty strong. Miss Allardyce screamed.

'Who are you?' said one of the men.

'I am the Colonel Sahib's son, and my order is that you go at once. You black men are frightening the Miss Sahib. One of you must run into cantonments and take the news that the Miss Sahib has hurt herself, and that the Colonel's son is here with her.'

'Put our feet into the trap?' was the laughing reply. 'Hear this boy's speech!'

'Say that I sent you – I, the Colonel's son. They will give you money.'

'What is the use of this talk? Take up the child and the girl, and we can at least ask for the ransom. Ours are the villages on the heights,' said a voice in the background.

These *were* the Bad Men – worse than Goblins – and it needed all Wee Willie Winkie's training to prevent him from bursting into tears. But he felt that to cry before a native, excepting only his mother's *ayah*, would be an infamy greater than any mutiny. Moreover, he, as future Colonel of the 195th, had that grim Regiment at his back.

'Are you going to carry us away?' said Wee Willie Winkie, very blanched and uncomfortable.

'Yes, my little Sahib Bahadur,' said the tallest of the men, 'and eat you afterwards.'

'That is child's talk,' said Wee Willie Winkie. 'Men do not eat men.'

A yell of laughter interrupted him, but he went on firmly – 'And if you do carry us away, I tell you that all my Regiment will come up in a day and kill you all without leaving one. Who will take my message to the Colonel Sahib?'

Speech in any vernacular – and Wee Willie Winkie had a colloquial acquaintance with three – was easy to the boy who could not yet manage his 'r's' and 'th's' aright.

Another man joined the conference, crying: 'O foolish men! What this babe says is true. He is the heart's heart of those white troops. For the sake of peace let them go both, for if he be taken, the Regiment will break loose and gut the valley. *Our* villages are in the valley, and we shall not escape. That Regiment are devils. They broke Khoda Yar's breastbone with kicks when he tried to take the rifles; and if we touch this child they will fire and rape and plunder for a month, till nothing remains. Better to send a man back to take the message, and get a reward. I say that this child is their God, and that they will spare none of us, nor our women, if we harm him.'

It was Din Mahommed, the dismissed groom of the Colonel, who made the diversion, and an angry and heated discussion followed. Wee Willie Winkie, standing over Miss Allardyce, waited the upshot. Surely his 'Wegiment', his own 'Wegiment', would not desert him if they knew of his extremity.

The riderless pony brought the news to the 195th, though there had been consternation in the Colonel's household for an hour before. The little beast came in through the parade-ground in front of the main barracks, where the men were settling down to play Spoil-five till the afternoon. Devlin, the Colour-Sergeant of E Company, glanced at the empty saddle and tumbled through the barrack-rooms, kicking up each Room Corporal as he passed. 'Up, ye beggars! There's something happened to the Colonel's son,' he shouted.

'He couldn't fall off! S'elp me, 'e *couldn't* fall off,' blubbered a drummer-boy. 'Go an' hunt acrost the river. He's over there if he's anywhere, an' maybe those Pathans have got 'im. For the love o' Gawd, don't look for 'im in the nullahs! Let's go over the river.'

'There's sense in Mott yet,' said Devlin. 'E Company, double out to the river – sharp!'

So E Company, in its shirt-sleeves mainly, doubled for the dear life, and in the rear toiled the perspiring Sergeant, adjuring it to double yet faster. The cantonment was alive with the men of the 195th hunting for Wee Willie Winkie, and the Colonel finally overtook E Company, far too exhausted to swear, struggling in the pebbles of the river-bed.

Up the hill under which Wee Willie Winkie's Bad Men were discussing the wisdom of carrying off the child and the girl, a look-out fired two shots.

'What have I said?' shouted Din Mahommed. 'There is the warning! The *pulton* are out already and are coming across the plain. Get away! Let us not be seen with the boy.'

The men waited for an instant, and then, as another shot was fired, withdrew into the hills, silently as they had appeared.

'Ve Wegiment is coming,' said Wee Willie Winkie confidently to Miss Allardyce, 'and it's all wight. Don't cwy!'

He needed the advice himself, for ten minutes later, when his father came up, he was weeping bitterly with his head in Miss Allardyce's lap.

And the men of the 195th carried him home with shouts and rejoicings; and Coppy, who had ridden a horse into a lather, met him, and, to his intense disgust, kissed him openly in the presence of the men.

But there was balm for his dignity. His father assured him that not only would the breaking of arrest be condoned, but that the good-conduct badge would be restored as soon as his mother could sew it on his blouse-sleeve. Miss Allardyce had told the Colonel a story that made him proud of his son.

'She belonged to you, Coppy,' said Wee Willie Winkie, indicating Miss Allardyce with a grimy forefinger. 'I *knew* she didn't ought to go acwoss ve wiver, and I knew ve Wegiment would come to me if I sent Jack home.'

'You're a hero, Winkie,' said Coppy – 'a *pukka* hero!'

'I don't know what vat means,' said Wee Willie Winkie, 'but you mustn't call me Winkie any no more. I'm Percival Will'am Will'ams.'

And in this manner did Wee Willie Winkie enter into his manhood.

Little Tobrah

'Prisoner's head did not reach to the top of the dock,' as the English newspapers say. This case, however, was not reported because nobody cared by so much as a hempen rope for the life or death of Little Tobrah. The accessors in the red court-house sat upon him all through the long hot afternoon, and whenever they asked him a question he salaamed and whined. Their verdict was that the evidence was inconclusive, and the Judge concurred. It was true that the dead body of Little Tobrah's sister had been found at the bottom of the well, and Little Tobrah was the only human being within a half mile radius at the time; but the child might have fallen in by accident. Therefore Little Tobrah was acquitted, and told to go where he pleased. This permission was not so generous as it sounds, for he had nowhere to go to, nothing in particular to eat, and nothing whatever to wear.

He trotted into the court-compound, and sat upon the well-kerb, wondering whether an unsuccessful dive into the black water below would end in a forced voyage across the other Black Water. A groom put down an emptied nose-bag on the bricks, and Little Tobrah, being hungry, set himself to scrape out what wet grain the horse had overlooked.

'O Thief – and but newly set free from the terror of the Law! Come along!' said the groom, and Little Tobrah was led by the ear to a large and fat Englishman, who heard the tale of the theft.

'Hah!' said the Englishman three times (only he said a stronger word). 'Put him into the net and take him home.' So Little Tobrah was thrown into the net of the cart, and, nothing doubting that he should be stuck like a pig, was driven to the Englishman's house. 'Hah!' said the Englishman as before.

'Wet grain, by Jove! Feed the little beggar, some of you, and we'll make a riding-boy of him! See? Wet grain, good Lord!'

'Give an account of yourself,' said the Head of the Grooms to Little Tobrah after the meal had been eaten, and the servants lay at ease in their quarters behind the house. 'You are not of the groom caste, unless it be for the stomach's sake. How came you into the court, and why? Answer, little devil's spawn!'

'There was not enough to eat,' said Little Tobrah calmly. 'This is a good place.'

'Talk straight talk,' said the Head Groom, 'or I will make you clean out the stable of that large red stallion who bites like a camel.'

'We be *Telis*, oil-pressers,' said Little Tobrah, scratching his toes in the dust. 'We were *Telis* – my father, my mother, my brother, the elder by four years, myself, and the sister.'

'She who was found dead in the well?' said one who had heard something of the trial.

'Even so,' said Little Tobrah gravely. 'She who was found dead in the well. It befell upon a time, which is not in my memory, that the sickness came to the village where our oil-press stood, and first my sister was smitten as to her eyes, and went without sight, for it was *mata* – the small-pox. Thereafter, my father and my mother died of that same sickness, so we were alone – my brother who had twelve years, I who had eight, and the sister who could not see. Yet there were the bullock and the oil-press remaining, and we made shift to press the oil as before. But Surjun Dass, the grain-seller, cheated us in his dealings; and it was always a stubborn bullock to drive. We put marigold flowers for the Gods upon the neck of the bullock, and upon the great grinding-beam that rose through the roof; but we gained nothing thereby, and Surjun Dass was a hard man.'

'*Bapri-bap*,' muttered the grooms' wives, 'to cheat a child so! But *we* know what the *bunnia*-folk are, sisters.'

'The press was an old press, and we were not strong men – my brother and I; nor could we fix the neck of the beam firmly in the shackle.'

'Nay, indeed,' said the gorgeously clad wife of the Head Groom, joining the circle. 'That is a strong man's work. When I was a maid in my father's house—'

'Peace, woman,' said the Head Groom. 'Go on, boy.'

'It is nothing,' said Little Tobrah. 'The big beam tore down the roof upon a day which is not in my memory, and with the roof fell much of the hinder wall, and both together upon our bullock, whose back was broken. Thus we had neither home, nor press, nor bullock – my brother, myself, and the sister who was blind. We went crying away from that place, hand-in-hand, across the fields; and our money was seven annas and six pice. There was a famine in the land. I do not know the name of the land. So, on a night when we were sleeping, my brother took the five annas that remained to us and ran away. I do not know whither he went. The curse of my father be upon him. But I and the sister begged food in the villages, and there was none to give. Only all men said – "Go to the Englishmen and they will give." I did not know what the Englishmen were; but they said that they were white, living in tents. I went forward; but I cannot say whither I went, and there was no more food for myself or the sister. And upon a hot night, she weeping and calling for food, we came to a well, and I bade her sit upon the kerb, and thrust her in, for, in truth, she could not see; and it is better to die than to starve.'

'Ai! Ahi!' wailed the grooms' wives in chorus; 'he thrust her in, for it is better to die than to starve!'

'I would have thrown myself in also, but that she was not dead and called to me from the bottom of the well, and I was afraid and ran. And one came out of the crops saying that I had killed her and defiled the well, and they took me before an Englishman, white and terrible, living in a tent, and me he sent here. But there were no witnesses, and it is better to die than to starve. She, furthermore, could not see with her eyes, and was but a little child.'

'Was but a little child,' echoed the Head Groom's wife. 'But who art thou, weak as a fowl and small as a day-old colt, what art *thou*?'

'I who was empty am now full,' said Little Tobrah, stretching himself upon the dust. 'And I would sleep.'

The groom's wife spread a cloth over him while Little Tobrah slept the sleep of the just.

The Tomb
of His Ancestors

Some people will tell you that if there were but a single loaf of bread in all India it would be divided equally between the Plowdens, the Trevors, the Beadons, and the Rivett-Carnacs. That is only one way of saying that certain families serve India generation after generation as dolphins follow in line across the open sea.

Let us take a small and obscure case. There has been at least one representative of the Devonshire Chinns in or near Central India since the days of Lieutenant-Fireworker Humphrey Chinn, of the Bombay European Regiment, who assisted at the capture of Seringapatam in 1799. Alfred Ellis Chinn, Humphrey's younger brother, commanded a regiment of Bombay Grenadiers from 1804 to 1813, when he saw some mixed fighting; and in 1834 John Chinn of the same family – we will call him John Chinn the First – came to light as a level-headed administrator in time of trouble at a place called Mundesur. He died young, but left his mark on the new country, and the Honourable the Board of Directors of the Honourable the East India Company embodied his virtues in a stately resolution, and paid for the expenses of his tomb among the Satpura hills.

He was succeeded by his son, Lionel Chinn, who left the little old Devonshire home just in time to be severely wounded in the Mutiny. He spent his working life within a hundred and fifty miles of John Chinn's grave, and rose to the command of a regiment of small, wild hill-men, most of whom had known his father. His son John was born in the small thatched-roofed, mud-walled cantonment, which is even today eighty miles from the nearest railway, in the heart of a scrubby, tigerish country. Colonel Lionel Chinn served thirty years and retired. In the

Canal his steamer passed the outward-bound troopship, carrying his son eastward to the family duties.

The Chinns are luckier than most folk, because they know exactly what they must do. A clever Chinn passes for the Bombay Civil Service, and gets away to Central India, where everybody is glad to see him. A dull Chinn enters the Police Department or the Woods and Forests, and sooner or later, he, too, appears in Central India, and that is what gave rise to the saying 'Central India is inhabited by Bhils, Mairs, and Chinns, all very much alike.' The breed is small-boned, dark, and silent, and the stupidest of them are good shots. John Chinn the Second was rather clever, but as the eldest son he entered the army, according to Chinn tradition. His duty was to abide in his father's regiment, for the term of his natural life, though the corps was one which most men would have paid heavily to avoid. They were irregulars, small, dark, and blackish, clothed in rifle-green with black-leather trimmings; and friends called them the 'Wuddars', which means a race of low-caste people who dig up rats to eat. But the Wuddars did not resent it. They were the only Wuddars, and their points of pride were these:

Firstly, they had fewer English officers than any native regiment. Secondly, their subalterns were not mounted on parade, as is the general rule, but walked at the head of their men. A man who can hold his own with the Wuddars at their quickstep must be sound in wind and limb. Thirdly, they were the most *pukka shikarries* (out-and-out hunters) in all India. Fourthly – up to one hundredthly – they were the Wuddars – Chinn's Irregular Bhil Levies of the old days, but now, henceforward and for ever, the Wuddars.

No Englishman entered their mess except for love or through family usage. The officers talked to their soldiers in a tongue not two hundred white folk in India understood; and the men were their children, all drawn from the Bhils, who are, perhaps, the strangest of the many strange races in India. They were, and at heart are, wild men, furtive, shy, full of untold superstitions. The races whom we call natives of the country

found the Bhil in possession of the land when they first broke
into that part of the world thousands of years ago. The books
call them Pre-Aryan, Aboriginal, Dravidian, and so forth; and,
in other words, that is what the Bhils call themselves. When a
Rajput chief, whose bards can sing his pedigree backwards for
twelve hundred years, is set on the throne, his investiture is not
complete till he has been marked on the forehead with blood
from the veins of a Bhil. The Rajputs say the ceremony has no
meaning, but the Bhil knows that it is the last, last shadow of
his old rights as the long-ago owner of the soil.

Centuries of oppression and massacre made the Bhil a cruel
and half-crazy thief and cattle-stealer, and when the English
came he seemed to be almost as open to civilisation as the tigers
of his own jungles. But John Chinn the First, father of Lionel,
grandfather of our John, went into his country, lived with him,
learned his language, shot the deer that stole his poor crops,
and won his confidence, so that some Bhils learned to plough
and sow, while others were coaxed into the Company's service
to police their friends.

When they understood that standing in line did not mean
instant execution, they accepted soldiering as a cumbrous but
amusing kind of sport, and were zealous to keep the wild Bhils
under control. That was the thin edge of the wedge. John Chinn
the First gave them written promises that, if they were good
from a certain date, the Government would overlook previous
offences: and since John Chinn was never known to break his
word – he promised once to hang a Bhil locally esteemed in-
vulnerable, and hanged him in front of his tribe for seven
proved murders – the Bhils settled down as steadily as they
knew how. It was slow, unseen work, of the sort that is being
done all over India today; and though John Chinn's only
reward came, as I have said, in the shape of a grave at Government expense, the little people of the hills never forgot him.

Colonel Lionel Chinn knew and loved them too, and they
were very fairly civilised, for Bhils, before his service ended.
Many of them could hardly be distinguished from low-caste
Hindoo farmers; but in the south, where John Chinn the First

was buried, the wildest still clung to the Satpura ranges, cherishing a legend that some day Jan Chinn, as they called him, would return to his own. In the meantime they mistrusted the white man and his ways. The least excitement would stampede them, plundering at random, and now and then killing; but if they were handled discreetly they grieved like children, and promised never to do it again.

The Bhils of the regiment – the uniformed men – were virtuous in many ways, but they needed humouring. They felt bored and homesick unless taken after tigers as beaters; and their cold-blooded daring – all Wuddars shoot tigers on foot: it is their caste-mark – made even the officers wonder. They would follow up a wounded tiger as unconcernedly as though it were a sparrow with a broken wing; and this through a country full of caves and rifts and pits, where a wild beast could hold a dozen men at his mercy. Now and then some little man was brought to barracks with his head smashed in or his ribs torn away; but his companions never learned caution; they contented themselves with settling the tiger.

Young John Chinn was decanted at the verandah of the Wuddars' lonely mess-house from the back seat of a two-wheeled cart, his gun-cases cascading all round him. The slender, little, hooky-nosed boy looked forlorn as a strayed goat when he slapped the white dust off his knees, and the cart jolted down the glaring road. But in his heart he was contented. After all, this was the place where he had been born, and things were not much changed since he had been sent to England, a child, fifteen years ago.

There were a few new buildings, but the air and the smell and the sunshine were the same; and the little green men who crossed the parade-ground looked very familiar. Three weeks ago John Chinn would have said he did not remember a word of the Bhil tongue, but at the mess-door he found his lips moving in sentences that he did not understand – bits of old nursery rhymes, and tail-ends of such orders as his father used to give the men.

The Colonel watched him come up the steps, and laughed.

'Look!' he said to the Major. 'No need to ask the young un's breed. He's a *pukka* Chinn. Might be his father in the Fifties over again.'

'Hope he'll shoot as straight,' said the Major. 'He's brought enough ironmongery with him.'

'Wouldn't be a Chinn if he didn't. Watch him blowin' his nose. Regular Chinn beak. Flourishes his handkerchief like his father. It's the second edition – line for line.'

'Fairy tale, by Jove!' said the Major, peering through the slats of the jalousies. 'If he's the lawful heir, he'll . . . Now old Chinn could no more pass that chick without fiddling with it than . . .'

'His son!' said the Colonel, jumping up.

'Well, I be blowed!' said the Major. The boy's eye had been caught by a split reed screen that hung on a slew between the verandah pillars, and mechanically he had tweaked the edge to set it level. Old Chinn had sworn three times a day at that screen for many years; he could never get it to his satisfaction. His son entered the anteroom in the middle of a five-fold silence. They made him welcome for his father's sake and, as they took stock of him, for his own. He was ridiculously like the portrait of the Colonel on the wall, and when he had washed a little of the dust from his throat he went to his quarters with the old man's short, noiseless jungle-step.

'So much for heredity,' said the Major. 'That comes of three generations among the Bhils.'

'And the men know it,' said a Wing-officer. 'They've been waiting for this youth with their tongues hanging out. I am persuaded that, unless he absolutely beats 'em over the head, they'll lie down by companies and worship him.'

'Nothin' like havin' a father before you,' said the Major. 'I'm a parvenu with my chaps. I've only been twenty years in the regiment, and my revered parent he was a simple squire. There's no getting at the bottom of a Bhil's mind. Now, *why* is the superior bearer that young Chinn brought with him flee-ing across country with his bundle?' He stepped into the verandah, and shouted after the man – a typical new-joined subaltern's servant who speaks English and cheats his master.

'What is it?' he called.

'Plenty bad men here. I going, sar,' was the reply. 'Have taken Sahib's keys, and say will shoot.'

'Doocid lucid – doocid convincin'. How those up-country thieves can leg it! He has been badly frightened by some one.' The Major strolled to his quarters to dress for mess.

Young Chinn, walking like a man in a dream, had fetched a compass round the entire cantonment before going to his own tiny cottage. The captain's quarters, in which he had been born, delayed him for a little; then he looked at the well on the parade-ground, where he had sat of evenings with his nurse, and at the ten-by-fourteen church, where the officers went to service if a chaplain of any official creed happened to come along. It seemed very small as compared with the gigantic building he used to stare up at, but it was the same place.

From time to time he passed a knot of silent soldiers, who saluted. They might have been the very men who had carried him on their backs when he was in his first knickerbockers. A faint light burned in his room, and, as he entered, hands clasped his feet, and a voice murmured from the floor.

'Who is it?' said young Chinn, not knowing he spoke in the Bhil tongue.

'I bore you in my arms, Sahib, when I was a strong man and you were a small one – crying, crying, crying! I am your servant, as I was your father's before you. We are all your servants.'

Young Chinn could not trust himself to reply, and the voice went on:

'I have taken your keys from that fat foreigner, and sent him away; and the studs are in the shirt for mess. Who should know, if I do not know? And so the baby has become a man, and forgets his nurse; but my nephew shall make a good servant, or I will beat him twice a day.'

Then there rose up, with a rattle, as straight as a Bhil arrow, a little white-haired wizened ape of a man, with medals and orders on his tunic, stammering, saluting, and trembling.

Behind him a young and wiry Bhil, in uniform, was taking the trees out of Chinn's mess-boots.

Chinn's eyes were full of tears. The old man held out his keys.

'Foreigners are bad people. He will never come back again. We are all servants of your father's son. Has the Sahib forgotten who took him to see the trapped tiger in the village across the river, when his mother was so frightened and he was so brave?'

The scene came back to Chinn in great magic-lantern flashes. 'Bukta!' he cried; and all in a breath: 'You promised nothing should hurt me. *Is* it Bukta?'

The man was at his feet a second time. 'He has not forgotten. He remembers his own people as his father remembered. Now can I die. But first I will live and show the Sahib how to kill tigers. That *that* yonder is my nephew. If he is not a good servant, beat him and send him to me, and I will surely kill him, for now the Sahib is with his own people. Ai, Jan *baba* – Jan *baba*! My Jan *baba*! I will stay here and see that this does his work well. Take off his boots, fool. Sit down upon the bed, Sahib, and let me look. It *is* Jan *baba*!'

He pushed forward the hilt of his sword as a sign of service, which is an honour paid only to viceroys, governors, generals, or to little children whom one loves dearly. Chinn touched the hilt mechanically with three fingers, muttering he knew not what. It happened to be the old answer of his childhood, when Bukta in jest called him the little General Sahib.

The Major's quarters were opposite Chinn's, and when he heard his servant gasp with surprise he looked across the room. Then the Major sat on the bed and whistled; for the spectacle of the senior native commissioned officer of the regiment, an 'unmixed' Bhil, a Companion of the Order of British India, with thirty-five years' spotless service in the army, and a rank among his own people superior to that of many Bengal princelings, valeting the last-joined subaltern, was a little too much for his nerves.

The throaty bugles blew the Mess-call that has a long legend behind it. First a few piercing notes like the shrieks of beaters in a far-away cover, and next, large, full, and smooth, the refrain of the wild song: 'And oh, and oh, the green pulse of Mundore – Mundore!'

'All little children were in bed when the Sahib heard that call last,' said Bukta, passing Chinn a clean handkerchief. The call brought back memories of his cot under the mosquito-netting, his mother's kiss, and the sound of footsteps growing fainter as he dropped asleep among his men. So he hooked the dark collar of his new mess-jacket, and went to dinner like a prince who has newly inherited his father's crown.

Old Bukta swaggered forth curling his whiskers. He knew his own value, and no money and no rank within the gift of the Government would have induced him to put studs in young officers' shirts, or to hand them clean ties. Yet, when he took off his uniform that night, and squatted among his fellows for a quiet smoke, he told them what he had done, and they said that he was entirely right. Thereat Bukta propounded a theory which to a white mind would have seemed raving insanity; but the whispering, level-headed little men of war considered it from every point of view, and thought that there might be a great deal in it.

At mess under the oil-lamps the talk turned as usual to the unfailing subject of *shikar* – big game shooting of every kind and under all sorts of conditions. Young Chinn opened his eyes when he understood that each one of his companions had shot several tigers in the Wuddar style – on foot, that is – making no more of the business than if the brute had been a dog.

'In nine cases out of ten,' said the Major, 'a tiger is almost as dangerous as a porcupine. But the tenth time you come home feet first.'

That set all talking, and long before midnight Chinn's brain was in a whirl with stories of tigers – man-eaters and cattle-killers each pursuing his own business as methodically as clerks in an office; new tigers that had lately come into such-and-such a district; and old, friendly beasts of great cunning, known by nicknames in the mess – such as 'Puggy', who was lazy, with huge paws, and 'Mrs. Malaprop', who turned up when you never expected her, and made female noises. Then they spoke of Bhil superstitions, a wide and picturesque field, till young Chinn hinted that they must be pulling his leg.

''Deed we aren't,' said a man on his left. 'We know all about you. You're a Chinn and all that, and you've a sort of vested right here; but if you don't believe what we're telling you, what will you do when old Bukta begins his stories? He knows about ghost-tigers, and tigers that go to a hell of their own; and tigers that walk on their hind feet; and your grandpapa's riding-tiger, as well. Odd he hasn't spoken of that yet.'

'You know you've an ancestor buried down Satpura way, don't you?' said the Major, as Chinn smiled irresolutely.

'Of course I do,' said Chinn, who had the chronicle of the Book of Chinn by heart. It lies in a worn old ledger on the Chinese lacquer table behind the piano in the Devonshire home, and the children are allowed to look at it on Sundays.

'Well, I wasn't sure. Your revered ancestor, my boy, according to the Bhils, has a tiger of his own – a saddle-tiger that he rides round the country whenever he feels inclined. *I* don't call it decent in an ex-Collector's ghost; but that is what the Southern Bhils believe. Even our men, who might be called moderately cool, don't care to beat that country if they hear that Jan Chinn is running about on his tiger. It is supposed to be a clouded animal – not stripy, but blotchy, like a tortoise-shell tom-cat. No end of a brute, it is, and a sure sign of war or pestilence or – or something. There's a nice family legend for you.'

'What's the origin of it, d'you suppose?' said Chinn.

'Ask the Satpura Bhils. Old Jan Chinn was a mighty hunter before the Lord. Perhaps it was the tiger's revenge, or perhaps he's huntin' 'em still. You must go to his tomb one of these days and inquire. Bukta will probably attend to that. He was asking me before you came whether by any ill-luck you had already bagged your tiger. If not, he is going to enter you under his own wing. Of course, for you of all men it's imperative. You'll have a first-class time with Bukta.'

The Major was not wrong. Bukta kept an anxious eye on young Chinn at drill, and it was noticeable that the first time the new officer lifted up his voice in an order the whole line quivered. Even the Colonel was taken aback, for it might have been Lionel Chinn returned from Devonshire with a new lease of life. Bukta had continued to develop his peculiar theory among his intimates, and it was accepted as a matter of faith in the lines, since every word and gesture on young Chinn's part so confirmed it.

The old man arranged early that his darling should wipe out the reproach of not having shot a tiger; but he was not content to take the first or any beast that happened to arrive. In his own villages he dispensed the high, low, and middle justice, and when his people – naked and fluttered – came to him with word of a beast marked down, he bade them send spies to the kills and the watering-places, that he might be sure the quarry was such an one as suited the dignity of such a man.

Three or four times the reckless trackers returned, most truthfully saying that the beast was mangy, undersized – a tigress worn with nursing, or a broken-toothed old male – and Bukta would curb young Chinn's impatience.

At last, a noble animal was marked down – a ten-foot cattle-killer with a huge roll of loose skin along the belly, glossy-hided, full-frilled about the neck, whiskered, frisky, and young. He had slain a man in pure sport, they said.

'Let him be fed,' quoth Bukta, and the villagers dutifully drove out cows to amuse him, that he might lie up near by.

Princes and potentates have taken ship to India and spent great moneys for the mere glimpse of beasts one-half as fine as this of Bukta's.

'It is not good,' said he to the Colonel, when he asked for shooting-leave, 'that my Colonel's son who may be – that my Colonel's son should lose his maidenhead on any small jungle beast. That may come after. I have waited long for this which is a tiger. He has come in from the Mair country. In seven days we will return with the skin.'

The mess gnashed their teeth enviously. Bukta, had he

chosen, might have invited them all. But he went out alone with Chinn, two days in a shooting-cart and a day on foot, till they came to a rocky, glary valley with a pool of good water in it. It was a parching day, and the boy very naturally stripped and went in for a bathe, leaving Bukta by the clothes. A white skin shows far against brown jungle, and what Bukta beheld on Chinn's back and right shoulder dragged him forward step by step with staring eyeballs.

'I'd forgotten it isn't decent to strip before a man of his position,' thought Chinn, flouncing in the water. 'How the little devil stares! What is it, Bukta?'

'The Mark!' was the whispered answer.

'It is nothing. You know how it is with my people!' Chinn was annoyed. The dull-red birth-mark on his shoulder, something like a conventionalised Tartar cloud, had slipped his memory, or he would not have bathed. It occurred, so they said at home, in alternate generations, appearing, curiously enough, eight or nine years after birth, and, save that it was part of the Chinn inheritance, would not be considered pretty. He hurried ashore, dressed again, and went on till they met two or three Bhils, who promptly fell on their faces. 'My people,' grunted Bukta, not condescending to notice them. 'And so your people, Sahib. When I was a young man we were fewer, but not so weak. Now we are many, but poor stock. As may be remembered. How will you shoot him, Sahib? From a tree; from a shelter which my people shall build; by day or by night?'

'On foot and in the daytime,' said young Chinn.

'That was your custom, as I have heard,' said Bukta to himself. 'I will get news of him. Then you and I will go to him. I will carry one gun. You have yours. There is no need of more. What tiger shall stand against *thee*?'

He was marked down by a little water-hole at the head of a ravine, full-gorged and half asleep in the May sunlight. He was walked up like a partridge, and he turned to do battle for his life. Bukta made no motion to raise his rifle, but kept his eyes on Chinn, who met the shattering roar of the charge with a single shot – it seemed to him hours as he sighted – which tore through the throat, smashing the backbone below the neck and between the shoulders. The brute crouched, choked, and fell, and before Chinn knew well what had happened Bukta bade him stay still while he paced the distance between his feet and the ringing jaws.

'Fifteen,' said Bukta. 'Short paces. No need for a second shot, Sahib. He bleeds cleanly where he lies, and we need not spoil the skin. I said there would be no need of these, but they came – in case.'

Suddenly the sides of the ravine were crowned with the heads of Bukta's people – a force that could have blown the ribs out of the beast had Chinn's shot failed; but their guns were hidden, and they appeared as interested beaters, some five or six, waiting the word to skin. Bukta watched the life fade from the wild eyes, lifted one hand, and turned on his heel.

'No need to show that *we* care,' said he. 'Now, after this, we can kill what we choose. Put out your hand, Sahib.'

Chinn obeyed. It was entirely steady, and Bukta nodded. 'That also was your custom. My men skin quickly. They will carry the skin to cantonments. Will the Sahib come to my poor village for the night and, perhaps, forget that I am his officer?'

'But those men – the beaters. They have worked hard, and perhaps—'

'Oh, if they skin clumsily, we will skin them. They are my people. In the Lines I am one thing. Here I am another.'

This was very true. When Bukta doffed uniform and reverted to the fragmentary dress of his own people, he left his civilisation of drill in the next world. That night, after a little talk with his subjects, he devoted to an orgy; and a Bhil orgy is a thing not to be safely written about. Chinn, flushed with triumph, was in the thick of it, but the meaning of the mysteries was hidden. Wild folk came and pressed about his knees with offerings. He gave his flask to the elders of the village. They grew eloquent, and wreathed him about with flowers. Gifts and loans, not all seemly, were thrust upon him, and infernal music rolled and maddened round red fires, while singers sang songs of the ancient times, and danced peculiar dances. The aboriginal liquors are very potent, and Chinn was compelled to taste them often, but, unless the stuff had been drugged, how came he to fall asleep suddenly, and to waken late the next day – half a march from the village?

'The Sahib was very tired. A little before dawn he went to sleep,' Bukta explained. 'My people carried him here, and now it is time we should go back to cantonments.'

The voice, smooth and deferential, the step, steady and silent, made it hard to believe that only a few hours before Bukta was yelling and capering with naked fellow-devils of the scrub.

'My people were very pleased to see the Sahib. They will never forget. When next the Sahib goes out recruiting, he will go to my people, and they will give him as many men as we need.'

Chinn kept his own counsel, except as to the shooting of the tiger, and Bukta embroidered that tale with a shameless tongue. The skin was certainly one of the finest ever hung up in the mess, and the first of many. When Bukta could not accompany his boy on shooting-trips, he took care to put him in good hands, and Chinn learned more of the mind and desire of the wild Bhil in his marches and campings, by talks at twilight or at wayside pools, than an uninstructed man could have come at in a lifetime.

Presently his men in the regiment grew bold to speak of their relatives – mostly in trouble – and to lay cases of tribal custom before him. They would say, squatting in his verandah at twilight, after the easy, confidential style of the Wuddars, that such-and-such a bachelor had run away with such-and-such a wife at a far-off village. Now, how many cows would Chinn Sahib consider a just fine? Or, again, if written order came from the Government that a Bhil was to repair to a walled city of the plains to give evidence in a law-court, would it be wise to disregard that order? On the other hand, if it were obeyed, would the rash voyager return alive?

'But what have I to do with these things?' Chinn demanded of Bukta, impatiently. 'I am a soldier. I do not know the Law.'

'Hoo! Law is for fools and white men. Give them a large and

loud order and they will abide by it. Thou art their Law.'

'But wherefore?'

Every trace of expression left Bukta's countenance. The idea might have smitten him for the first time. 'How can I say?' he replied. 'Perhaps it is on account of the name. A Bhil does not love strange things. Give them orders, Sahib – two, three, four words at a time such as they can carry away in their heads. That is enough.'

Chinn gave orders then, valiantly, not realising that a word spoken in haste before mess became the dread unappealable law of villages beyond the smoky hills – was, in truth, no less than the Law of Jan Chinn the First, who, so the whispered legend ran, had come back to earth to oversee the third generation in the body and bones of his grandson.

There could be no sort of doubt in this matter. All the Bhils knew that Jan Chinn reincarnated had honoured Bukta's village with his presence after slaying his first – in this life – tiger; that he had eaten and drunk with the people, as he was used; and – Bukta must have drugged Chinn's liquor very deeply – upon his back and right shoulder all men had seen the same angry red Flying Cloud that the high Gods had set on the flesh of Jan Chinn the First when first he came to the Bhil. As concerned the foolish white world which has no eyes, he was a slim and young officer in the Wuddars; but his own people knew he was Jan Chinn, who had made the Bhil a man; and, believing, they hastened to carry his words, careful never to alter them on the way.

Because the savage and the child who plays lonely games have one horror of being laughed at or questioned, the little folk kept their convictions to themselves; and the Colonel, who thought he knew his regiment, never guessed that each one of the six hundred quick-footed, beady-eyed rank-and-file, at attention beside their rifles, believed serenely and unshakenly that the subaltern on the left flank of the line was a demi-god twice born – tutelary deity of their land and people. The Earth-gods themselves had stamped the incarnation, and who would dare to doubt the handiwork of the Earth-gods?

Chinn, being practical above all things, saw that his family name served him well in the lines and in camp. His men gave no trouble – one does not commit regimental offences with a god in the chair of justice – and he was sure of the best beaters in the district when he needed them. They believed that the protection of Jan Chinn the First cloaked them, and were bold in that belief beyond the utmost daring of excited Bhils.

His quarters began to look like an amateur natural-history museum, in spite of duplicate heads and horns and skulls that he sent home to Devonshire. The people, very humanly, learned the weak side of their god. It is true he was unbribable, but bird-skins, butterflies, beetles, and, above all, news of big game pleased him. In other respects, too, he lived up to the Chinn tradition. He was fever-proof. A night's sitting out over a tethered goat in a damp valley, that would have filled the Major with a month's malaria, had no effect on him. He was, as they said, 'salted before he was born'.

Now, in the autumn of his second year's service an uneasy rumour crept out of the earth and ran about among the Bhils. Chinn heard nothing of it till a brother-officer said across the mess-table: 'Your revered ancestor's on the rampage in the Satpura country. You'd better look him up.'

'I don't want to be disrespectful, but I'm a little sick of my revered ancestor. Bukta talks of nothing else. What's the old boy supposed to be doing now?'

'Riding cross-country by moonlight on his processional tiger. That's the story. He's been seen by about two thousand Bhils, skipping along the tops of the Satpuras, and scaring people to death. They believe it devoutly, and all the Satpura chaps are worshipping away at his shrine – tomb, I mean – like good 'uns. You really ought to go down there. Must be a queer thing to see your grandfather treated as a god.'

'What makes you think there's any truth in the tale?' said Chinn.

'Because all our men deny it. They say they've never heard of Chinn's tiger. Now that's a manifest lie, because every Bhil has.'

'There's only one thing you've overlooked,' said the Colonel, thoughtfully. 'When a local god reappears on earth it's always an excuse for trouble of some kind; and those Satpura Bhils are about as wild as your grandfather left them, young 'un. It means something.'

'Meanin' they may go on the war-path?' said Chinn.

'Can't say – as yet. Shouldn't be surprised a little bit.'

'I haven't been told a syllable.'

'Proves it all the more. They are keeping something back.'

'Bukta tells me everything, too, as a rule. Now, why didn't he tell me that?'

Chinn put the question directly to the old man that night, and the answer surprised him.

'Why should I tell what is well known? Yes, the Clouded Tiger is out in the Satpura country.'

'What do the wild Bhils think that it means?'

'They do not know. They wait. Sahib, what *is* coming? Say only one little word, and we will be content.'

'We? What have tales from the south, where the jungly Bhils live, to do with drilled men?'

'When Jan Chinn wakes is no time for any Bhil to be quiet.'

'But he has not waked, Bukta.'

'Sahib' – the old man's eyes were full of tender reproof – 'if he does not wish to be seen, why does he go abroad in the moonlight? We know he is awake, but we do not know what he desires. Is it a sign for all the Bhils, or one that concerns the Satpura folk alone? Say one little word, Sahib, that I may carry it to the lines, and send on to our villages. Why does Jan Chinn ride out? Who has done wrong? Is it pestilence? Is it murrain? Will our children die? Is it a sword? Remember, Sahib, we are thy people and thy servants, and in this life I bore thee in my arms – not knowing.'

'Bukta has evidently looked on the cup this evening,' Chinn thought; 'but if I can do anything to soothe the old chap I must. It's like the Mutiny rumours on a small scale.'

He dropped into a deep wicker chair, over which was thrown his first tiger-skin, and his weight on the cushion flapped the clawed paws over his shoulders. He laid hold of them mechanically as he spoke, drawing the painted hide, cloak-fashion, about him.

'Now will I tell the truth, Bukta,' he said, leaning forward, the dried muzzle on his shoulder, to invent a specious lie.

'I see that it is the truth,' was the answer, in a shaking voice.

'Jan Chinn goes abroad among the Satpuras, riding on the Clouded Tiger, ye say? Be it so. Therefore the sign of the wonder is for the Satpura Bhils only, and does not touch the Bhils who plough in the north and east, the Bhils of the Khandesh, or any others, except the Satpura Bhils, who, as we know, are wild and foolish.'

'It is, then, a sign for *them*. Good or bad?'

'Beyond doubt, good. For why should Jan Chinn make evil to those whom he has made men? The nights over yonder are hot; it is ill to lie in one bed over long without turning, and Jan Chinn would look again upon his people. So he rises, whistles his Clouded Tiger, and goes abroad a little to breathe the cool air. If the Satpura Bhils kept to their villages, and did not wander after dark, they would not see him. Indeed, Bukta, it is no more than that he would see the light again in his own country. Send this news south, and say that it is my word.'

Bukta bowed to the floor. 'Good Heavens!' thought Chinn, 'and this blinking pagan is a first-class officer, and as straight as a die! I may as well round it off neatly.' He went on:

'If the Satpura Bhils ask the meaning of the sign, tell them that Jan Chinn would see how they kept their old promises of good living. Perhaps they have plundered; perhaps they mean to disobey the orders of the Government; perhaps there is a dead man in the jungle; and so Jan Chinn has come to see.'

'Is he, then, angry?'

'Bah! Am *I* ever angry with my Bhils? I say angry words, and threaten many things. *Thou* knowest, Bukta. I have seen thee smile behind thy hand. I know, and thou knowest. The Bhils are my children. I have said it many times.'

'Ay. We be thy children,' said Bukta.

'And no otherwise is it with Jan Chinn, my father's father.

He would see the land he loved and the people once again. It is a good ghost, Bukta. I say it. Go and tell them. And I do hope devoutly,' he added, 'that it will calm 'em down.' Flinging back the tiger-skin, he rose with a long, unguarded yawn that showed his well-kept teeth.

Bukta fled, to be received in the lines by a knot of panting inquirers.

'It is true,' said Bukta. 'He wrapped himself in the skin and spoke from it. He would see his own country again. The sign is not for us; and, indeed, he is a young man. How should he lie idle of nights? He says his bed is too hot and the air is bad. He goes to and fro for the love of night-running. He has said it.'

The grey-whiskered assembly shuddered.

'He says the Bhils are his children. Ye know he does not lie. He has said it to me.'

'But what of the Satpura Bhils? What means the sign for them?'

'Nothing. It is only night-running, as I have said. He rides to see if they obey the Government, as he taught them to do in his first life.'

'And what if they do not?'

'He did not say.'

The light went out in Chinn's quarters.

'Look,' said Bukta. 'Now he goes away. None the less it is a good ghost, as he has said. How shall we fear Jan Chinn, who made the Bhil a man? His protection is on us; and ye know Jan Chinn never broke a protection spoken or written on paper. When he is older and has found him a wife he will lie in his bed till morning.'

A commanding officer is generally aware of the regimental state of mind a little before the men; and this is why the Colonel said a few days later that some one had been putting the fear of God into the Wuddars. As he was the only person officially entitled to do this, it distressed him to see such unanimous virtue. 'It's too good to last,' he said. 'I only wish I could find out what the little chaps mean.'

The explanation, as it seemed to him, came at the change of

the moon, when he received orders to hold himself in readiness to 'allay any possible excitement' among the Satpura Bhils, who were, to put it mildly, uneasy because a paternal Government had sent up against them a Mahratta State-educated vaccinator, with lancets, lymph, and an officially registered calf. In the language of State, they had 'manifested a strong objection to all prophylactic measures', and 'forcibly detained the vaccinator', and 'were on the point of neglecting or evading their tribal obligations'.

'That means they are in a blue funk – same as they were at census-time,' said the Colonel; 'and if we stampede them into the hills we'll never catch 'em, in the first place, and, in the second, they'll whoop off plundering till further orders. Wonder who the God-forsaken idiot is who is trying to vaccinate a Bhil? I knew trouble was coming. One good thing is that they'll only use local corps, and we can knock up something we'll call a campaign, and let them down easy. Fancy us potting our best beaters because they don't want to be vaccinated! They're only crazy with fear.'

'Don't you think, sir,' said Chinn the next day, 'that perhaps you could give me a fortnight's shooting-leave?'

'Desertion in the face of the enemy, by Jove!' The Colonel laughed. 'I might, but I'd have to antedate it a little, because we're warned for service, as you might say. However, we'll assume that you applied for leave three days ago, and are now well on your way south.'

'I'd like to take Bukta with me.'

'Of course, yes. I think that will be the best plan. You've some kind of hereditary influence with the little chaps, and they may listen to you when a glimpse of our uniforms would drive them wild. You've never been in that part of the world before, have you? Take care they don't send you to your family vault in your youth and innocence. I believe you'll be all right if you can get 'em to listen to you.'

'I think so, sir; but if – if they should accidentally put an – make asses of 'emselves – they might, you know – I hope you'll represent that they were only frightened. There isn't an ounce of real vice in 'em, and I should never forgive myself if any one of – of my name got them into trouble.'

The Colonel nodded, but said nothing.

Chinn and Bukta departed at once. Bukta did not say that, ever since the official vaccinator had been dragged into the hills by indignant Bhils, runner after runner had skulked up to the lines, entreating, with forehead in the dust, that Jan Chinn should come and explain this unknown horror that hung over his people.

The portent of the Clouded Tiger was now too clear. Let Jan Chinn comfort his own, for vain was the help of mortal man. Bukta toned down these beseechings to a simple request for Chinn's presence. Nothing would have pleased the old man better than a rough-and-tumble campaign against the Satpuras, whom he, as an 'unmixed' Bhil, despised; but he had a duty to all his nation as Jan Chinn's interpreter, and he devoutly believed that forty plagues would fall on his village if he tampered with that obligation. Besides, Jan Chinn knew all things, and he rode the Clouded Tiger.

They covered thirty miles a day on foot and pony, raising the blue wall-like line of the Satpuras as swiftly as might be. Bukta was very silent.

They began the steep climb a little after noon, but it was near sunset ere they reached the stone platform clinging to the side of a rifted, jungle-covered hill, where Jan Chinn the First was laid, as he had desired, that he might overlook his people. All India is full of neglected graves that date from the beginning of the eighteenth century – tombs of forgotten colonels of corps long since disbanded; mates of East Indiamen who went on shooting expeditions and never came back; factors, agents, writers, and ensigns of the Honourable the East India Company by hundreds and thousands and tens of thousands. English folk forget quickly, but natives have long memories, and if a man has done good in his life it is remembered after his death. The weathered marble four-square tomb of Jan Chinn was hung about with wild flowers and nuts, packets of wax and honey, bottles of native spirits, and infamous cigars, with buffalo horns and plumes of dried grass. At one end was a rude clay image of a white man, in the old-fashioned top-hat, riding on a bloated tiger.

Bukta salaamed reverently as they approached. Chinn bared his head and began to pick out the blurred inscription. So far as he could read it ran thus – word for word, and letter for letter:

TO THE MEMORY OF JOHN CHINN, ESQ.

Late Collector of . . . .
. . . ithout Bloodshed or . . . error of Authority
Employ . . . only . . . eans of Conciliat . . . and Confiden . . .
Accomplished the . . . tire Subjection . . .
a Lawless and Predatory Peop . . .
. . . taching them to . . . ish Government
by a Conque . . . over . . . Minds
The most perma . . . and rational Mode of Domini . . .
. . . Governor-General and Counc . . . engal . . .
have ordered thi . . . . erected
. . . arted this Life Aug. 19, 184 . . . Ag . . .

On the other side of the grave were ancient verses, also very worn. As much as Chinn could decipher said:

            . . . the savage band
Forsook their Haunts and b . . . is Command
. . . mended . . . rals check a . . . st for spoil
And . . . s . . . ing Hamlets prove his gene . . . toil
Humanit . . . survey . . . ights restore . . .
A nation . . . ield . . . subdued without a Sword.

For some little time he leaned on the tomb thinking of this dead man of his own blood, and of the house in Devonshire; then, nodding to the plains; 'Yes; it's a big work – all of it – even my little share. He must have been worth knowing. . . . Bukta, where are my people?'

'Not here, Sahib. No man comes here except in full sun. They wait above. Let us climb and see.'

But Chinn, remembering the first law of Oriental diplomacy,

in an even voice answered: 'I have come this far only because the Satpura folk are foolish, and dared not visit our lines. Now bid them wait on me *here*. I am not a servant, but the master of Bhils.'

'I go – I go,' clucked the old man. Night was falling, and at any moment Jan Chinn might whistle up his dreaded steed from the darkening scrub.

Now for the first time in a long life Bukta disobeyed a lawful command and deserted his leader; for he did not come back, but pressed to the flat table-top of the hill, and called softly. Men stirred all about him – little trembling men with bows and arrows who had watched the two since noon.

'Where is he?' whispered one.

'At his own place. He bids you come,' said Bukta.

'Now?'

'Now.'

'Rather let him loose the Clouded Tiger upon us. We do not go.'

'Nor I, though I bore him in my arms when he was a child in this his life. Wait here till the day.'

'But surely he will be angry.'

'He will be very angry, for he has nothing to eat. But he has said to me many times that the Bhils are his children. By sunlight I believe this, but – by moonlight I am not so sure. What folly have ye Satpura pigs compassed that ye should need him at all?'

'One came to us in the name of the Government with little ghost-knives and a magic calf, meaning to turn us into cattle by the cutting off of our arms. We were greatly afraid, but we did not kill the man. He is here, bound – a black man; and we think he comes from the West. He said it was an order to cut us all with knives – especially the women and the children. We did not hear that it was an order, so we were afraid, and kept to our hills. Some of our men have taken ponies and bullocks from the plains, and others pots and cloths and earrings.'

'Are any slain?'

'By our men? Not yet. But the young men are blown to and fro by many rumours like flames upon a hill. I sent runners asking for Jan Chinn lest worse should come to us. It was this fear that he foretold by the sign of the Clouded Tiger.'

'He says it is otherwise,' said Bukta; and he repeated, with amplifications, all that young Chinn had told him at the conference of the wicker chair.

'Think you,' said the questioner, at last, 'that the Government will lay hands on us?'

'Not I,' Bukta rejoined. 'Jan Chinn will give an order, and ye will obey. The rest is between the Government and Jan Chinn. I myself know something of the ghost-knives and the scratching. It is a charm against the Smallpox. But how it is done I cannot tell. Nor need that concern you.'

'If he stand by us and before the anger of the Government we will most strictly obey Jan Chinn, except – except we do not go down to that place tonight.'

They could hear young Chinn below them shouting for Bukta; but they cowered and sat still, expecting the Clouded Tiger. The tomb had been holy ground for nearly half a century. If Jan Chinn chose to sleep there, who had better right? But they would not come within eyeshot of the place till broad day.

At first Chinn was exceedingly angry, till it occurred to him that Bukta most probably had a reason (which, indeed, he had), and his own dignity might suffer if he yelled without answer. He propped himself against the foot of the grave, and, alternately dozing and smoking, came through the warm night proud that he was a lawful, legitimate, fever-proof Chinn.

He prepared his plan of action much as his grandfather would have done; and when Bukta appeared in the morning with a most liberal supply of food, said nothing of the over-night desertion. Bukta would have been relieved by an outburst of human anger; but Chinn finished his victual leisurely, and a cheroot, ere he made any sign.

'They were very much afraid,' said Bukta, who was not too bold himself. 'It remains only to give orders. They say they will obey if thou wilt only stand between them and the Government.'

'That I know,' said Chinn, strolling slowly to the table-land. A few of the elder men stood in an irregular semicircle in an open glade; but the ruck of people – women and children – were hidden in the thicket. They had no desire to face the first anger of Jan Chinn the First.

Seating himself on a fragment of split rock, he smoked his cheroot to the butt, hearing men breathe hard all about him. Then he cried, so suddenly that they jumped:

'Bring the man that was bound!'

A scuffle and a cry were followed by the appearance of a Hindoo vaccinator, quaking with fear, bound hand and foot, as the Bhils of old were accustomed to bind their human sacrifices. He was pushed cautiously before the presence; but young Chinn did not look at him.

'I said – the man that *was* bound. Is it a jest to bring me one tied like a buffalo? Since when could the Bhil bind folk at his pleasure? Cut!'

Half a dozen hasty knives cut away the thongs, and the man crawled to Chinn, who pocketed his case of lancets and tubes of lymph. Then, sweeping the semicircle with one comprehensive forefinger, and in the voice of compliment, he said, clearly and distinctly: 'Pigs!'

'Ai!' whispered Bukta. 'Now he speaks. Woe to foolish people!'

'I have come on foot from my house' (the assembly shuddered) 'to make clear a matter which any other than a Satpura Bhil would have seen with both eyes from a distance. Ye know the Smallpox, who pits and scars your children so that they look like wasp-combs. It is an order of the Government that whoso is scratched on the arm with these little knives which I hold up is charmed against Her. All Sahibs are thus charmed, and very many Hindoos. This is the mark of the charm. Look!'

He rolled back his sleeve to the armpit and showed the white scars of the vaccination-mark on the white skin. 'Come, all, and look.'

A few daring spirits came up, and nodded their heads wisely. There was certainly a mark, and they knew well what other dread marks were hidden by the shirt. Merciful was Jan Chinn, that he had not then and there proclaimed his godhead.

'Now all these things the man whom ye bound told you.'

'I did – a hundred times; but they answered with blows,' groaned the operator, chafing his wrists and ankles.

'But, being pigs, ye did not believe; and so came I here to save you, first from Smallpox, next from a great folly of fear, and lastly, it may be, from the rope and the jail. It is no gain to me; it is no pleasure to me; but for the sake of that one who is yonder, who made the Bhil a man' – he pointed down the hill – 'I, who am of his blood, the son of his son, come to turn your people. And I speak the truth, as did Jan Chinn.'

The crowd murmured reverently, and men stole out of the thicket by twos and threes to join it. There was no anger in their god's face.

'These are my orders. (Heaven send they'll take 'em, but I seem to have impressed them so far!) I myself will stay among you while this man scratches your arms with knives, after the order of the Government. In three, or it may be five or seven days, your arms will swell and itch and burn. That is the power of Smallpox fighting in your base blood against the orders of the Government. I will therefore stay among you till I see that Smallpox is conquered, and I will not go away till the men and the women and the little children show me upon their arms such marks as I have even now showed you. I bring with me two very good guns, and a man whose name is known among beasts and men. We will hunt together, I and he, and your young men and the others shall eat and lie still. This is my order.'

There was a long pause while victory hung in the balance. A white-haired old sinner, standing on one uneasy leg, piped up:

'There are ponies and some few bullocks and other things for which we need a *kowl* [protection]. They were *not* taken in the way of trade.'

The battle was won, and John Chinn drew a breath of relief.

The young Bhils had been raiding, but if taken swiftly all could be put straight.

'I will write a *kowl* as soon as the ponies, the bullocks, and the other things are counted before me and sent back whence they came. But first we will put the Government mark on such as have not been visited by Smallpox.' In an undertone, to the vaccinator: 'If you show you are afraid you'll never see Poona again, my friend.'

'There is not sufficient ample supply of vaccine for all this population,' said the man. 'They have destroyed the offeecial calf.'

'They won't know the difference. Scrape 'em all round, and give me a couple of lancets; I'll attend to the elders.'

The aged diplomat who had demanded protection was the first victim. He fell to Chinn's hand, and dared not cry out. As soon as he was freed he dragged up a companion, and held him fast, and the crisis became, as it were, a child's sport; for the vaccinated chased the unvaccinated to treatment, vowing that all the tribe must suffer equally. The women shrieked, and the children ran howling; but Chinn laughed, and waved the pink-tipped lancet.

'It is an honour,' he cried. 'Tell them, Bukta, how great an honour it is that I myself should mark them. Nay, I cannot mark every one – the Hindoo must also do his work – but I will touch all marks that he makes, so there will be an equal virtue in them. Thus do the Rajputs stick pigs. Ho, brother with one eye! Catch that girl and bring her to me. She need not run away yet, for she is not married, and I do not seek her in marriage. She will not come? Then she shall be shamed by her little brother, a fat boy, a bold boy. He puts out his arm like a soldier. Look! *He* does not flinch at the blood. Some day he shall be in my regiment. And now, mother of many, we will lightly touch thee, for Smallpox has been before us here. It is a true thing, indeed, that this charm breaks the power of Mata. There will be no more pitted faces among the Satpuras, and so ye can ask many cows for each maid to be wed.'

And so on and so on – quick-poured showman's patter,

sauced in the Bhil hunting proverbs and tales of their own brand of coarse humour – till the lancets were blunted and both operators worn out.

But, nature being the same the world over, the unvaccinated grew jealous of their marked comrades, and came near to blows about it. Then Chinn declared himself a court of justice, no longer a medical board, and made formal inquiry into the late robberies.

'We are the thieves of Mahadeo,' said the Bhils, simply. 'It is our fate, and we were frightened. When we are frightened we always steal.'

Simply and directly as children, they gave in the tale of the plunder, all but two bullocks and some spirits that had gone a-missing (these Chinn promised to make good out of his own pocket), and ten ringleaders were despatched to the lowlands with a wonderful document, written on the leaf of a note-book, and addressed to an assistant district superintendent of police. There was warm calamity in that note, as Jan Chinn warned them, but anything was better than loss of liberty.

Armed with this protection, the repentant raiders went down-hill. They had no desire whatever to meet Mr. Dundas Fawne of the Police, aged twenty-two, and of a cheerful countenance, nor did they wish to revisit the scene of their robberies. Steering a middle course, they ran into the camp of the one Government chaplain allowed to the various irregular corps through a district of some fifteen thousand square miles, and stood before him in a cloud of dust. He was by way of being a priest they knew, and what was more to the point, a good sportsman who paid his beaters generously.

When he read Chinn's note he laughed, which they deemed a lucky omen, till he called up policemen, who tethered the ponies and the bullocks by the piled house-gear, and laid stern hands upon three of that smiling band of the thieves of Mahadeo. The chaplain himself addressed them magisterially with a riding-whip. That was painful, but Jan Chinn had prophesied it. They submitted, but would not give up the written protection, fearing the jail. On their way back they met Mr. D. Fawne, who had heard about the robberies, and was not pleased.

'Certainly,' said the eldest of the gang, when the second interview was at an end, 'certainly Jan Chinn's protection has saved us our liberty, but it is as though there were many beatings in one small piece of paper. Put it away.'

One climbed into a tree, and stuck the letter into a cleft forty feet from the ground, where it could do no harm. Warmed, sore, but happy, the ten returned to Jan Chinn next day, where he sat among uneasy Bhils, all looking at their right arms, and all bound under terror of their god's disfavour not to scratch.

'It was a good *kowl*,' said the leader. 'First the chaplain, who laughed, took away our plunder, and beat three of us, as was promised. Next, we met Fawne Sahib, who frowned, and asked for the plunder. We spoke the truth, and so he beat us all, one after another, and called us chosen names. He then gave us these two bundles' – they set down a bottle of whisky and a box of cheroots – 'and we came away. The *kowl* is left in a tree, because its virtue is that so soon as we show it to a Sahib we are beaten.'

'But for that *kowl*,' said Jan Chinn, sternly, 'ye would all have been marching to jail with a policeman on either side. Ye come now to serve as beaters for me. These people are unhappy, and we will go hunting till they are well. Tonight we will make a feast.'

It is written in the chronicles of the Satpura Bhils, together with many other matters not fit for print, that through five days, after the day that he had put his mark upon them, Jan Chinn the First hunted for his people; and on the five nights of those days the tribe was gloriously and entirely drunk. Jan Chinn bought country spirits of an awful strength, and slew wild pig and deer beyond counting, so that if any fell sick they might have two good reasons.

Between head- and stomach-aches they found no time to think of their arms, but followed Jan Chinn obediently through the jungles, and with each day's returning confidence men, women, and children stole away to their villages as the little army passed by. They carried news that it was good and right to be scratched with ghost-knives; that Jan Chinn was indeed reincarnated as a god of free food and drink, and that of all nations the Satpura Bhils stood first in his favour, if they would only refrain from scratching. Henceforward that kindly demi-god would be connected in their minds with great gorgings and the vaccine and lancets of a paternal Government.

'And tomorrow I go back to my home,' said Jan Chinn to his faithful few, whom neither spirits, over-eating, nor swollen glands could conquer. It is hard for children and savages to behave reverently at all times to the idols of their make-belief, and they had frolicked excessively with Jan Chinn. But the reference to his home cast a gloom on the people.

'And the Sahib will not come again?' said he who had been vaccinated first.

'That is to be seen,' answered Chinn, warily.

'Nay, but come as a white man – come as a young man whom we know and love; for, as thou alone knowest, we are a weak people. If we again saw thy – thy horse—' They were picking up their courage.

'I have no horse. I came on foot – with Bukta, yonder. What is this?'

'Thou knowest – the Thing that thou hast chosen for a night-horse.' The little men squirmed in fear and awe.

'Night-horse? Bukta, what is this last tale of children?'

Bukta had been a silent leader in Chinn's presence since the night of his desertion, and was grateful for a chance-flung question.

'They know, Sahib,' he whispered. 'It is the Clouded Tiger. That that comes from the place where thou didst once sleep. It is thy horse – as it has been these three generations.'

'My horse! That was a dream of the Bhils!'

'It is no dream. Do dreams leave the tracks of broad pugs on earth? Why make two faces before thy people? They know of the night-ridings, and they – and they—'

'Are afraid, and would have them cease.'

Bukta nodded. 'If thou hast no further need of him. He is thy horse.'

'The thing leaves a trail, then?' said Chinn.

'We have seen it. It is like a village road under the tomb.'

'Can ye find and follow it for me?'

'By daylight – if one comes with us, and, above all, stands near by.'

'I will stand close, and we will see to it that Jan Chinn does not ride any more.'

The Bhils shouted the last words again and again.

From Chinn's point of view the stalk was nothing more than an ordinary one – down hill, through split and crannied rocks, unsafe, perhaps, if a man did not keep his wits by him, but no worse than twenty others he had undertaken. Yet his men – they refused absolutely to beat, and would only trail – dripped sweat at every move. They showed the marks of enormous pugs that ran, always down hill, to a few hundred feet below Jan Chinn's tomb, and disappeared in a narrow-mouthed cave. It was an insolently open road, a domestic highway, beaten without thought of concealment.

'The beggar might be paying rent and taxes,' Chinn muttered ere he asked whether his friend's taste ran to cattle or man.

'Cattle,' was the answer. 'Two heifers a week. We drive them for him at the foot of the hill. It is his custom. If we did not, he might seek us.'

'Blackmail and piracy,' said Chinn. 'I can't say I fancy going into the cave after him. What's to be done?'

The Bhils fell back as Chinn lodged himself behind a rock with his rifle ready. Tigers, he knew, were shy beasts, but one who had been long cattle-fed in this sumptuous style might prove overbold.

'He speaks!' someone whispered from the rear. 'He knows, too.'

'Well, of *all* the infernal cheek!' said Chinn. There was an angry growl from the cave – a direct challenge.

'Come out, then,' Chinn shouted. 'Come out of that! Let's have a look at you.'

The brute knew well enough that there was some connection between brown nude Bhils and his weekly allowance; but the white helmet in the sunlight annoyed him, and he did not approve of the voice that broke his rest. Lazily as a gorged snake he dragged himself out of the cave, and stood yawning and blinking at the entrance. The sunlight fell upon his flat right side, and Chinn wondered. Never had he seen a tiger marked after this fashion. Except for his head, which was staringly barred, he was dappled – not striped, but dappled like a child's rocking-horse in rich shades of smoky black on red gold. That portion of his belly and throat which should have been white was orange, and his tail and paws were black.

He looked leisurely for some ten seconds, and then deliberately lowered his head, his chin dropped and drawn in, staring intently at the man. The effect of this was to throw forward the round arch of his skull, with two broad bands across it, while below the bands glared the unwinking eyes; so that, head on, as he stood, he showed something like a diabolically scowling pantomime-mask. It was a piece of natural mesmerism that he had practised many times on his quarry, and though Chinn was by no means a terrified heifer, he stood for a while, held by the extraordinary oddity of the attack. The head – the body seemed to have been packed away behind it – the ferocious, skull-like head, crept nearer, to the switching of an angry tail-tip in the grass. Left and right the Bhils had scattered to let Jan Chinn subdue his own horse.

'My word!' he thought. 'He's trying to frighten me!' and fired between the saucer-like eyes, leaping aside upon the shot.

A big coughing mass, reeking of carrion, bounded past him up the hill, and he followed discreetly. The tiger made no attempt to turn into the jungle: he was hunting for sight and breath – nose up, mouth open, the tremendous fore-legs scattering the gravel in spurts.

'Scuppered!' said John Chinn, watching the flight. 'Now if he was a partridge he'd tower. Lungs must be full of blood.'

The brute had jerked himself over a boulder and fallen out of sight the other side. John Chinn looked over with a ready barrel. But the red trail led straight as an arrow even to his grandfather's tomb, and there, among the smashed spirit bottles and the fragments of the mud image, the life left with a flurry and a grunt.

'If my worthy ancestor could see that,' said John Chinn, 'he'd have been proud of me. Eyes, lower jaw, and lungs. A very nice shot.' He whistled for Bukta as he drew the tape over the stiffening bulk.

'Ten – six – eight – by Jove! It's nearly eleven – call it eleven. Fore-arm, twenty-four – five – seven and a half. A short tail, too; three feet one. But *what* a skin! Oh, Bukta! Bukta! The men with the knives swiftly.'

'Is he beyond question dead?' said an awe-stricken voice behind a rock.

'That was not the way I killed my first tiger,' said Chinn. 'I did not think that Bukta would run. I had no second gun.'

'It – it is the Clouded Tiger,' said Bukta, unheeding the taunt. 'He is dead.'

Whether all the Bhils, vaccinated and unvaccinated, of the Satpuras had lain by to see the kill, Chinn could not say; but the whole hill's flank rustled with little men, shouting, singing, and stamping. And yet, till he had made the first cut in the splendid skin, not a man would take a knife; and, when the shadows fell, they ran from the red-stained tomb, and no persuasion would bring them back till dawn. So Chinn spent a second night in the open, guarding the carcass from jackals, and thinking about his ancestor.

He returned to the lowlands to the triumphal chant of an escorting army three hundred strong, the Mahratta vaccinator close at his elbow, and the rudely dried skin a trophy before him. When that army suddenly and noiselessly disappeared, as quail in high corn, he argued he was near civilisation, and a turn in the road brought him upon the camp of a wing of his own corps. He left the skin on a cart-tail for the world to see, and sought the Colonel.

'They're perfectly right,' he explained earnestly. 'There isn't an ounce of vice in 'em. They were only frightened. I've vaccinated the whole boiling, and they like it awfully. What are – what are we doing here, sir?'

'That's what I'm trying to find out,' said the Colonel. 'I don't know yet whether we're a piece of a brigade or a police force. However, I think we'll call ourselves a police force. How did you manage to get a Bhil vaccinated?'

'Well, sir,' said Chinn, 'I've been thinking it over, and, as far as I can make out, I've got a sort of hereditary influence over 'em.'

'So I know, or I wouldn't have sent you; but *what*, exactly?'

'It's rather rummy. It seems, from what I can make out, that I'm my own grandfather reincarnated, and I've been disturbing the peace of the country by riding a pad-tiger of nights. If I hadn't done that, I don't think they'd have objected to the vaccination; but the two together were more than they could stand. And so, sir, I've vaccinated 'em, and shot my tiger-horse as a sort o' proof of good faith. You never saw such a skin in your life.'

The Colonel tugged his moustache thoughtfully. 'Now, how the deuce,' said he, 'am I to include that in my report?'

Indeed, the official version of the Bhils' anti-vaccination stampede said nothing about Lieutenant John Chinn, his god-ship. But Bukta knew, and the corps knew, and every Bhil in the Satpura hills knew.

And now Bukta is zealous that John Chinn shall swiftly be wedded and impart his powers to a son; for if the Chinn succession fails, and the little Bhils are left to their own imaginings, there will be fresh trouble in the Satpuras.

Georgie Porgie

Georgie Porgie, pudding and pie,
Kissed the girls and made them cry.
When the girls came out to play
Georgie Porgie ran away.

If you will admit that a man has no right to enter his drawing-room early in the morning, when the housemaid is setting things right and clearing away the dust, you will concede that civilised people who eat out of China and own card-cases have no right to apply their standard of right and wrong to an unsettled land. When the place is made fit for their reception, by those men who are told off to the work, they can come up, bringing in their trunks their own society and the Decalogue, and all the other apparatus. Where the Queen's Law does not carry, it is irrational to expect an observance of other and weaker rules. The men who run ahead of the cars of Decency and Propriety, and make the jungle ways straight, cannot be judged in the same manner as the stay-at-home folk of the ranks of the regular *Tchin*.

Not many months ago the Queen's Law stopped a few miles north of Thayetmyo on the Irrawaddy. There was no very strong Public Opinion up to that limit, but it existed to keep men in order. When the Government said that the Queen's Law must carry up to Bhamo and the Chinese border the order was given, and some men whose desire was to be ever a little in advance of the rush of Respectability flocked forward with the troops. These were the men who could never pass examinations, and would have been too pronounced in their ideas for the administration of bureau-worked Provinces. The Supreme

Government stepped in as soon as might be, with codes and regulations, and all but reduced New Burma to the dead Indian level; but there was a short time during which strong men were necessary and ploughed a field for themselves.

Among the forerunners of Civilisation was Georgie Porgie, reckoned by all who knew him a strong man. He held an appointment in Lower Burma when the order came to break the Frontier, and his friends called him Georgie Porgie because of the singularly Burmese-like manner in which he sang a song whose first line is something like the words 'Georgie Porgie'. Most men who have been in Burma will know the song. It means: 'Puff, puff, puff, puff, great steamboat!' Georgie sang it to his banjo, and his friends shouted with delight, so that you could hear them far away in the teak-forest.

When he went to Upper Burma he had no special regard for God or Man, but he knew how to make himself respected, and to carry out the mixed Military–Civil duties that fell to most men's share in those months. He did his office work and entertained, now and again, the detachments of fever-shaken soldiers who blundered through his part of the world in search of a flying party of dacoits. Sometimes he turned out and dressed down dacoits on his own account; for the country was still smouldering and would blaze when least expected. He enjoyed these charivaris, but the dacoits were not so amused. All the officials who came in contact with him departed with the idea that Georgie Porgie was a valuable person, well able to take care of himself, and, on that belief, he was left to his own devices.

At the end of a few months he wearied of his solitude, and cast about for company and refinement. The Queen's Law had hardly begun to be felt in the country, and Public Opinion, which is more powerful than the Queen's Law, had yet to come. Also, there was a custom in the country which allowed a white man to take to himself a wife of the Daughters of Heth upon due payment. The marriage was not quite so binding as is the *nikkah* ceremony among Mohammedans, but the wife was very pleasant.

When all our troops are back from Burma there will be a proverb in their mouths, 'As thrifty as a Burmese wife', and pretty English ladies will wonder what in the world it means.

The headman of the village next to Georgie Porgie's post had a fair daughter who had seen Georgie Porgie and loved him from afar. When news went abroad that the Englishman with the heavy hand who lived in the stockade was looking for a housekeeper, the headman came in and explained that, for five hundred rupees down, he would entrust his daughter to Georgie Porgie's keeping, to be maintained in all honour, respect, and comfort, with pretty dresses, according to the custom of the country. This thing was done, and Georgie Porgie never repented it.

He found his rough-and-tumble house put straight and made comfortable, his hitherto unchecked expenses cut down by one-half, and himself petted and made much of by his new acquisition, who sat at the head of his table and sang songs to him and ordered his Madrassee servants about, and was in every way as sweet and merry and honest and winning a little woman as the most exacting of bachelors could have desired. No race, men say who know, produces such good wives and heads of households as the Burmese. When the next detachment tramped by on the war-path the Subaltern in command found at Georgie Porgie's table a hostess to be deferential to, a woman to be treated in every way as one occupying an assured position. When he gathered his men together next dawn and replunged into the jungle he thought regretfully of the nice little dinner and the pretty face, and envied Georgie Porgie from the bottom of his heart. Yet *he* was engaged to a girl at Home, and that is how some men are constructed.

The Burmese girl's name was not a pretty one; but as she was promptly christened Georgina by Georgie Porgie, the blemish did not matter. Georgie Porgie thought well of the petting and the general comfort, and vowed that he had never spent five hundred rupees to a better end.

After three months of domestic life a great idea struck him. Matrimony – English matrimony – could not be such a bad thing after all. If he were so thoroughly comfortable at the Back of Beyond with this Burmese girl who smoked cheroots, how much more comfortable would he be with a sweet English maiden who would not smoke cheroots, and would play upon a piano instead of a banjo? Also he had a desire to return to his kind, to hear a Band once more, and to feel how it felt to wear a dress-suit again. Decidedly, Matrimony would be a very good thing. He thought the matter out at length of evenings, while Georgina sang to him, or asked him why he was so silent, and whether she had done anything to offend him. As he thought, he smoked, and as he smoked he looked at Georgina, and in his fancy turned her into a fair, thrifty, amusing, merry, little English girl, with hair coming low down on her forehead, and perhaps a cigarette between her lips. Certainly, not a big, thick, Burma cheroot, of the brand that Georgina smoked. He would wed a girl with Georgina's eyes and most of her ways. But not all. She could be improved upon. Then he blew thick smoke-wreaths through his nostrils and stretched himself. He would taste marriage. Georgina had helped him to save money, and there were six months' leave due to him.

'See here, little woman,' he said, 'we must put by more money for these next three months. I want it.' That was a direct slur on Georgina's housekeeping; for she prided herself on her thrift; but since her God wanted money she would do her best.

'You want money?' she said with a little laugh. 'I *have* money. Look!' She ran to her own room and fetched out a small bag of rupees. 'Of all that you give me, I keep back some. See! One hundred and seven rupees. Can you want more money than that? Take it. It is my pleasure if you use it.' She spread out the money on the table and pushed it towards him with her quick, little, pale yellow fingers.

Georgie Porgie never referred to economy in the household again.

Three months later, after the dispatch and receipt of several mysterious letters which Georgina could not understand, and hated for that reason, Georgie Porgie said that he was going away, and she must return to her father's house and stay there.

Georgina wept. She would go with her God from the world's end to the world's end. Why should she leave him? She loved him.

'I am only going to Rangoon,' said Georgie Porgie. 'I shall be back in a month, but it is safer to stay with your father. I will leave you two hundred rupees.'

'If you go for a month, what need of two hundred? Fifty are more than enough. There is some evil here. Do not go, or at least let me go with you.'

Georgie Porgie does not like to remember that scene even at this date. In the end he got rid of Georgina by a compromise of seventy-five rupees. She would not take more. Then he went by steamer and rail to Rangoon.

The mysterious letters had granted him six months' leave. The actual flight and an idea that he might have been treacherous hurt severely at the time, but as soon as the big steamer was well out into the blue, things were easier, and Georgina's face, and the queer little stockaded house, and the memory of the rushes of shouting dacoits by night, the cry and struggle of the first man that he had ever killed with his own hand, and a hundred other more intimate things, faded and faded out of Georgie Porgie's heart, and the vision of approaching England took its place. The steamer was full of men on leave, all rampantly jovial souls who had shaken off the dust and sweat of Upper Burma and were as merry as schoolboys. They helped Georgie Porgie to forget.

Then came England with its luxuries and decencies and comforts, and Georgie Porgie walked in a pleasant dream upon pavements of which he had nearly forgotten the ring, wondering why men in their senses ever left Town. He accepted his keen delight in his furlough as the reward of his services. Providence further arranged for him another and greater delight – all the pleasures of a quiet English wooing, quite different from the brazen business of the East, when half the community stand back and bet on the result, and the other half wonder what Mrs. So-and-So will say to it.

It was a pleasant girl and a perfect summer, and a big country-house near Petworth where there are acres and acres of purple heather and high-grassed water-meadows to wander through. Georgie Porgie felt that he had at last found something worth the living for, and naturally assumed that the next thing to do was to ask the girl to share his life in India. She, in her ignorance, was willing to go. On this occasion there was no bartering with a village headman. There was a fine middle-class wedding in the country, with a stout Papa and a weeping Mamma, and a best man in purple and fine linen, and six snub-nosed girls from the Sunday School to throw roses on the path between the tombstones up to the Church door. The local paper described the affair at great length, even down to giving the hymns in full. But that was because the Direction were starving for want of material.

Then came a honeymoon at Arundel, and the Mamma wept copiously before she allowed her one daughter to sail away to India under the care of Georgie Porgie the Bridegroom. Beyond any question, Georgie Porgie was immensely fond of his wife, and she was devoted to him as the best and greatest man in the world. When he reported himself at Bombay he felt justified in demanding a good station for his wife's sake; and, because he had made a little mark in Burma and was beginning to be appreciated, they allowed him nearly all that he asked for, and posted him to a station which we will call Sutrain. It stood upon several hills, and was styled officially a 'Sanitarium', for the good reason that the drainage was utterly neglected. Here Georgie Porgie settled down, and found married life come very naturally to him. He did not rave, as do many bridegrooms, over the strangeness and delight of seeing his own true love sitting down to breakfast with him every morning 'as though it were the most natural thing in the world'. 'He had been there before', as the Americans say, and, checking the merits of his own present Grace by those of Georgina, he was more and more inclined to think that he had done well.

But there was no peace or comfort across the Bay of Bengal,

under the teak-trees where Georgina lived with her father, waiting for Georgie Porgie to return. The headman was old, and remembered the war of '51. He had been to Rangoon, and knew something of the ways of the *Kullahs*. Sitting in front of his door in the evenings, he taught Georgina a dry philosophy which did not console her in the least.

The trouble was that she loved Georgie Porgie just as much as the French girl in the English History books loved the priest whose head was broken by the King's bullies. One day she disappeared from the village, with all the rupees that Georgie Porgie had given her, and a very small smattering of English – also gained from Georgie Porgie.

The headman was angry at first, but lit a fresh cheroot and said something uncomplimentary about the sex in general. Georgina had started on a search for Georgie Porgie, who might be in Rangoon, or across the Black Water, or dead, for aught that she knew. Chance favoured her. An old Sikh policeman told her that Georgie Porgie had crossed the Black Water. She took a steerage-passage from Rangoon and went to Calcutta, keeping the secret of her search to herself.

In India every trace of her was lost for six weeks, and no one knows what trouble of heart she must have undergone.

She reappeared, four hundred miles north of Calcutta, steadily heading northwards, very worn and haggard, but very fixed in her determination to find Georgie Porgie. She could not understand the language of the people; but India is infinitely charitable, and the women-folk along the Grand Trunk gave her food. Something made her believe that Georgie Porgie was to be found at the end of that pitiless road. She may have seen a sepoy who knew him in Burma, but of this no one can be certain. At last, she found a regiment on the line of march, and met there one of the many subalterns whom Georgie Porgie had invited to dinner in the far off, old days of the dacoit-hunting. There was a certain amount of amusement among the tents when Georgina threw herself at the man's feet and began to cry. There was no amusement when her story was told; but a collection was made, and that was more to the point. One of the subalterns knew of Georgie Porgie's whereabouts, but not of his marriage. So he told Georgina and she went her way joyfully to the north, in a railway carriage where there was rest for tired feet and shade for a dusty little head. The marches from the train through the hills into Sutrain were trying, but Georgina had money, and families journeying in bullock-carts gave her help. It was an almost miraculous journey, and Georgina felt sure that the good spirits of Burma were looking after her. The hill-road to Sutrain is a chilly stretch, and Georgina caught a bad cold. Still there was Georgie Porgie at the end of all the trouble to take her up in his arms and pet her, as he used to do in the old days when the stockade was shut for the night and he had approved of the evening meal. Georgina went forward as fast as she could; and her good spirits did her one last favour.

An Englishman stopped her, in the twilight just at the turn of the road into Sutrain, saying, 'Good Heavens! What are you doing here?'

He was Gillis, the man who had been Georgie Porgie's assistant in Upper Burma, and who occupied the next post to Georgie Porgie's in the jungle. Georgie Porgie had applied to have him to work with at Sutrain because he liked him.

'I have come,' said Georgina simply. 'It was such a long way, and I have been months in coming. Where is his house?'

Gillis gasped. He had seen enough of Georgina in the old times to know that explanations would be useless. You cannot explain things to the Oriental. You must show.

'I'll take you there,' said Gillis, and he led Georgina off the road, up the cliff, by a little pathway, to the back of a house set on a platform cut into the hillside.

The lamps were just lit, but the curtains were not drawn. 'Now look,' said Gillis, stopping in front of the drawing-room window. Georgina looked and saw Georgie Porgie and the Bride.

She put her hand up to her hair, which had come out of its top-knot and was straggling about her face. She tried to set her ragged dress in order, but the dress was past pulling straight, and she coughed a queer little cough, for she really had taken a very bad cold. Gillis looked, too, but while Georgina only looked at the Bride once, turning her eyes always on Georgie Porgie, Gillis looked at the Bride all the time.

'What are you going to do?' said Gillis, who held Georgina by the wrist, in case of any unexpected rush into the lamplight. 'Will you go in and tell that English woman that you lived with her husband?'

'No,' said Georgina faintly. 'Let me go. I am going away. I swear that I am going away.' She twisted herself free and ran off into the dark.

'Poor little beast!' said Gillis, dropping on to the main road. 'I'd ha' given her something to get back to Burma with. What a narrow shave though! And that angel would never have forgiven it.'

This seems to prove that the devotion of Gillis was not entirely due to his affection for Georgie Porgie.

The Bride and the Bridegroom came out into the verandah after dinner, in order that the smoke of Georgie Porgie's cheroots might not hang in the new drawing-room curtains.

'What is that noise down there?' said the Bride. Both listened.

'Oh,' said Georgie Porgie, 'I suppose some brute of a hill-man has been beating his wife.'

'Beating – his – wife! How ghastly!' said the Bride. 'Fancy *your* beating *me*!' She slipped an arm round her husband's waist, and, leaning her head against his shoulder, looked out across the cloud-filled valley in deep content and security.

But it was Georgina crying, all by herself, down the hillside, among the stones of the watercourse where the washermen wash the clothes.

At the End of the Passage

The sky is lead and our faces are red,
  And the gates of Hell are opened and riven,
  And the winds of Hell are loosened and driven,
And the dust flies up in the face of Heaven,
  And the clouds come down in a fiery sheet,
Heavy to raise and hard to be borne.
  And the soul of man is turned from his meat,
Turned from the trifles for which he has striven
  Sick in his body, and heavy hearted,
  And his soul flies up like the dust in the sheet
  Breaks from his flesh and is gone and departed,
  As the blasts they blow on the cholera-horn.

Himalayan

Four men, each entitled to 'life, liberty, and the pursuit of happiness', sat at a table playing whist. The thermometer marked – for them – one hundred and one degrees of heat. The room was darkened till it was only just possible to distinguish the pips of the cards and the very white faces of the players. A tattered, rotten punkah of whitewashed calico was puddling the hot air and whining dolefully at each stroke. Outside lay gloom of a November day in London. There was neither sky, sun, nor horizon – nothing but a brown purple haze of heat. It was as though the earth were dying of apoplexy.

From time to time clouds of tawny dust rose from the ground without wind or warning, flung themselves tablecloth-wise among the tops of the parched trees, and came down again. Then a whirling dust-devil would scutter across the plain for a couple of miles, break, and fall outward, though there was nothing to check its flight save a long low line of piled railway-sleepers white with the dust, a cluster of huts made of mud, condemned rails, and canvas, and the one squat four-roomed bungalow that belonged to the assistant engineer in charge of a section of the Gaudhari State line then under construction.

The four, stripped to the thinnest of sleeping-suits, played whist crossly, with wranglings as to leads and returns. It was not the best kind of whist, but they had taken some trouble to arrive at it. Mottram of the Indian Survey had ridden thirty and railed one hundred miles from his lonely post in the desert since the night before; Lowndes of the Civil Service, on special duty in the political department, had come as far to escape for an instant the miserable intrigues of an impoverished native State whose king alternately fawned and blustered for more money from the pitiful revenues contributed by hard-wrung peasants and despairing camel-breeders; Spurstow, the doctor of the line, had left a cholera-stricken camp of coolies to look after itself for forty-eight hours while he associated with white men once more. Hummil, the assistant engineer, was the host. He stood fast and received his friends thus every Sunday if they could come in. When one of them failed to appear, he would send a telegram to his last address, in order that he might know whether the defaulter were dead or alive. There are very many places in the East where it is not good or kind to let your acquaintances drop out of sight even for one short week.

The players were not conscious of any special regard for each other. They squabbled whenever they met; but they ardently desired to meet, as men without water desire to drink. They were lonely folk who understood the dread meaning of loneliness. They were all under thirty years of age – which is too soon for any man to possess that knowledge.

'Pilsener?' said Spurstow, after the second rubber, mopping his forehead.

'Beer's out, I'm sorry to say, and there's hardly enough soda-water for tonight,' said Hummil.

'What filthy bad management!' Spurstow snarled.

'Can't help it. I've written and wired; but the trains don't come through regularly yet. Last week the ice ran out – as Lowndes knows.'

'Glad I didn't come. I could ha' sent you some if I had known, though. Phew! it's too hot to go on playing bumble-puppy.' This with a savage scowl at Lowndes, who only laughed. He was a hardened offender.

Mottram rose from the table and looked out of a chink in the shutters.

'What a sweet day!' said he.

The company yawned all together and betook themselves to an aimless investigation of all Hummil's possessions – guns, tattered novels, saddlery, spurs, and the like. They had fingered them a score of times before, but there was really nothing else to do.

'Got anything fresh?' said Lowndes.

'Last week's *Gazette of India*, and a cutting from a home paper. My father sent it out. It's rather amusing.'

'One of those vestrymen that call 'emselves M.P.'s again, is it?' said Spurstow, who read his newspapers when he could get them.

'Yes. Listen to this. It's to your address, Lowndes. The man was making a speech to his constituents, and he piled it on. Here's a sample, "And I assert unhesitatingly that the Civil Service in India is the preserve – the pet preserve – of the aristocracy of England. What does the democracy – what do the masses – get from that country, which we have step by step fraudulently annexed? I answer, nothing whatever. It is farmed with a single eye to their own interests by the scions of the aristocracy. They take good care to maintain their lavish scale of incomes, to avoid or stifle any inquiries into the nature and conduct of their administration, while they themselves force the unhappy peasant to pay with the sweat of his brow for all the luxuries in which they are lapped."' Hummil waved the cutting above his head. ''Ear! 'ear!' said his audience.

Then Lowndes, meditatively, 'I'd give – I'd give three

months' pay to have that gentleman spend one month with me and see how the free and independent native prince works things. Old Timbersides' – this was his flippant title for an honoured and decorated feudatory prince – 'has been wearing my life out this week past for money. By Jove, his latest performance was to send me one of his women as a bribe!'

'Good for you! Did you accept it?' said Mottram.

'No. I rather wish I had now. She was a pretty little person, and she yarned away to me about the horrible destitution among the king's women-folk. The darlings haven't had any new clothes for nearly a month, and the old man wants to buy a new drag from Calcutta – solid silver railings and silver lamps, and trifles of that kind. I've tried to make him understand that he has played the deuce with the revenues for the last twenty years and must go slow. He can't see it.'

'But he has the ancestral treasure-vaults to draw on. There must be three millions at least in jewels and coin under his palace,' said Hummil.

'Catch a native king disturbing the family treasure! The priests forbid it except as the last resort. Old Timbersides has added something like a quarter of a million to the deposit in his reign.'

'Where the mischief does it all come from?' said Mottram.

'The country. The state of the people is enough to make you sick. I've known the taxmen wait by a milch-camel till the foal was born and then hurry off the mother for arrears. And what can I do? I can't get the court clerks to give me any accounts; I can't raise anything more than a fat smile from the commander-in-chief when I find out the troops are three months in arrears; and old Timbersides begins to weep when I speak to him. He has taken to the King's Peg heavily – liqueur brandy for whisky, and Heidsieck for soda-water.'

'That's what the Rao of Jubela took to. Even a native can't last long at that,' said Spurstow. 'He'll go out.'

'And a good thing, too. Then I suppose we'll have a council of regency, and a tutor for the young prince, and hand him back his kingdom with ten years' accumulations.'

'Whereupon that young prince, having been taught all the

vices of the English, will play ducks and drakes with the money and undo ten years' work in eighteen months. I've seen that business before,' said Spurstow. 'I should tackle the king with a light hand if I were you, Lowndes. They'll hate you quite enough under any circumstances.'

'That's all very well. The man who looks on can talk about the light hand; but you can't clean a pig-sty with a pen dipped in rose-water. I know my risks; but nothing has happened yet. My servant's an old Pathan, and he cooks for me. They are hardly likely to bribe him, and I don't accept food from my true friends, as they call themselves. Oh, but it's weary work! I'd sooner be with you, Spurstow. There's shooting near your camp.'

'Would you? I don't think it. About fifteen deaths a day don't incite a man to shoot anything but himself. And the worst of it is that the poor devils look at you as though you ought to save them. Lord knows, I've tried everything. My last attempt was empirical, but it pulled an old man through. He was brought to me apparently past hope, and I gave him gin and Worcester sauce with cayenne. It cured him; but I don't recommend it.'

'How do the cases run generally?' said Hummil.

'Very simply indeed. Chlorodyne, opium pill, chlorodyne, collapse, nitre, bricks to the feet, and then – the burning-ghaut. The last seems to be the only thing that stops the trouble. It's black cholera, you know. Poor devils! But, I will say, little Bunsee Lal, my apothecary, works like a demon. I've recommended him for promotion if he comes through it all alive.'

'And what are your chances, old man?' said Mottram.

'Don't know; don't care much; but I've sent the letter in. What are you doing with yourself generally?'

'Sitting under a table in the tent and spitting on the sextant to keep it cool,' said the man of the survey. 'Washing my eyes to avoid ophthalmia, which I shall certainly get, and trying to make a sub-surveyor understand that an error of five degrees in an angle isn't quite so small as it looks. I'm altogether alone, y'know, and shall be till the end of the hot weather.'

'Hummil's the lucky man,' said Lowndes, flinging himself into a long chair. 'He has an actual roof – torn as to the ceiling-cloth, but still a roof – over his head. He sees one train daily. He can get beer and soda-water and ice 'em when God is good. He has books, pictures,' – they were torn from the *Graphic* – 'and the society of the excellent sub-contractor Jevins, besides the pleasure of receiving us weekly.'

Hummil smiled grimly. 'Yes, I'm the lucky man, I suppose. Jevins is luckier.'

'How? Not—'

'Yes. Went out. Last Monday.'

'By his own hand?' said Spurstow quickly, hinting the suspicion that was in everybody's mind. There was no cholera near Hummil's section. Even fever gives a man at least a week's grace, and sudden death generally implied self-slaughter.

'I judge no man this weather,' said Hummil. 'He had a touch of the sun, I fancy; for last week, after you fellows had left, he came in to the verandah and told me that he was going home to see his wife, in Market Street, Liverpool, that evening.

'I got the apothecary in to look at him, and we tried to make him lie down. After an hour or two he rubbed his eyes and said he believed he had had a fit – hoped he hadn't said anything rude. Jevins had a great idea of bettering himself socially. He was very like Chucks in his language.'

'Well?'

'Then he went to his own bungalow and began cleaning a rifle. He told the servant that he was going to shoot buck in the morning. Naturally he fumbled with the trigger, and shot himself through the head – accidentally. The apothecary sent in a report to my chief, and Jevins is buried somewhere out there. I'd have wired to you, Spurstow, if you could have done anything.'

'You're a queer chap,' said Mottram. 'If you'd killed the man yourself you couldn't have been more quiet about the business.'

'Good Lord! what does it matter?' said Hummil calmly. 'I've got to do a lot of his overseeing work in addition to my own. I'm the only person that suffers. Jevins is out of it – by pure accident, of course, but out of it. The apothecary was going to write a long screed on suicide. Trust a babu to drivel when he gets the chance.'

'Why didn't you let it go in as suicide?' said Lowndes.

'No direct proof. A man hasn't many privileges in this country, but he might at least be allowed to mishandle his own rifle. Besides, some day I may need a man to smother up an accident to myself. Live and let live. Die and let die.'

'You take a pill,' said Spurstow, who had been watching Hummil's white face narrowly. 'Take a pill, and don't be an ass. That sort of talk is skittles. Anyhow, suicide is shirking your work. If I were Job ten times over, I should be so interested in what was going to happen next that I'd stay on and watch.'

'Ah! I've lost that curiosity,' said Hummil.

'Liver out of order?' said Lowndes feelingly.

'No. Can't sleep. That's worse.'

'By Jove, it is!' said Mottram. 'I'm that way every now and then, and the fit has to wear itself out. What do you take for it?'

'Nothing. What's the use? I haven't had ten minutes' sleep since Friday morning.'

'Poor chap! Spurstow, you ought to attend to this,' said Mottram. 'Now you mention it, your eyes are rather gummy and swollen.'

Spurstow, still watching Hummil, laughed lightly. 'I'll patch him up, later on. Is it too hot, do you think, to go for a ride?'

'Where to?' said Lowndes wearily. 'We shall have to go away at eight, and there'll be riding enough for us then. I hate a horse when I have to use him as a necessity. Oh, heavens! what is there to do?'

'Begin whist again, at chick points ['a chick' is supposed to be eight shillings] and a gold mohur on the rub,' said Spurstow promptly.

'Poker. A month's pay all round for the pool – no limit – and fifty-rupee raises. Somebody would be broken before we got up,' said Lowndes.

'Can't say that it would give me any pleasure to break any man in this company,' said Mottram. 'There isn't enough excitement in it, and it's foolish.' He crossed over to the worn and battered little camp-piano – wreckage of a married household that had once held the bungalow – and opened the case.

'It's used up long ago,' said Hummil. 'The servants have picked it to pieces.'

The piano was indeed hopelessly out of order, but Mottram managed to bring the rebellious notes into a sort of agreement, and there rose from the ragged keyboard something that might once have been the ghost of a popular music-hall song. The men in the long chairs turned with evident interest as Mottram banged the more lustily.

'That's good!' said Lowndes. 'By Jove! the last time I heard that song was in '79, or thereabouts, just before I came out.'

'Ah!' said Spurstow with pride, 'I was home in '80.' And he mentioned a song of the streets popular at that date.

Mottram executed it roughly. Lowndes criticised and volunteered emendations. Mottram dashed into another ditty, not of the music-hall character, and made as if to rise.

'Sit down,' said Hummil. 'I didn't know that you had any music in your composition. Go on playing until you can't think of anything more. I'll have that piano tuned up before you come again. Play something festive.'

Very simple indeed were the tunes to which Mottram's art and the limitations of the piano could give effect, but the men listened with pleasure, and in the pauses talked all together of what they had seen or heard when they were last at home. A dense dust-storm sprung up outside, and swept roaring over the house, enveloping it in the choking darkness of midnight, but Mottram continued unheeding, and the crazy tinkle reached the ears of the listeners above the flapping of the tattered ceiling-cloth.

In the silence after the storm he glided from the more directly personal songs of Scotland, half humming them as he played, into the Evening Hymn.

'Sunday,' said he, nodding his head.

'Go on. Don't apologise for it,' said Spurstow.

Hummil laughed long and riotously. 'Play it, by all means. You're full of surprises today. I didn't know you had such a gift of finished sarcasm. How does that thing go?'

Mottram took up the tune.

'Too slow by half. You miss the note of gratitude,' said Hummil. 'It ought to go to the "Grasshopper's Polka" – this way.' And he chanted, *prestissimo*—

'Glory to thee, my God, this night,
For all the blessings of the light.

'That shows we really feel our blessings. How does it go on? –

'If in the night I sleepless lie,
My soul with sacred thoughts supply;
May no ill dreams disturb my rest—

'Quicker, Mottram!—

'Or powers of darkness me molest!

'Bah! what an old hypocrite you are!'

'Don't be an ass,' said Lowndes. 'You are at full liberty to make fun of anything else you like, but leave that hymn alone. It's associated in my mind with the most sacred recollections—'

'Summer evenings in the country – stained-glass window, – light going out, and you and she jamming your heads together over one hymnbook,' said Mottram.

'Yes, and a fat old cockchafer hitting you in the eye when you walked home. Smell of hay, and a moon as big as a bandbox sitting on the top of a haycock; bats – roses – milk and midges,' said Lowndes.

'Also mothers. I can just recollect my mother singing me to sleep with that when I was a little chap,' said Spurstow.

The darkness had fallen on the room. They could hear Hummil squirming in his chair.

'Consequently,' said he testily, 'you sing it when you are seven fathoms deep in Hell! It's an insult to the intelligence of the Deity to pretend we're anything but tortured rebels.'

'Take *two* pills,' said Spurstow; 'that's tortured liver.'

'The usually placid Hummil is in a vile bad temper. I'm sorry for his coolies tomorrow,' said Lowndes, as the servants brought in the lights and prepared the table for dinner.

As they were settling into their places about the miserable goat-chops, and the smoked tapioca pudding, Spurstow took occasion to whisper to Mottram, 'Well done, David!'

'Look after Saul, then,' was the reply.

'What are you two whispering about?' said Hummil suspiciously.

'Only saying that you are a damned poor host. This fowl can't be cut,' returned Spurstow with a sweet smile. 'Call this a dinner?'

'I can't help it. You don't expect a banquet, do you?'

Throughout that meal Hummil contrived laboriously to insult directly and pointedly all his guests in succession, and at each insult Spurstow kicked the aggrieved persons under the table; but he dared not exchange a glance of intelligence with either of them. Hummil's face was white and pinched, while his eyes were unnaturally large. No man dreamed for a moment of resenting his savage personalities, but as soon as the meal was over they made haste to get away.

'Don't go. You're just getting amusing, you fellows. I hope I haven't said anything that annoyed you. You're such touchy devils.' Then, changing the note into one of almost abject entreaty, Hummil added, 'I say, you surely aren't going?'

'In the language of the blessed Jorrocks, where I dines I sleeps,' said Spurstow. 'I want to have a look at your coolies tomorrow, if you don't mind. You can give me a place to lie down in, I suppose?'

The others pleaded the urgency of their several duties next day, and, saddling up, departed together, Hummil begging them to come next Sunday. As they jogged off, Lowndes unbosomed himself to Mottram –

'. . . And I never felt so like kicking a man at his own table in my life. He said I cheated at whist, and reminded me I was in debt! Told you you were as good as a liar to your face! You aren't half indignant enough over it.'

'Not I,' said Mottram. 'Poor devil! Did you ever know old Hummy behave like that before or within a hundred miles of it?'

'That's no excuse. Spurstow was hacking my shin all the time, so I kept a hand on myself. Else I should have—'

'No, you wouldn't. You'd have done as Hummy did about Jevins; judge no man this weather. By Jove! the buckle of my bridle is hot in my hand! Trot out a bit, and 'ware ratholes.'

Ten minutes' trotting jerked out of Lowndes one very sage remark when he pulled up, sweating from every pore –

'Good thing Spurstow's with him tonight.'

'Ye-es. Good man, Spurstow. Our roads turn here. See you again next Sunday, if the sun doesn't bowl me over.'

'S'pose so, unless old Timbersides' finance minister manages to dress some of my food. Good-night, and – God bless you!'

'What's wrong now?'

'Oh, nothing.' Lowndes gathered up his whip, and, as he flicked Mottram's mare on the flank, added, 'You're not a bad little chap – that's all.' And the mare bolted half a mile across the sand, on the word.

In the assistant engineer's bungalow Spurstow and Hummil smoked the pipe of silence together, each narrowly watching the other. The capacity of a bachelor's establishment is as elastic as its arrangements are simple. A servant cleared away the dining-room table, brought in a couple of rude native bedsteads made of tape strung on a light wood frame, flung a square of cool Calcutta matting over each, set them side by side, pinned two towels to the punkah so that their fringes should just sweep clear of the sleeper's nose and mouth, and announced that the couches were ready.

The men flung themselves down, ordering the punkah-coolies by all the power of Hell to pull. Every door and window was shut, for the outside air was that of an oven. The atmosphere within was only 104°, as the thermometer bore witness, and heavy with the foul smell of badly-trimmed kerosene lamps; and this stench, combined with that of native tobacco, baked brick, and dried earth, sends the heart of many a strong man down to his boots, for it is the smell of the Great Indian Empire when she turns herself for six months into a house of torment. Spurstow packed his pillows craftily so that he reclined rather than lay, his head at a safe elevation above his feet. It is not good to sleep on a low pillow in the hot weather if you happen to be of thick-necked build, for you may pass with lively snores and gugglings from natural sleep into the deep slumber of heat-apoplexy.

'Pack your pillows,' said the doctor sharply, as he saw Hummil preparing to lie down at full length.

The night-light was trimmed; the shadow of the punkah wavered across the room, and the '*flick*' of the punkah-towel and the soft whine of the rope through the wall-hole followed it. Then the punkah flagged, almost ceased. The sweat poured from Spurstow's brow. Should he go out and harangue the coolie? It started forward again with a savage jerk, and a pin came out of the towels. When this was replaced, a tomtom in the coolie-lines began to beat with the steady throb of a swollen artery inside some brain-fevered skull. Spurstow turned on his side and swore gently. There was no movement on Hummil's part. The man had composed himself as rigidly as a corpse, his hands clinched at his sides. The respiration was too hurried for any suspicion of sleep. Spurstow looked at the set face. The jaws were clinched, and there was a pucker round the quivering eyelids.

'He's holding himself as tightly as ever he can,' thought Spurstow. 'What in the world is the matter with him? – Hummil!'

'Yes,' in a thick constrained voice.

'Can't you get to sleep?'

'No.'

'Head hot? Throat feeling bulgy? or how?'

'Neither, thanks. I don't sleep much, you know.'

'Feel pretty bad?'

'Pretty bad, thanks. There is a tomtom outside, isn't there?

I thought it was my head at first . . . Oh, Spurstow, for pity's sake give me something that will put me asleep – sound asleep – if it's only for six hours!' He sprang up, trembling from head to foot. 'I haven't been able to sleep naturally for days, and I can't stand it! – I can't stand it!'

'Poor old chap!'

'That's no use. Give me something to make me sleep. I tell you I'm nearly mad. I don't know what I say half my time. For three weeks I've had to think and spell out every word that has come through my lips before I dared say it. Isn't that enough to drive a man mad? I can't see things correctly now, and I've lost my sense of touch. My skin aches – my skin aches! Make me sleep. Oh, Spurstow, for the love of God make me sleep sound. It isn't enough merely to let me dream. Let me sleep!'

'All right, old man, all right. Go slow; you aren't half as bad as you think.'

The flood-gates of reserve once broken, Hummil was clinging to him like a frightened child. 'You're pinching my arm to pieces.'

'I'll break your neck if you don't do something for me. No, I didn't mean that. Don't be angry, old fellow.' He wiped the sweat off himself as he fought to regain composure. 'I'm a bit restless and off my oats, and perhaps you could recommend some sort of sleeping mixture – bromide of potassium.'

'Bromide of skittles! Why didn't you tell me this before? Let go of my arm, and I'll see if there's anything in my cigarette-case to suit your complaint.' Spurstow hunted among his day-clothes, turned up the lamp, opened a little silver cigarette-case, and advanced on the expectant Hummil with the daintiest of fairy squirts.

'The last appeal of civilisation,' said he, 'and a thing I hate to use. Hold out your arm. Well, your sleeplessness hasn't ruined your muscle; and what a thick hide it is! Might as well inject a buffalo subcutaneously. Now in a few minutes the morphia will begin working. Lie down and wait.'

A smile of unalloyed and idiotic delight began to creep over Hummil's face. 'I think,' he whispered – 'I think I'm going off now. Gad! it's positively heavenly! Spurstow, you must give me that case to keep; you—' The voice ceased as the head fell back.

'Not for a good deal,' said Spurstow to the unconscious form. 'And now, my friend, sleeplessness of your kind being very apt to relax the moral fibre in little matters of life and death, I'll just take the liberty of spiking your guns.'

He paddled into Hummil's saddle-room in his bare feet and uncased a twelve-bore rifle, an express, and a revolver. Of the first he unscrewed the nipples and hid them in the bottom of a saddlery-case; of the second he abstracted the lever, kicking it behind a big wardrobe. The third he merely opened, and knocked the doll-head bolt of the grip up with the heel of a riding-boot.

'That's settled,' he said, as he shook the sweat off his hands. 'These little precautions will at least give you time to turn. You have too much sympathy with gun-room accidents.'

And as he rose from his knees, the thick muffled voice of Hummil cried in the doorway, 'You fool!'

Such tones they use who speak in the lucid intervals of delirium to their friends a little before they die.

Spurstow started, dropping the pistol. Hummil stood in the doorway, rocking with helpless laughter.

'That was awf'ly good of you, I'm sure,' he said, very slowly, feeling for his words. 'I don't intend to go out by my own hand at present. I say, Spurstow, that stuff won't work. What shall I do? What shall I do?' And panic terror stood in his eyes.

'Lie down and give it a chance. Lie down at once.'

'I daren't. It will only take me half-way again, and I shan't be able to get away this time. Do you know it was all I could do to come out just now? Generally I am as quick as lightning; but you had clogged my feet. I was nearly caught.'

'Oh yes, I understand. Go and lie down.'

'No, it isn't delirium; but it was an awfully mean trick to play on me. Do you know I might have died?'

As a sponge rubs a slate clean, so some power unknown to Spurstow had wiped out of Hummil's face all that stamped it for the face of a man, and he stood at the doorway in the expression of his lost innocence. He had slept back into terrified childhood.

'Is he going to die on the spot?' thought Spurstow. Then, aloud, 'All right, my son. Come back to bed, and tell me all about it. You couldn't sleep; but what was all the rest of the nonsense?'

'A place – a place down there,' said Hummil, with simple sincerity. The drug was acting on him by waves, and he was flung from the fear of a strong man to the fright of a child as his nerves gathered sense or were dulled.

'Good God! I've been afraid of it for months past, Spurstow. It has made every night hell to me; and yet I'm not conscious of having done anything wrong.'

'Be still, and I'll give you another dose. We'll stop your nightmares, you unutterable idiot!'

'Yes, but you must give me so much that I can't get away. You must make me quite sleepy – not just a little sleepy. It's so hard to run then.'

'I know it; I know it. I've felt it myself. The symptoms are exactly as you describe.'

'Oh, don't laugh at me, confound you! Before this awful sleeplessness came to me I've tried to rest on my elbow and put a spur in the bed to sting me when I fell back. Look!'

'By Jove! the man has been rowelled like a horse! Ridden by the nightmare with a vengeance! And we all thought him sensible enough. Heaven send us understanding! You like to talk, don't you?'

'Yes, sometimes. Not when I'm frightened. *Then* I want to run. Don't you?'

'Always. Before I give you your second dose try to tell me exactly what your trouble is.'

Hummil spoke in broken whispers for nearly ten minutes, while Spurstow looked into the pupils of his eyes and passed his hand before them once or twice.

At the end of the narrative the silver cigarette-case was produced, and the last words that Hummil said as he fell back for the second time were, 'Put me quite to sleep; for if I'm caught I die – I die!'

'Yes, yes; we all do that sooner or later – thank Heaven who has set a term to our miseries,' said Spurstow, settling the cushions under the head. 'It occurs to me that unless I drink something I shall go out before my time. I've stopped sweating, and – I wear a seventeen-inch collar.' He brewed himself scalding hot tea, which is an excellent remedy against heat-apoplexy if you take three or four cups of it in time. Then he watched the sleeper.

'A blind face that cries and can't wipe its eyes, a blind face that chases him down corridors! H'm! Decidedly, Hummil ought to go on leave as soon as possible; and, sane or otherwise, he undoubtedly did rowel himself most cruelly. Well, Heaven send us understanding!'

At mid-day Hummil rose, with an evil taste in his mouth, but an unclouded eye and a joyful heart.

'I was pretty bad last night, wasn't I?' said he.

'I have seen healthier men. You must have had a touch of the sun. Look here: if I write you a swingeing medical certificate, will you apply for leave on the spot?'

'No.'

'Why not? You want it.'

'Yes, but I can hold on till the weather's a little cooler.'

'Why should you, if you can get relieved on the spot?'

'Burkett is the only man who could be sent; and he's a born fool.'

'Oh, never mind about the line. You aren't so important as all that. Wire for leave, if necessary.'

Hummil looked very uncomfortable.

'I can hold on till the Rains,' he said evasively.

'You can't. Wire to headquarters for Burkett.'

'I won't. If you want to know why, particularly, Burkett is married, and his wife's just had a kid, and she's up at Simla, in the cool, and Burkett has a very nice billet that takes him into Simla from Saturday to Monday. That little woman isn't at all well. If Burkett was transferred she'd try to follow him.

If she left the baby behind she'd fret herself to death. If she came – and Burkett's one of those selfish little beasts who are always talking about a wife's place being with her husband – she'd die. It's murder to bring a woman here just now. Burkett hasn't the physique of a rat. If he came here he'd go out; and I know she hasn't any money, and I'm pretty sure she'd go out too. I'm salted in a sort of way, and I'm not married. Wait till the Rains, and then Burkett can get thin down here. It'll do him heaps of good.'

'Do you mean to say that you intend to face – what you have faced, till the Rains break?'

'Oh, it won't be so bad, now you've shown me a way out of it. I can always wire to you. Besides, now I've once got into the way of sleeping, it'll be all right. Anyhow, I shan't put in for leave. That's the long and the short of it.'

'My great Scott! I thought all that sort of thing was dead and done with.'

'Bosh! You'd do the same yourself. I feel a new man, thanks to that cigarette-case. You're going over to camp now, aren't you?'

'Yes; but I'll try to look you up every other day, if I can.'

'I'm not bad enough for that. I don't want you to bother. Give the coolies gin and ketchup.'

'Then you feel all right?'

'Fit to fight for my life, but not to stand out in the sun talking to you. Go along, old man, and bless you!'

Hummil turned on his heel to face the echoing desolation of his bungalow, and the first thing he saw standing in the verandah was the figure of himself. He had met a similar apparition once before, when he was suffering from overwork and the strain of the hot weather.

'This is bad – already,' he said, rubbing his eyes. 'If the thing slides away from me all in one piece, like a ghost, I shall know it is only my eyes and stomach that are out of order. If it walks – my head is going.'

He approached the figure, which naturally kept at an unvarying distance from him, as is the use of all spectres that are born of overwork. It slid through the house and dissolved into swimming specks within the eyeball as soon as it reached the burning light of the garden. Hummil went about his business till even. When he came in to dinner he found himself sitting at the table. The vision rose and walked out hastily. Except that it cast no shadow it was in all respects real.

No living man knows what that week held for Hummil. An increase of the epidemic kept Spurstow in camp among the coolies, and all he could do was to telegraph to Mottram, bidding him to go to the bungalow and sleep there. But Mottram was forty miles away from the nearest telegraph, and knew nothing of anything save the needs of the survey till he met, early on Sunday morning, Lowndes and Spurstow heading towards Hummil's for the weekly gathering.

'Hope the poor chap's in a better temper,' said the former, swinging himself off his horse at the door. 'I suppose he isn't up yet.'

'I'll just have a look at him,' said the doctor. 'If he's asleep there's no need to wake him.'

And an instant later, by the tone of Spurstow's voice calling upon them to enter, the men knew what had happened. There was no need to wake him.

The punkah was still being pulled over the bed, but Hummil had departed this life at least three hours.

The body lay on its back, hands clinched by the side, as Spurstow had seen it lying seven nights previously. In the staring eyes was written terror beyond the expression of any pen.

Mottram, who had entered behind Lowndes. bent over the dead and touched the forehead lightly with his lips. 'Oh, you lucky, lucky devil!' he whispered.

But Lowndes had seen the eyes, and withdrew shuddering to the other side of the room.

'Poor chap! poor old chap! And the last time I met him I was angry. Spurstow, we should have watched him. Has he—?'

Deftly Spurstow continued his investigations, ending by a search round the room.

'No, he hasn't,' he snapped. 'There's no trace of anything. Call the servants.'

They came, eight or ten of them, whispering and peering over each other's shoulders.

'When did your Sahib go to bed?' said Spurstow.

'At eleven or ten, we think,' said Hummil's personal servant.

'He was well then? But how should you know?'

'He was not ill, as far as our comprehension extended. But he had slept very little for three nights. This I know, because I saw him walking much, and specially in the heart of the night.'

As Spurstow was arranging the sheet, a big straight-necked hunting spur tumbled on the ground. The doctor groaned. The personal servant peeped at the body.

'What do you think, Chuma?' said Spurstow, catching the look on the dark face.

'Heaven-born, in my poor opinion, this that was my master has descended into the Dark Places, and there has been caught because he was not able to escape with sufficient speed. We have the spur for evidence that he fought with Fear. Thus have I seen men of my race do with thorns when a spell was laid upon them to overtake them in their sleeping hours and they dared not sleep.'

'Chuma, you're a mud-head. Go out and prepare seals to be set on the Sahib's property.'

'God has made the Heaven-born. God has made me. Who are we, to inquire into the dispensations of God? I will bid the other servants hold aloof while you are reckoning the tale of the Sahib's property. They are all thieves, and would steal.'

'As far as I can make out, he died from – oh, anything; stoppage of the heart's action, heat-apoplexy, or some other visitation,' said Spurstow to his companions. 'We must make an inventory of his effects, and so on.'

'He was scared to death,' insisted Lowndes. 'Look at those eyes! For pity's sake don't let him be buried with them open!'

'Whatever it was, he's clear of all the trouble now,' said Mottram softly.

Spurstow was peering into the open eyes.

'Come here,' said he. 'Can you see anything there?'

'I can't face it!' whimpered Lowndes. 'Cover up the face!

Is there any fear on earth that can turn a man into that likeness? It's ghastly. Oh, Spurstow, cover it up!'

'No fear – on earth,' said Spurstow. Mottram leaned over his shoulder and looked intently.

'I see nothing except some grey blurs in the pupil. There can be nothing there, you know.'

'Even so. Well, let's think. It'll take half a day to knock up any sort of coffin; and he must have died at midnight. Lowndes, old man, go out and tell the coolies to break ground next to Jevins's grave. Mottram, go round the house with Chuma and see that the seals are put on things. Send a couple of men to me here, and I'll arrange.'

The strong-armed servants when they returned to their own kind told a strange story of the doctor Sahib vainly trying to call their master back to life by magic arts – to wit, the holding of a little green box that clicked to each of the dead man's eyes, and of a bewildered muttering on the part of the doctor Sahib, who took the little green box away with him.

The resonant hammering of a coffin-lid is no pleasant thing to hear, but those who have experience maintain that much more terrible is the soft swish of the bed-linen, the reeving and unreeving of the bed-tapes, when he who has fallen by the roadside is apparelled for burial, sinking gradually as the tapes are tied over, till the swaddled shape touches the floor and there is no protest against the indignity of hasty disposal.

At the last moment Lowndes was seized with scruples of conscience. 'Ought you to read the service – from beginning to end?' said he to Spurstow.

'I intend to. You're my senior as a civilian. You can take it if you like.'

'I didn't mean that for a moment. I only thought if we could get a chaplain from somewhere – I'm willing to ride anywhere – and give poor Hummil a better chance. That's all.'

'Bosh!' said Spurstow, as he framed his lips to the tremendous words that stand at the head of the burial service.

*   *   *

After breakfast they smoked a pipe in silence to the memory of the dead. Then Spurstow said absently—

''Tisn't in medical science.'

'What?'

'Things in a dead man's eye.'

'For goodness' sake leave that horror alone!' said Lowndes. 'I've seen a native die of pure fright when a tiger chivied him. I know what killed Hummil.'

'The deuce you do! I'm going to try to see.' And the doctor retreated into the bath-room with a Kodak camera. After a few minutes there was the sound of something being hammered to pieces, and he emerged, very white indeed.

'Have you got a picture?' said Mottram. 'What does the thing look like?'

'It was impossible, of course. You needn't look, Mottram. I've torn up the films. There was nothing there. It was impossible.'

'That,' said Lowndes, very distinctly, watching the shaking hand striving to relight the pipe, 'is a damned lie.'

Mottram laughed uneasily. 'Spurstow's right,' he said. 'We're all in such a state now that we'd believe anything. For pity's sake let's try to be rational.'

There was no further speech for a long time. The hot wind whistled without, and the dry trees sobbed. Presently the daily train, winking brass, burnished steel, and spouting steam, pulled up panting in the intense glare. 'We'd better go on on that,' said Spurstow. 'Go back to work. I've written my certificate. We can't do any more good here, and work'll keep our wits together. Come on.'

No one moved. It is not pleasant to face railway journeys at mid-day in June. Spurstow gathered up his hat and whip, and, turning in the doorway, said—

'There may be Heaven – there must be Hell.
 Meantime, there is our life here. We-ell?'

Neither Mottram nor Lowndes had any answer to the question.

Joseph Conrad

'Conrad is among the very greatest novelists in the language – or any language' F. R. LEAVIS in The Great Tradition

Lord Jim 50p

The novel by which Conrad is most often remembered by perhaps a majority of readers, and the first considerable novel he wrote.

The Secret Agent: A Simple Tale 40p

Based on anarchist and terrorist activities in London, this novel has been described by Dr. Leavis as 'indubitably a classic and a masterpiece'.

Victory: An Island Tale 50p

In his critical biography of the author, Jocelyn Baines places this tragic story of the Malay Archipelago 'among Conrad's best novels'.

Nostromo: A Tale of the Seaboard 60p

His story of revolution in South America, which Arnold Bennett regarded as 'one of the greatest novels of any age'.

Under Western Eyes 45p

An atmosphere of ominous suspense hangs over this story of revolutionaries, set in Switzerland and Russia.

The Rover 40p

Conrad's last completed novel which recalls, with its Mediterranean setting, memories of the first sea Conrad had ever known.

Selected bestsellers

☐ **Let Sleeping Vets Lie** James Herriot 50p
☐ **Jaws** Peter Benchley 60p
☐ **Slay-Ride** Dick Francis 45p
☐ **The Tower** Richard Martin Stern 50p
   (filmed as *The Towering Inferno*)
☐ **Open Season** David Osborn 50p
☐ **The Man with the Golden Gun** Ian Fleming 40p
☐ **Gold** Wilbur Smith 40p
☐ **Airport** Arthur Hailey 50p
☐ **Mandingo** Kyle Onstott 50p
☐ **Royal Flash** George MacDonald Fraser 40p
☐ **The Poseidon Adventure** Paul Gallico 60p
☐ **Penmarric** Susan Howatch 75p
☐ **Lady of Quality** Georgette Heyer 50p
☐ **The Frightened Bride** Barbara Cartland 40p
☐ **Fuzz** Ed McBain 30p
☐ **Jonathan Livingston Seagull** Richard Bach 50p
☐ **The Spy Who Came In from the Cold** John le Carré 40p
☐ **Princess of Celle** Jean Plaidy 60p
☐ **Bury My Heart at Wounded Knee** Dee Brown 95p
☐ **The Little Prince** Antoine de Saint-Exupéry 35p
☐ **The Maltese Falcon** Dashiell Hammett 45p

All these books are available at your bookshop or newsagent;
or can be obtained direct from the publisher
Just tick the titles you want and fill in the form below

Pan Books Cavaye Place London SW10 9PG
Send purchase price plus 15p for the first book and 5p for
each additional book, to allow for postage and packing

Name (block letters) ————————————————

Address ——————————————————————

————————————————————————————

While every effort is made to keep prices low, it is sometimes
necessary to increase prices at short notice. Pan Books reserve
the right to show on covers new retail prices which may differ
from those advertised in the text or elsewhere